Einstein's COMPASS

A YA TIME TRAVELER ADVENTURE

EINSTEIN'S COMPASS

Copyright © 2019 by Modern Mystic Media, LLC

ISBN: 978-0-9988308-8-9 (paperback)
ISBN: 978-0-9988308-9-6 (ebook)
ISBN: 978-0-9988308-7-2 (audiobook)

LEXILE® 860

Names: Blair, Grace, 1950- author. | Bright, Laren, 1950- author.
Title: Einstein's compass : a YA time traveler adventure / Grace Blair &
Laren Bright.

Description: [Lubbock, Texas] : [Modern Mystic Media], [2019] | Interest age level: 012-018. | Summary: "How did Albert Einstein come up with his world-changing theories of light and time? Did he explore spiritual realms and other dimensions, go back to an ancient lifetime on Atlantis, and escape the clutches of a giant evil, human-dragon who was after his compass? Did his supernatural compass guide his discoveries?"--Provided by publisher.

Identifiers: ISBN 9780998830889 (paperback) | ISBN 9780998830896 (ebook)

Subjects: LCSH: Einstein, Albert, 1879-1955--Juvenile fiction. | Atlantis (Leg-endary place)--Juvenile fiction. | Supernatural--Juvenile fiction. | Time travel--Juvenile fiction. | CYAC: Einstein, Albert, 1879-1955--Fiction. | Atlantis (Legendary place)--Fiction. | Supernatural--Fiction. | Time travel--Fiction. | LCGFT: Paranormal fiction.

Classification: LCC PZ7.1.B57 Ei 2019 (print) | LCC PZ7.1.B57 (ebook) | DDC [Fic]--dc23

Einstein's COMPASS

A YA TIME TRAVELER ADVENTURE

Grace Blair & Laren Bright

Table of Contents

"There are only two ways to live your life. One is as though nothing is a miracle. The other is as though everything is a miracle."

— Albert Einstein

fee
a

Prolog

Circa 10,400 BCE – The Islands of Pose

T he earth tremor stopped Raka
Atlantean healer priest raised
his violet eyes and searched the landsc
turbance. He shrugged when he discov
then continued his way toward the cou
Raka did not understand was that the
an earthly shudder, but a spiritual c
walking toward the darkness that wa
and with his first step, the door of
Light had slammed shut to him. So, b
fallen Angel of Light.

* * *

A brisk summer afternoon sea breez
out Raka's shoulder-length blond h

9

nzed man of twenty-five was handsome,
He smiled as he swept a hand through his
a hidden pocket in his cloak to check the
ad stolen from the Temple of Healing.

e vial triggered memories that he found
. His hands curled into fists as he felt a
in the pit of his stomach. *All I do is run
nd boy for Uncle Thoth and my brother*
angrily. *Why won't Uncle Thoth show
stal works? He never includes me in the
. Until I can control my "impulses," they
y to the more buried secrets of Light.*

into a snarl at the thought. *My grand-
ty god Atlas! Admittedly, I am meant
m.*

entertaining thoughts like these for
had finally consumed him. His Con-
had constricted as the negativity grew.
er and frustration had built to the
hadowed his judgment and propelled
the dispirited Prince of Light was on
to meet with the Council of the Sons
o be placed in an elevated position in
hange for betraying his Atlantean
wasn't received in the way he de-
B.

Aryan was a military complex and the promised land of power, pomp, and ceremony. The Temple of Darkness was established by former Angels of Light who, like Raka, had become jealous of the energy in the Temple of Light that they could not access. They had rejected the discipline of the Light of God. The veils of Light that once surrounded the Angels of Light dimmed and the angels became as asleep to the Spirit within. The gross heaviness of fear descended around their bodies.

Throughout years, those attracted to the Temple of Darkness increased in number. Their separation from the Light created trepidation among the people of the world. As their following grew, the Council of the Sons of Belial and its army sought to insulate the five islands of Poseidon from outside invaders. The Atlanteans, following the inner spiritual Light, left the struggles for worldly power to the Council of the Sons of Belial and its warriors.

Atlantis, with The Temple of Light, was a garden of God's loving and a sanctuary from worldly stresses, a flourishing place of divine innocence and healing. People from the surrounding islands and the world at large came to refresh and restore themselves in body, mind, and spirit. The Sons of Belial knew the real driving force was the Spirit of life that lay on Atlantis. The invisible emanation of the Firestone crystal was the energy source of the planet.

Thanks to it, the circling satellites in space recharged the temples and cities around the world. The Council of Five of the Sons of Belial had their own ideas about what could be done with the planet's most potent energy source and lusted after the fire crystal.

General Tora-Fuliar was the leader of Aryan Island. Seven feet tall, blond and blue-eyed, the fortyish man was typical of his race. He and his cohort of four colonels had agreed to meet with the priest-scientist cum spy Raka, ostensibly to discuss his joining them. But their real purpose was to use his knowledge to wrest control of the Firestone crystal from the Atlanteans, whom they considered weak and inferior. The secret meeting would take place in Belial, the cliff fortress with towering walls that overlooked the Atlantic Ocean.

Arriving at the fortress, Raka was met at its massive twin gates by four Aryan soldiers who had been told to expect him. As they beckoned him inside, the priest of Light saw carcasses of wild boar strewn across an enormous marble altar and recognized what they meant. He held his breath as the stink of foul, stale blood and dark purpose filled the air. The blond, blue-eyed warriors checked Raka for weapons, and he smirked as his precious vial eluded their search. The guards escorted Raka through a second gate inside the fortress to the southern tower. He was led into a vast, foreboding, windowless chamber that had been carved out of the island's living rock. His eyes narrowed at the pentagram painted in blood in the middle of the torch-lit room. The dark energy of the animal sacrifice held during the full moon of the previous night lingered in it.

At the far end of the war room, the symbol of the Black Sun hung behind the general's massive desk, which was hewn from dark obsidian that had been formed in a volcanic cataclysm eons ago. Covering the fifteen-foot-high walls to the right of the writing table hung maps of the world. The general and his colonels were seated on severe, straight-backed ebony chairs around a polished black marble table. Dressed in black linen trousers and tan shirts with the Black Sun symbol on each collar and black alligator boots, the five somehow managed to appear casual despite their rigidity.

Raka strode up to the black table to greet the ruling council of the Sons of Belial. Taking in the scene, he thought to himself that while the five appeared relaxed, there was a tension in the room. To Raka, they resembled nothing more than a pack of wolves ready to leap. He straightened his golden silk garment and smiled, nodding to the general. "I am honored that you agreed to meet with me, General."

As the general stood, he sniffed as if taking in Raka's scent, then inclined his head. "Welcome. We have been looking forward to this meeting." He motioned to Raka to sit down across from them. Raka's eyes scanned the room as he settled warily into his chair. The dark and barbarous energy of the council made him uncomfortable. The general forced a smile that didn't reach his eyes and began. "We understand you want to *help* us."

Raka inhaled profoundly and adjusted his energy field to withstand the negative force emanating from those present. Nodding, he replied, "If you recall, at the Temple of Healing I used energy healing stones to alleviate your pain a few months ago. You had sustained a back injury in a rather unfortunate incident."

The general frowned but grunted in agreement.

"You stayed with us on Atlantis for several days to recuperate, and each time I came to treat you, you questioned me about the Firestone energy crystal."

The general nodded. "I did."

"Its value is obvious, but tell me what your interest in it is."

The general was not about to reveal his real intention to an untested outsider, so he said, "The firestone crystal is possibly one of the most important artifacts on the planet. You Atlanteans are focused on research and your

14

sciences and arts. You are ill-prepared to defend the Firestone from those who would use it for their own gain."

Raka nodded in understanding as the general continued. "We Aryans are strong. The Firestone should be guarded by our soldiers. After all, it is the energy source for all of the planet." The general leaned in as if to thrust his argument forward. "The council and the Sons of Belial are best suited to protect the crystal and you healers of Atlantis. We know that unless we are taught the mysteries of the crystal, disaster could be imminent."

Raka saw the energy around the general's body turn dark with flares of red, and he recognized the lust for power. He was also aware the general was not telling him everything. No surprise there. The healer was not some ignorant novice; he knew the warrior wanted to use the firestone crystal to enhance the Aryan's military might— and his own power. He was aware that with the Firestone, they could be invincible. And that they could and most likely would use this power to attempt to control the Atlanteans and take dominance over the entire planet. Despite his hopes for forming an alliance with the Sons of Belial, Raka now accepted that it would be a long time before these people trusted him—if they ever would. He wondered if he would even survive after he delivered what they wanted. He sighed inwardly, conceding to himself that this was not going to go the way he had hoped.

Still, he would play along for a while. Looking the general in the eye, he said, "General, I believe I could assist you in gaining access to the firestone crystal."

The general and his colonels nodded with interest as Raka continued. "But there are other things I might do for you. I noticed the beasts you have sacrificed to absorb their power. What if you could have even greater physical power than that you leech from the boars you kill?"

The colonels murmured, and the general's eyes narrowed. He glanced at his minions, who could barely conceal their grins as each entertained his own twisted fantasy of power.

Raka continued with a sly smile, "Yes, I assumed you would be interested." He leaned back, appearing casual and said, "Of course, if I were to assist you, then I would want something in return."

The general leaned forward. "Of course. What do you want?"

Raka pulled the vial from his pocket and held it up as he said with a sneer, "I wanted to be a part of you. But how can I trust any of you when you lie to my face? I am not about to turn over the power of the crystal to someone who would deceive me."

The general's face darkened, but before he or the council could react, Raka pulled off the vial's stopper and downed the contents in one gulp.

In truth, Raka was not sure what to expect. The vial had been received from a planet in the Draconian constellation with which Atlantis had become allied. As part of their treaty, the Draconian had been supplying the healers of Atlantis with a solution of their DNA. Mere drops mixed with herbs could regenerate a limb or restore the nearly depleted life force of an injured or sick patient. The amount Raka had just swallowed had never been tried before.

The instant the liquid touched his tongue, Raka's body began to change. The five Sons of Belial were frozen in place as Raka's body began writhing and twisting.

A scream tore from deep within Raka's throat, and with a shudder, the healer of Light's form began to shift. His soft human feet started to swell and extrude wicked-looking claws. His skin became rough and toughened. The thick leather straps of his sandals burst with a snap. His legs contracted and bent into a reptilian shape, even as his torso elongated and a tail sinuously extended from the base of his spine. His pink flesh turned a greyish green, then scales emerged from his chest, arms, and neck. His supple lips thinned, and a long serpentine tongue darted out from between them. He tasted the air with his new senses. As he transformed, his airways and throat opened wide. Raka collapsed to the ground, shuddering in ecstatic agony as the pain of bone, sinew, and flesh reconfiguring itself consumed him.

Finally breaking free of their horrific fascination, the council reacted, and the war room erupted into pandemonium. Drawn by the shouts, a score of soldiers bearing spear and shields rushed into the chamber. It was a credit to their intensive training that the scene that greeted their eyes caused them but a moment's pause. With crisp precision the soldiers spaced themselves around the writhing reptile and thrust their spears forward, their points forming a 360-degree-barrier.

But they were already too late; Raka's vulnerability had passed. His transformation into a twelve-foot dragon was complete. He was fully awake and ready to take control. The former Healer of Light felt intoxicated with raw power and luxuriated in it. Almost casually, he stretched out the reptilian claws at the end of his fingers and with a flick of his arm sliced open one of the warriors from chin to belt. His long, slithery tongue sensed the blood and offal much more thoroughly than before. With his reptile vision, the dim light in the room became bright. Awed beyond belief, Raka began to realize what his quest for power had wrought. He threw his head back and laughed as the guards' spears bounced harmlessly off his thick, scaly hide.

The air was electric with his power. He glanced disdainfully at his attackers. Sneering at their puniness, he walked toward the warriors. With a swipe of his tail, he knocked the legs out from under several of them, sending them crashing to the floor. As the others slowed to avoid tripping over their fallen comrades, Raka inhaled, then spewed a blast of fire that blackened and crisped the skin of the soldiers remaining at the front of the charge.

Despite his momentary victory, Raka knew more troops would soon descend upon the chamber. Enough of them, and he might be subdued. With bursts of fire blazing from his mouth, he cleared a path for himself. His eye sought the general and his colonels and found them huddled behind the stone table, which they had upended. "Now you see the power of Raka!" he exulted. "I will be back to claim my seat at the head of the council once you realize you have no choice but to kneel at my feet." Letting loose a final blast of fire that was absorbed by the thick marble tabletop, Raka ran from the room.

Raka fled through the rock hallways of the fortress until he came to the far wall that rose out of the eastern edge of the island. He gazed over the edge and found himself looking into the angry breakers crashing into the jagged rocks more than a hundred feet below. There was nowhere else to go. Cursing himself for not studying the island better, he prepared to defend himself. As the soldiers started pounding toward the parapet where he stood, Raka saw he had no choice. Exhaling a last massive blast of flame to buy another few seconds, Raka jumped up on the low wall and flung himself off into the air. He appeared to hover there for a moment before plummeting down and out of sight.

A cheer broke from the soldiers' throats but was quickly stifled as the irate general stormed out among them. "Where is he?" The soldiers feared the general's reaction, but one finally pointed to the far ledge.

Shaking his head in disapproval at the soldiers' incompetence, he strode to the parapet and stared down at the rocks below, hoping to see the ruined remains of the dragon's body. But he saw no trace of Raka's remains. He turned and screamed for the soldiers to get down to the rocks and find the dragon's body.

Sometime later, an exhausted captain of the guard hesitantly approached the general. "We've searched every nook and cranny below the cliffs, sir." The general raised his eyebrows in question. The guard captain shook his head and looked at his feet. "Nothing."

The general snorted but did not appear too surprised. Heartened by the lack of response, the captain frowned and said, "I thought we brought a priest in to see you, sir. Where did the dragon come from?"

The general's eyes narrowed. "That's not the question, Captain. What you should be asking is, where did it go?"

* * *

Swimming furiously under the water, Raka tried to process what had taken place. His jump from the cliff had been a risk, but it had paid off. After just a moment of unconsciousness after the impact, his body had quickly restored itself enough for him to escape into the sea. Now he found himself barely bruised. He was shaken from his meeting with the Sons of Belial and wanted nothing more than to sequester himself for a while and consider his new body. He also needed to plan his next moves. The remote caves of Aryan Island would suit that purpose, he decided.

With his new strength and supernatural speed, he quickly arrived at his destination; an underground cavern near the shore where he and his brother, Arka, had camped when they were children hunting for crystals. Dragging himself to a pool of water fed by a natural spring, Raka stared at his image. The once handsome, blue-eyed priest/scientist with shoulder-length golden hair was now a twelve-foot-long, flesh-eating changeling. His beady red eyes widened as he shook his head in disbelief. He snorted at his grotesque body. Unsure of what to expect, he gently touched the black four-inch horns on the top of his head. Spongy, he thought. He gazed with some approval, though, at his massive arms.

He turned to find short, black, spiny wings on his back and a long tail protruding from the base of his spine. With his razor-sharp alligator talons, he jabbed and pinched his armored dark-greenish skin. No tenderness, no marks or blood surfaced. He opened his mouth to examine his long, rough, but slimy reptilian tongue and the wickedly sharp bony ridge behind his lips, more like a raptor's beak than anything else.

His quick self-inspection complete, Raka found himself both horrified and fascinated. He now had so much raw physical power, but... At what cost? His mind reeling, the dragon paced. "Can I fix this and return to normal?" He considered everything he knew about the Draconian DNA, which had been used for healing and even regeneration of organs and limbs. In every case he had studied or been involved with, there had never been a report of reversal of the effects it produced. As the consequences of his rash actions finally dawned on him, Raka collapsed onto the cavern's sandy floor and sobbed. When his frustration and grief finally dissipated late into the night, he succumbed to his exhaustion and fell asleep.

* * *

Raka sat in his grotto on a battered wooden armchair that had washed up on the shore of his hideaway cove. For the last day or so he had done little but experiment with his new form and new powers. He had begun to develop a healthy respect for his strength and the seeming indestructibility of his body. He had come to grips with the realization that there was no going back.

Truth be told, he was beginning to think he wouldn't have wanted to go back even if it were possible. He had not been appreciated. Neither his uncle Thoth nor his twin, Arka, had ever recognized his promise. "If only Arka had let me practice the mystical arts with him, I would have shown him what I could do. Fool! It's his fault I am here," Raka muttered to himself.

The day before his meeting with the Council, reflecting further, Raka remembered his quarrel with Arka.

Arka pointed to the container on the counter. "Where were you today? You were supposed to take the ruby crystals to the Temple of Healing. We had to cancel the treatments when they did not arrive."

Raka petulantly stared at the ground. "Something important came up." Then he looked up at Arka defiantly. "But I told Prensa to take the crystals to the temple. It's his fault the treatments were canceled, not mine."

Arka frowned. "Prensa? He is our cook, not your servant."

Arka shook his head as if to disperse Raka's weak excuse, then changed course. "The temple guard said he saw you walking with a female member of the Belial Brotherhood near the gardens. What were you doing there with her?"

"She wanted to know what we did in the Temple of Healing," Raka lied. "I showed her around the temple grounds." That wasn't all I showed her, Raka thought to himself with a lascivious smirk.

Arka could only shake his head in resignation.

The memory aroused Raka's anger, which brought him crashing back to the present. "I am meant to do important things, not just be an errand boy!" he shouted at the rock walls of the cavern.

With thoughts of revenge seething in his mind, he snatched at a rat that had the misfortune to scurry past. It was the first sustenance he'd had since the transformation—he hadn't really been hungry. He angrily tore a leg off and took a bite, the first food he'd had since changing form. As he swallowed, he felt something a transformation begins—short, gray hairs started to replace the scales on his arm. Raka stopped chewing and watched the shift. He was a changeling, he realized, but the transformation didn't end with his dragon form. Tossing the still squirming rat aside, he plucked a beetle off the cave wall and bit down on it with a sickening crunch. A moment later, his skin began hardening into a chitinous shell. Concentrating, he found he was able to control, or even halt, the changes to his structure.

The thought of changing into other forms intrigued him. His mind flooded with information he had learned in his healing energy classes. Raka felt something else as he sorted through what was happening. It was a sort of knowing, an intuition. Could be this be from the dragon DNA he had ingested? He thought back over his transformation.

He discovered that his eyes were now acutely sensitive. He could see in total darkness and normal light. His memory, too, had sharpened. He could repeat his entire meeting with the council verbatim. His memories were much more vivid. He recalled his rage at his uncle and brother and felt it with new intensity. In fact, he could muster no feelings of compassion or love at all. Glancing at the writhing rat whose leg he had bitten off, he studied its suffering. This excited his killing instinct. It took an effort not to inflict further pain on the creature. He craved more of the rat's blood, and he speculated that human blood and organs would be a delicacy. A burst of intuition revealed that eating an entire human body and drinking its blood would transform him into a doppelganger of that person. He would have to test out how long this would last, but he suspected it would hold until he decided to take on another form.

As he discovered more of the strengths his new form provided, Raka reveled in the thought that he had nothing to fear. Then, an ancestral memory—perhaps connected to his dragon DNA—flared in his mind. He saw many of his fellow reptiles trapped in a burning structure, writhing in agony. Fear welled up in him at this vivid memory. He had at least one vulnerability: fire. Raka tore himself away from the vision and shakily drew in a deep breath to calm his trembling body. "Enough wasting time on what I fear. Now it's time to plan for the future and my revenge on Arka and his ilk." That is the task worthy of my new, transformed self, he thought.

* * *

Since Raka's meeting with the council, the focus of the Aryan laboratory had moved to DNA and using it for transformation. General Tora-Fuliar envisioned an army of Draconian soldiers with which he could conquer the world. The council leader visited the lab each week for a progress report and was increasingly frustrated at the lack of results. DNA experiments required creative scientists, and creativity was not something the militaristic Aryans were noted for. It was evident that the best talent came from Atlantis. An aggressive recruitment campaign was mounted there.

The Light healers on Atlantis were primarily motivated by their desire to serve the higher Light of God with love. This intention provided them with the clarity to heal from a pure state of giving. Loving came forward and lifted the healer and the patient. The healer's material needs—food, shelter, and clothing—came as a part of their serving. The glamour of substantial gains and recognition offered by the Aryans, however, began to distract them from the reward of serving. Increasingly generous offers seduced the Atlantean Light workers away from the healing temples to the Aryan DNA research labs. Even some high priests sold their knowledge and healing secrets to the dark empire.

The DNA experiments on Aryan required a high-quality controlled food source. Scientists used everything from cows to mice. But the trials were not without challenge. The Aryan's successes in cloning had sparked fierce debates among scientists and the public. The people of Atlantis questioned the morality of cloning plants, animals, and possibly humans. But few knew that cloning was just a cover for a secret project of DNA experiments combining animal and human DNA. On the surface, it was producing novelty animals that had become big business on Aryan. Wealthy families and even countries were buying hybrids like Minotaur and Centaurs.

The clone business on Aryan also played into Raka's plan for revenge. Once he had become adept at using his new body, he made his way back to the city. He set up an observation outpost in an abandoned structure in the remote industrial area where the DNA research complex was located. Now that he had a plan, he could afford to be patient. For several weeks he watched the movements of the scientists, military, and guards.

The general routinely showed up alone in his golden anti-gravity vehicle at the end of the workweek, parking away from the building to avoid attention. He appeared to be meeting with Dr. Aimee, the director of the science facility, for progress reports on his new military species.

As days—then weeks—passed, Raka's patience started to wear thin. If progress weren't made soon, even the general would realize that he wasn't going to be able to produce an army of warriors like Raka—an army Raka fully intended to take over. Pacing in his ramshackle hideout, with a heightened awareness of everything around him, Raka sensed the time was approaching for him make his move. He felt increasingly impatient, believing he would soon know the moment to strike.

By the time the general returned to the facility, Raka was nearly bursting out of his skin. It took incredible self-control to hold himself back and merely observe. His senses perked up as he saw the general storm out of the facility. The man appeared furious, a sure sign he had received more bad news. The irate general made his way to his flyer and slammed its door. Raka couldn't believe his eyes; the general had caught his hand in the door. Even from this distance, Raka could hear the general bellow in pain as he jumped out of the vehicle, blood spurting from his self-inflicted wound. Raka immediately smelled the warm, precious blood, urging him into a frenzy. The general's screams pushed Raka over the edge, and he burst from his hiding place, streaking across the open field toward the wounded, infuriated man.

The general was not aware of Raka's presence until it was too late. A brutal blow from Raka's tail rendered his victim unconscious. Raka with his razor-like talons grabbed the general by the collar. With his brute dragon strength, the dragon picked up the general like a ragdoll and flew back to his hiding place. Inside, he threw the general onto a battered table. The stunned man moaned as he struggled back to consciousness. When the general's vision cleared, his eyes grew wide at the sight of the dragon standing above him, foul saliva dripping from the creature's lips fell on his head. "Wha…"

Raka grinned and put one of his talons to his lips. "Shhh, General, not that anyone can hear you in here." He reached out a hand-like claw offering to help the general sit up. Reflexively, the general grasped Raka's nail and struggled to a sitting position. Raka slowly placed his other claw on the general's shoulder. Then, with a ghastly smile, Raka viciously yanked the general's hand and ripped the general's entire arm from its socket. As his victim screamed in terror and agony, Raka regarded the arm thoughtfully. He began to gnaw on it with relish. The general lived long enough to see Raka devour his other arm and start on his legs. He did not live long enough to see Raka transform into a perfect replica of the man he was consuming.

As Raka finished licking the last of the general's blood from the floor, he heaved a contented sigh. He lay down to rest and recover once the transformation was complete. He closed his eyes, reveling in the thoughts of what he could do now as the head of the Aryan Military Council.

* * *

1446 BCE – Egypt

Concealed by the dark of the new moon and disguised as members of the Pharaoh's Imperial Guard, Moses, with his two priests, furtively made his way toward the most sacred sanctuary of the temple of Thebes. His eyes darted here and there as he scanned the corridor. He knew the consequences would be grave—likely deadly—if they were caught in the forbidden area. Even so, he would not be deterred. The stakes were too high. He must secure the holy relics if the Israelites were to have a chance of surviving the exodus from Egypt. Despite the high risk of his task, he found the calming techniques he had learned in his studies assisted him in staying focused and reasonably calm.

The three men clung to the shadows, silently moving along the temple walls from the main sanctuary, crossing the twelve smaller rooms toward the Mother Sanctuary. The scent of sandalwood greeted them as Moses opened the door to the forbidden room and the three slipped inside. The incense and a single lamp burned to clear the sacred chamber from the rituals of the day. Carefully closing the door behind them, Moses wiped the sweat from his brow on the sleeve of his robe, then paused as his eyes adjusted to the dim light. From across the chamber, he could feel the radiant energy of the precious Shamir Stone contained within the golden chest he had been instructed to construct in a dream. He had no idea what the box would be used for, but the vision was so profound that he did not question it for a moment. For now, keeping his people's holy relics in it seemed appropriate, though there was plenty more room inside the chest.

Illuminated by the light of his lamp, statues of men with the heads of beasts, each representing an Egyptian deity, lined the walls on either side of the chamber. Starting with the figure on the right, Moses and his companions bowed low, placing the palms of their hands on top of their feet. They paid their respects to every figure, starting with the wall to the right and moving in order around the temple until they stood before the altar.

As Moses ascended the alabaster steps to the altar, the golden headdress and cloak of the Imperial Guard protected him from the potent and dangerous energies of the God Stone within the chest. Used in the art of healing, the power within the Stone contained all the colors of the spectrum. Only an experienced hierophant of the temple could touch it. An Atlantean priest had inscribed upon the Shamir Stone the whole of the symbolic esoteric teaching throughout the ages of man as well as the force to vanquish any enemy of God.

At one time in his learning, Moses had been in service to the Temple of Isis, where he had learned the ancient Atlantean teachings, language, and hieroglyphics. As he approached the golden chest, he raised the palms of his hands toward it and began to chant the ancient names of God inwardly. With each sacred name, his vibration grew until his wave matched that of the precious God Stone within the chest.

On the altar near the chest was a covering with hieroglyphics meant to keep the stone's energy safely contained within the box when it was transported. Moses, now in harmony with the relic and still chanting, reverently began dressing the golden Ark. To his right, he noticed a small, round, shiny object. Curious, he picked it up. There were twelve small, brilliant gems in two conjoined loops atop the circular device. He could feel the pulsing energy in harmony with that of the stone within the Ark. With no time to determine how—or if—the round device was connected to it, Moses secured the object alongside the golden chest with the threads attached to the covering.

Jehovah said to Moses, "Tell the people of Israel that everyone who wants to may bring me an offering from this list: gold, silver, bronze, blue cloth, purple cloth, scarlet

cloth, fine-twined linen, goat's hair, red-dyed rams' skins, acacia wood, olive oil for the lamps, spice for the anointing oil and for the fragrant incense, onyx stones, stones to be set in the ephod and in the breastplate.

For I want the people of Israel to make me a sacred Temple where I can live among them. This home of mine shall be a pavilion–a Tabernacle."

After Jehovah inspected the building of the temple, He then said to Moses, "Put together the Tabernacle on the first day of the month. In it, place the sacred marble stone, the Ten Commandments; and install the veil to enclose the Ark of the Covenant within the Holy of Holies."

~Exodus 25

A bead of sweat made its way down his forehead as the tension grew within Moses. He knew the neophytes from the temple would soon be coming to begin their day. Turning from the altar, he motioned for the two men to take their places at either end of the chest. Reverently, they approached and grasped the handles, then made their way carefully down the altar steps.

Though outwardly calm, Moses felt as if every fiber of his being was tense and tuned for the sounds of people approaching. The men's disguises would do them little good if anyone saw them carrying the chest. Moses paused at the door and carefully peered down the corridor. The false dawn preceding the morning had not yet appeared. Yet. But Moses knew its arrival was imminent.

Taking another calming breath, Moses motioned for the men to follow him and they retraced their steps. Scant steps away from the archway that opened to the desert and their freedom, the men froze at the sound of movement nearby. A heartbeat later, a rat scurried across the corridor and disappeared into a crack in the stone wall.

Moses let out a breath he had not been aware he had been holding and motioned the men forward through the archway. In moments, they had disappeared into the early morning blackness.

* * *

70 AD – Jerusalem

The Temple Mount was enveloped in flames.

Blood covered the floor and poured down the steps. The number of the slain was inconceivable. There were so many grotesquely butchered bodies littered about that the attacking soldiers had to climb over them as they chased the few locals who still desperately tried to flee, their flickering hopes of survival brutally extinguished at the points of Roman swords and pikes. The sickening-sweet smell of burning flesh and acrid smoke filled the air as the hellish fires engulfed the temple. It seemed as if the whole city was ablaze.

Cloaked on the astral plane, Ezekiel stood in the Atlas, his one-man golden craft, as it circled the ruined city of Jerusalem. The messenger of God gazed through the Crystal Lux Portal, a doorway that opened to the inner dimensions of light. While Judea was in a battle for its life against Rome, the Traveler of Light and Wisdom was on a mission to keep the contents of the Ark of the Covenant safe. Resolute, he tightened his grasp on the controls of the Atlas, knowing he must secure the Ark before it was too late.

Ezekiel had drawn the plans for the Temple of Solomon. He knew in which secret tunnels lay the Ark of the Covenant, the chest Moses had been instructed to construct in a dream. The Holy of Holies had been forty cubits square and lined with gorgeous cedar panels. Now the wood had been reduced to char. There were exquisitely carved figures of cherubim, palm trees, and open flowers overlaid with gold in the chamber, the metal becoming too hot to touch. Chains and bracelets of gold closer to the flames were already melting into puddles of molten metal that leaked through the ruined floor of the

GRACE BLAIR & LAREN BRIGHT

Holy of Holies. Beyond the gaping, charred remnants of the olive-wood door sat the Ark of the Covenant. On the alabaster altar, it lay untouched.

Hidden within the gold-plated acacia chest rested the Shamir Stone. Next to the supernatural God Stone lay the tablets with the Ten Commandments Moses had received from God. The blue cloth covering the twin-winged cherubim was somehow still intact as if protected by a benevolent hand.

Before the Ark stood a living Draco Reptoid, a lean, towering Angel of Darkness. Twelve feet tall, his thin, bony wings furled midway up his back. Between his brow and the top of his skull were two chitinous horns. His burning, red eyes were riveted on the Ark, and an ichorous liquid escaped his lips as he salivated in anticipation. In one swift movement, the dark angel grasped and effortlessly lifted the Ark.

Before the creature could escape, Ezekiel uncloaked the Atlas, exposing its Light from the Holy of Holies. The demonic angel of darkness sneered as he turned, cringing from the Light, as Ezekiel uttered his prayer: "I ask for God's Light of the Holy Spirit to surround, fill, and protect this Ark of the Covenant and all its contents." As if stung, the angel of darkness dropped the Ark, but a beam of light from the Atlas caught it and held it suspended in midair. Raka raised his clawed fist in anger, spitting fire in contempt. His crimson wings unfurling, the dark angel cursed, "I will have the Ark. What I did with Atlantis will be nothing compared to what I can do once I possess it!"

Ezekiel touched the screen activating the Crystal Lux Portal. The holographic Portal opened, and the illumination beam pulled the Ark through the astral door. Distracted, neither Ezekiel nor the dragon saw a small, round brass object with twelve gems tumble from where it had been fastened to the cloth cover of the Ark.

The golden ship vanished as the tiny brass treasure tumbled below the floor into the dark abyss as the temple burned, then collapsed into itself.

Chapter 1
Spring 1885
A Gift

*T*he sun shone brightly, melting away the remnants of the dreary days of the Munich winter. From the arbor on the front porch of the Einstein home, fragrant purple wisteria blossomed. The garden was bursting into a riot of color with red tulips, yellow roses, blue cornflowers, and a multitude of other blossoms of various hues.

Albert had been down the street at his aunt's house. It was 1885, and the family was celebrating his cousin Benjamin's sixth birthday. Albert had turned six the month before and was therefore far worldlier than his "little" cousin, at least to his way of thinking. But he loved his cousin—almost as much as he enjoyed his aunt's apple strudel. In fact, he loved the pastry so much, he ran home after dessert and got sick all over the purple crocuses in his yard.

Pauline Einstein, young Albert's twenty-six-year-old mother, noticed him struggling to climb the porch stairs. Her brow furrowed as she opened the front door. His chubby cheeks flushed, Albert looked up with a sickly gaze and grasped his mother's hand. "Mama, I don't feel good," he moaned. Pauline knelt and kissed his head, then paused, frowning. "Albert, you're burning up!"

She pulled back her long muslin skirt, then scooped the boy into her arms and carried him upstairs to his bedroom. Albert had his own room, a pleasant chamber with tiny-blue-flowered wallpaper.

Albert fussed restlessly as Mama pulled off his necktie, ignoring the smell of sour vomit on his starched white shirt.

As Albert removed his pants, Pauline moistened a cloth from the washbasin and wiped Albert's face and hands. She dressed him in a long cotton nightshirt and tucked him under the covers. Albert fell asleep the second his head hit the goose down pillow. Mama sat in the chair next to his bed and stroked his hair. "Sleep, feel better, mein *liebst*." She stayed with him through the night, wiping his brow every few minutes to cool his fever. Albert slept fitfully, unaware of his mama's loving ministrations.

The next morning, Albert did not join the family for breakfast. Hermann, Albert's father, frowned at the dark circles under Pauline's eyes. "Is Albert doing better?"

Picking at her food, Pauline gave a heavy sigh and shook her head. "I'm worried. Albert has not awakened since yesterday when I put him to bed. His fever is still the same. I'm going to summon Dr. Weiss to examine him."

Upstairs, Albert lay unconscious, his spirit hovering over his bed. Disoriented, he saw his limp body below him. *What's happening to me?* He wondered. He saw a tall, brilliant-winged being at the foot of his bed. "It's all right, Albert. I am Angel Zerachiel." Albert stunned, struggled to find words. He felt a soft, warm glow from the Messenger of Light. The sick boy gazed at the luminous Being and said, "What is an angel?" Angel Zerachiel replied, "Angels are spiritual beings created by God to protect and guide humans. Each angel has a specific task or job." Albert responded, "Oh, do you have a special job too?" Zerachiel smiled, "I am an Angel of Healing. I care for children like you when they get sick.". Albert smiled and relaxed. His new friend was going to help him feel better.

* * *

Twisting the doorknob, Pauline ushered Dr. Klaus Weiss into Albert's room. Albert's spirit and Angel Zerachiel watched dispassionately as Dr. Weiss pulled his spectacles from the inside pocket of his tailored wool suit, pushed them up on his nose, and bent down to inspect the feverish boy.

After a couple minutes of gently poking, prodding, and listening, the doctor straightened and beckoned to Pauline. She moved toward him with a questioning look. "Albert is in the midst of working something through his body," Dr. Weiss stated.

"Is it serious, doctor?" Pauline asked, concern coloring her voice.

The doctor smiled reassuringly. "I don't think so. Give him willow bark for the fever." He took out a pad, uncapped his fountain pen, and spoke aloud as he wrote instructions for Pauline. "Steep about one teaspoon of the dried herb in two cups of boiling water for ten minutes, then strain." He opened his leather medical bag and pulled out a small tin container marked "Willow Bark." He handed the herbal remedy to Pauline. "You can also soothe his head with lavender and chamomile water."

Later that afternoon, Hermann came home early from work. He opened the door, which creaked slightly, and poked his head into the room. Pauline sat in the chair next to Albert's bed, spoon-feeding her son, who was propped up on pillows and looking better, but still quite weak.

Pauline turned at the sound and smiled at her husband. "The herbs Dr. Weiss recommended broke Albert's fever."

Hermann shared a wink with Pauline as he walked into the room and sat on the edge of the bed. He patted Albert's leg under the bedding. "I am so relieved to see you feeling better." Albert raised his tiny hand to acknowledge his papa. He did not remember the angel or leaving his body.

Hermann reached inside his moleskin pants and pulled out a round, brass object on a silver chain. The twelve gems on top glistened in the morning light. He dangled the unique object in the air in front of Albert's face.

Albert's eyes grew wide. "What is that, Papa?"

Hermann smiled, happy to see the illness was not severe enough to dampen Albert's curiosity. "This is a compass, Albert." A quizzical look came over the young boy's face. Hermann opened the brass cover to show Albert how the strange device worked.

Hermann's eyes glowed as he pointed to a thin arrow suspended above the face of the compass. "See this arrow?" Albert nodded, his eyes focused only on the object. "It always points north. This is because the tip is magnetic; it aligns itself with the Earth's magnetic field." Albert nodded, looking even closer. "The compass is for navigation, to help you find your way."

Mesmerized, Albert reached out and grasped the unique device. It felt heavy in his little hands. He twisted, turned, and gently shook it. No matter how he moved it, the needle mysteriously only pointed north. "Where did you get it, Papa?" Albert asked, still staring at the needle.

Hermann smiled. "A new customer, Count von Baden, gave it to me to pay for installing lighting in his castle. The compass has been in his family for many years."

"He must have been reluctant to give up such a treasure, Papa," Albert said, finally tearing his eyes away from the compass.

Hermann shrugged. "It was among a bunch of items he gave us to reduce the price for his job," Hermann said, his eyes twinkling. "And I thought you'd find it interesting." As Albert grinned, Hermann pointed to the cover of the object.

"See the twelve gemstones on top? This is a unique compass. Be sure and keep it safe."

"I will, Papa!" Albert said emphatically, his eyes drawn back to the device as if the magnetic needle pulled them. The excitement of receiving the new gadget gave Albert a spurt of energy, but it soon dissipated. Despite his best effort to continue examining his beautiful compass, Albert fell asleep under his parents' loving gaze.

Pauline reached out and touched Hermann's hand. "What a wonderful gift for Albert. He seems even better since you gave it to him."

Hermann smiled, pleased he was able to lessen his wife's concern.

In his sleep, Albert, too, smiled as he clutched the compass to his heart.

Chapter 2
Fall 1885
A Friend

*A*lbert's father was a partner in his brother Jacob's gas and electric supply company. One day, he took Albert to see an electrical lighting system the company had installed. The customer, Frederick Thomas, owned a local brewery, Munich Brau. The reason Hermann had dragged Albert along was that Thomas had a son, Johann, who was Albert's age. Both boys would soon begin first grade, and Hermann thought it would be good for the shy Albert to know at least one boy in his class.

Albert did not want to go with his father; he preferred the familiar routines at home. Being out in new places caused him to shut off inside. When the boys were introduced, Albert just stared at the floor and went into his own inner world. He thought boys his age were dull. He wanted to be alone.

Hermann forced a smile onto his lips. He reached down and shook Albert's shoulder. "Come, Albert, Johann wants to show you the new lights in the barn."

Albert knew his papa would not like it if he did not do as he suggested, so, reluctantly, his eyes still down, the reluctant guest shuffled over to Johann, wishing he could escape.

Unfazed by Albert's shyness, Johann encouraged him with a broad grin. "Wait 'til you see the lights! C'mon, I'll race you to the barn." Whooping, Johann burst out the kitchen door and ran toward the barn. Albert rolled his eyes. He ambled along, making his way across the yard.

Impatient, Johann bounced on his toes as he waited near the barn door for his guest. When Albert finally arrived, Johann flung open the barn door. Running inside, he jumped up onto a wooden box, reaching for a switch on the wall. "It's amazing to see," he said as he flipped the switch. In a moment, incandescent light flooded the spacious barn. The smell of fresh hay and saddle soap met Albert's nose. He noticed wooden beer barrels, stacked bales of hay, and horse carriages.

Unimpressed by the lighting, Albert pointed to the incandescent bulb and went into lecture mode. "When electrical current passes through a wire, it causes the wire to heat. The wire gets so hot that it glows and gives off light."

Johann looked at Albert in surprise, his blue eyes dancing with amazement. He could not believe what he was hearing. "How do you know that?"

This boy is interested in this? Albert thought to himself. Albert relaxed a bit and began to explain, encouraged that he seemed to have impressed Johann. "Papa takes me to work with him. He teaches me about electricity. He and my uncle want me to learn the lighting business and apprentice with them."

"No kidding?" Johann asked with obvious interest. "Is that what you want to do?"

Albert shrugged. "I don't know. I guess it could be okay."

Johann nodded, becoming thoughtful. "I know what you mean. My papa has plans for my brothers and me to take over the brewery. But I don't know if I want to do that, either." Another smile lit up Johann's face. "Hey, I know. I'll become a great brewer, and you can electrify all my breweries!"

Albert had to smile. Johann's friendliness and enthusiasm were infectious. Without warning, a lightbulb went off in the electrical expert's head. "Wait for a second," Albert said, tugging at a chain around his neck, pulling something out of his linen shirt. "Want to see something exciting?"

"More interesting than electric lights? You bet!" Johann nodded eagerly.

As Albert dangled a brass object on a silver chain, Johann's eyes grew large. "Wow, what is that?"

"It's a compass. My father gave it to me. Have you ever seen one before?"

Shaking his head, Johann guided Albert over to a bale of hay, and the two boys sat. "I haven't," Johann said, mesmerized by the fantastic device. "What does it do?"

Albert held out the gleaming brass compass with the twelve sparkling gems. So, Johann could see it better, he opened the top and rotated the compass. "See how the needle always points north no matter how I move the case?" His bright, brown eyes twinkled as the mystery of the unknown captured his soul. "Someday, I will understand why it does that."

Johann's blue eyes grew even more extensive. Not only had he never seen a compass before, he had never seen anything like it. Amid this fantastic day, Johann paused in thought. He had two older brothers, Francis and Daniel, who worked in the brewery, but they never talked like Albert did. His father, Frederick, a Lutheran, said the Einstein's were Jewish. Maybe that was the reason he knew so much.

Albert surrendered himself to the moment. He found

himself trusting his charming and friendly companion, and he allowed Johann to hold his cherished prize. Johann opened and closed the clasp. "Hey, come on!" said Johann, jumping to his feet. Their eyes glued to the compass, the two boys marched around the barn and watched the needle.

Content with their first parade, they returned to their seats on the hay bale and Johann returned the compass. Albert closed his eyes and held his precious gift to his chest. "Oh, I love my compass, and I love my Papa, who gave it to me." The compass tingled against Albert's chest. From inside the compass, a shimmer of light burst then radiated out about ten inches all around Albert's hand. Albert felt the unexpected warmth and opened his eyes to find a rainbow projecting from the gems. Above the compass floated a three-dimensional number 33. Johann, struck with wonder, squealed, "Look at that!"

Albert threw his hands up in surprise, dropping the compass onto the straw floor.

The boys sat mesmerized for what seemed like an eternity.

Behind them, the barn door opened. Papa Hermann hollered into the barn, "Albert, say goodbye to Johann! Your mama has dinner waiting."

Albert snatched up the enchanted instrument and

looked earnestly at his new friend. "Johann, you must never tell anyone what happened today. You promise?"

Speechless, Johann nodded his compliance.

Bonded by a special secret, neither boy had any inkling what a vital role the compass would play in the adventure of their lives.

Interlude

*O*n the dimension closest to Earth, sometimes called the astral realm, Moses, Ezekiel, Jesus, and Akhenaten floated in deep meditation. Known to those initiated into higher realms of Light as Mystical Travelers, they had gathered in the halls of the Crystal Temple for a sacred purpose.

The thread of Light of the Mystical Travelers on planet Earth dates back from the beginning of time through Egypt and into millennia to come. In the eighteenth dynasty through the reign of Akhenaten, hundreds of years before the time of Christ, evil practices had spread into many of the temples. Akhenaten, with great wisdom, endeavored to wipe out the deception through the worship of one God. Unfortunately, the great Pharaoh met his fate at the hands of Egyptian priests who were not eager to have their power diminished.

The next Mystical Travelers who came to influence events in the world, Moses, and Jesus, had prepared to endure tests of higher initiation. In Light centers and mystery schools around the planet, they studied and taught peace and compassion. The common man of the day could learn while still on Earth how to manifest Christ-consciousness.

As these four travelers meditated, the vibration of Ezekiel's Lux Crystal Portal interrupted the sublime moment, and they paused in the melodic sound of their chanting.

Bringing his awareness to the present moment, Ezekiel frowned and said, "The supernatural power of the Shamir Stone has been activated! How could that be? We contained the Ark of the Covenant at the fall of Jerusalem."

Leaning toward the image in the Portal, Ezekiel saw Albert and Johann playing with a round brass object. Above the relic floated the number 33.

"I think we have a situation to discuss," Ezekiel said thoughtfully. He touched his Portal, and the image of the two boys appeared on the larger screen in front of the room. The four looked at each other in surprise when they saw the 33.

Jesus reflected on the image. "Thirty-three, the number of a master teacher. He will need to develop a sincere devotion to bringing spiritual enlightenment to the world." Jesus could see into Albert's intense, dark eyes and read his essence. "He is a rare child who will be difficult to handle. He will need time and considerable effort to integrate his gift into his personality."

Through the Lux Crystal Portal, Ezekiel searched through the records of time for Albert Einstein. He saw the chaos and confusion spread across the planet as the world struggled with its transition into the industrial age. "Could this be the one to bridge across time and space and bring the theories of Light to mankind?" he wondered.

Ezekiel spoke again to the other travelers. "Albert Einstein was born on the day of infinity, March 14, 1879. Yes, he has the master number 33."

Moses considered the scene with the boys. "And he has a Shamir Stone? I thought we possessed the only remnant of that. What happened?"

On his Lux Crystal Portal, Ezekiel replayed his mission to rescue the Ark of the Covenant for the travelers.

Moses scrutinized the images on the Portal. In a moment, he pointed. "There, did you see a bright flash? Something fell out of the Ark."

"It looks like the same object that this boy has," Ezekiel said. "What is it?"

Moses cleared his throat, and the Light masters turned their gaze to him. "When I took the Ark from the temple, I found a round object with twelve gems on its top. I had no time to investigate it, but it was resonating with the relics in the Ark I had built."

Jesus raised his eyebrow. "Resonating?"

Moses nodded, "Yes. I didn't know what it was, but I believed it best to keep with our holy treasures."

Akhenaten's eyes widened in surprise. "Did you investigate this object?"

Moses shook his head. "I meditated on it from time to time, but it was not emanating the energy of the Shamir."

Jesus nodded. "Well, it is radiating a form of that energy now."

Ezekiel turned from his Portal with a sigh. "Apparently, there is a dormant fragment of the Shamir hidden in this compass device. It would only come awake when in contact with a being who was destined to have it."

Now Akhenaten frowned. "But the supernatural power of the Shamir Stone comes from those who live in the dimensions of Light far beyond Earth or this realm. The secret of building the mighty pyramids is within such a precious stone. This is not something to be taken lightly."

Jesus nodded. "We need to watch and protect the stone—and this young Albert Einstein."

Ezekiel agreed. "The forces of darkness will become aware of this, as we have. There is a being who has dedicated himself to acquiring the Shamir and using its power toward his own ends. Should he succeed..." Ezekiel knew he did not have to tell the travelers how disastrous that would be.

Chapter 3
The Dark Lord

On a dank underground cavern deep below Basel Germany's the Black Forest, Raka stirred. The instant the number 33 had appeared above Albert's compass, the power emanating from the device had awakened him from his centuries of slumber. His beady, red eyes began to glow as he came into consciousness, and his reptilian nostrils dilated as he tasted the air. The scent brought a smile to his lips, baring razor-sharp teeth. His eyes widening in disbelief, he shook his bony, horned head.

Not since the fall of Jerusalem had the twelve-foot angel of darkness smelled such power. "The Shamir Stone! It's been so long..."

The fallen dark angel yearned for vengeance, not just on his youthful nemesis, but also on Arka, his brother, who had become a high priest in Atlantis. Raka scowled at the thought of how Arka had so severely undermined his progress in Atlantis before he had taken on his dragon form.

Raka chuckled then, as his thoughts turned to how he had masterminded the destruction of Atlantis. *The priests of Light never saw it coming.* Wielding the giant six-sided Firestone crystal in the Temple of Light, it was he who caused the disintegration of the entire continent. *It felt good to beat my brother—and THEM—that day.*

Pulling himself from the stone slab upon which he had been sleeping, Raka began pacing as he considered the present. With a deep longing for the sacred stone, he sighed, "To get the Shamir I will have to blend in." He shuddered as he realized what that meant. *I will have to appear... human!* He thought, his mind spitting out the last word as if it had a foul taste.

With the supernatural stone of the ancients, Raka would rule the world. The deep, depraved, primal need impelled him to fight, destroy, and kill to acquire the power of the Stone of Light. *I've made many attempts, only to be thwarted by those Light Travelers and the restrictions of God's Law.* Determination building within him, the angel of darkness shrugged off his anger.

As powerful as he was, Raka knew there were constraints. While anything was possible, not everything was permitted, and if he violated the cosmic law, there would be a terrible price for him to pay. He knew he would have to be patient and plan well. Immortality released him from some of the chains that bound his human nemeses.

Rubbing his jaw, Raka began plotting.

Chapter 4
Raka's Transformation

*T*he headline in the *Stuttgart Zeitung* newspaper read,

LOCAL MAN MISSING

A search is underway for a young man who has disappeared in the Black Forest community of Stuttgart, southeast of Munich. He was last seen walking to university. The Black Forest Police have mounted an extensive search, though an early winter storm is expected to bring up to two inches of snow and freezing temperatures.

With a contented sigh, Raka wiped the last of the blond man's blood from his jaw. He had gorged on the bright, pure essence of a young human to step up his energetic matrix, which had degraded when he had become reptilian.

Raka had been surreptitiously observing the locals for weeks now, learning modern ways and studying their language. During that time, he had found an abandoned shack and furnished his cave with things inside of it that he would need when in human guise: a chair, table, and bed. In the dead of night, he had broken into the home of a well-to-do bachelor and relieved the puny human of some of his garments as he slept. Now, having consumed a human to regenerate the needed DNA, he was finally ready to make his transformation.

With a shudder, then a lurch, he began to shift. The claws of his feet became soft as human toes appeared. Hairy male legs replaced his stubby reptilian hind appendages, and his tail receded back into his body. Scales from his torso, arms, and neck melted into pink flesh. His long, slithery tongue withered until it could extend a scant inch or two beyond his lips. As he morphed, his airways constricted, and he grabbed at his throat, gasping for air. Writhing in ecstatic agony, then surrendering to the pain of bone, sinew, and flesh reconfiguring itself, he collapsed to the ground. Naked, he lay as motionless as death as he recovered from the ordeal.

Sometime later, Raka woke crunched in a fetal position and took in a breath. He had not been in human form for a very long time.

He slowly opened his eyes. The candlelight in the cave seemed dim to his human senses. Raka rolled onto all fours, then straightened his back, so he was kneeling on the hard rock of the cave floor. He explored his new weak and wingless form with soft, fleshy hands. He felt vulnerable. His appraisal complete, he gathered the strength of the anemic body and stood. The blood rushed from his head, and he stumbled sideways. He flung out an arm, seeking support, and braced himself on the cave wall, then staggered to a tattered armchair and sat with a thud.

The resulting cloud of dust set him coughing, and he cursed the frailty of humans. After a moment, he forced himself to stand again. This time, he maintained his equilibrium. No time to waste; he must dress and get going!

As a changeling, he was still able to keep the reptile glands in his throat. Rubbing them stimulated his adrenaline and made him feel powerful. He spat on his hand and smelled with delight the pungent reptilian saliva. "Potent as ever," he assessed, somewhat reassured.

Near the chair was a single bed with his new clothes. Struggling to master the musculature of this form he had not occupied for so long, he put on the pants, shirt, and jacket "liberated," and nodded in satisfaction as he slightly lengthened his legs and shortened his arms, so the garments fit perfectly. He also decided to alter his facial structure just enough that he would not be taken for the young man whose body he now inhabited. He had no interest in encountering people the fellow had known.

Completing his transformation and putting on the last of his clothing, Raka prepared for his first foray in this incarnation. He had no idea of how to knot the ridiculous piece of cloth humans called a necktie, so he stuffed it into his inside jacket pocket. Frowning, he muttered, "The dress of the Egyptians was simple. I hate these confining things."

The thought of Egypt reminded Raka of how he had manipulated Pharaoh Akhenaten's court. He smiled as he remembered deceiving the priests by promising them power if they would abandon the prophet of the One God. He recalled the delight he had experienced watching the duplicitous fools, Akhenaten's closest friends, murder the Egyptian king while he meditated.

Bringing himself out of his reverie, Raka went over to a wooden chest that contained one of his most prized possessions. It was something he'd had fabricated in another time and place, during one of his earlier forays in human form. Opening the finely crafted box, he picked up an ornate walking stick. Its handle was a dragon head of pure gold. A pair of flawless rubies was crafted to make fierce, glowing eyes, not unlike his own when he was in reptilian form.

The stick not only steadied him as he walked but had a hollow chamber hidden in its tip. Should he press on the ruby eyes in a certain way, the stick would transform into a weapon that would eject needles coated with his reptilian venom into his victim. He nodded in satisfaction at the craftsmanship. He had paid a fortune for the piece, but it was well worth it.

By human standards, he was a handsome blond male in his early thirties. Donning an ebony Homburg hat, Raka gazed at himself in the mirror near the bed. Familiarizing himself again with the muscles of his stubby human tongue, he practiced the new language.

When he felt he had mastered the new words, he went through the entire performance. His charismatic blue eyes twinkling, he touched his Homburg with his right hand. In flawless German, he spoke the greeting he had observed. "Hello, my name is Rudolf. How do you do?"

Raka grunted in satisfaction with his accomplishment. He was ready for his mission. Tilting his head, the dark angel sniffed to discern the scent of the Shamir Stone's power. In just a moment, he had identified the direction and set off at a brisk walk.

He reminded himself that his mission could take years. After all, there were cosmic laws that had to be observed. It wasn't as if he could just locate the Shamir, murder its possessor, and walk away. No, the ways of the universe were not quite that simple.

No matter. Raka would amuse himself meddling in the affairs of these humans until he could manipulate things to his advantage.

He could be patient. After all, he had... all the time in the world.

Chapter 5
Spring 1891
Triangles

*U*ncle Jakob found the twelve-year-old Albert sitting at the kitchen table, drawing triangles, again. Jacob was the youngest of five siblings.

Unlike Albert's father, Hermann, Jakob had been able to pursue higher education and had qualified as an engineer. Hermann had not resented his brother's opportunity, and together the two brothers built a successful company providing generators and electrical lighting to municipalities in southern Germany. Jakob oversaw the technical side while Hermann handled sales. Perhaps more essential to the partnership, Hermann was able to secure loans from his wife's side of the family.

Jakob's training and knowledge were regularly put to the test by Albert, who had an inexhaustible supply of questions. One day he was asking for details on how the generators worked. Then he had to know about the capacity of the wires that ran to the lighting fixtures. Most of all, Albert wanted to learn about light. But recently, geometry had become his focus.

"I see geometric shapes have captured your attention, nephew."

Albert nodded, his bright eyes eager. "Somehow, triangles seem to blend nature and science. I even see geometric designs in the flowers in the garden."

Jakob raised an eyebrow as he pulled up a chair across from his precocious nephew. "Hmm. Well, have you ever heard of Pythagoras?"

Albert reflected for a moment. "The name is familiar," he said hesitantly. "But I don't remember who he is." The look on Albert's face let Jakob know Albert wanted to know more.

Leaning forward, the learned man explained, "Pythagoras was a Greek mathematician who lived between 569 and 475 BC. He is sometimes called the first mathematician, meaning he was one of the first scientists on record to have made significant contributions to the field of mathematics." As Albert nodded, Jakob continued. "He was more than just a mathematician, though; he studied and worked with religion and philosophy. What's more, he was also a musician; he played the lyre."

Albert's hazel eyes danced with curiosity. "Now that's a man I would like to know more about!"

Jakob smiled and beckoned Albert to follow him to a nearby bookcase. After searching for a moment, he pulled a small book from the shelf and handed it to the boy. "When I saw you drawing triangles the other day, I knew it would not be long before you would want to explore the mystery of Pythagoras and his theories."

Albert grabbed the book and marched back to the table. He did not even notice Uncle Jakob had left, smiling and shaking his head. "Give that boy a book, and it is like tossing a sponge into a pail of water. He absorbs every drop of knowledge," he muttered to himself walking out the door.

The house was quiet as a church as Albert lost himself in the book on Pythagoras. Warm summer winds blew the yellow cotton curtains, and they flapped through the open window over the kitchen sink. The young mathematician's feet dangled from the wood-and-thatched chair at the rectangular table topped with butcher block. As he read, he began to realize that his uncle Jakob had given him his first real intellectual puzzle. Deep in thought, Albert was unaware that he had almost chewed through his pencil as he stared at the diagram of a right triangle. His eyebrows drawing closer and closer together as he read,

Albert became determined to prove the Pythagorean theorem.

Losing himself in his contemplation, Albert absent-
mindedly began playing with his compass as he turned
pages in the book. He would read a few paragraphs and
then gaze at the compass face, letting his mind wander in
speculation. There was no way for him to know that the
energy of the compass took his mind beyond space and
time. Albert was far away, and unaware of where he was
as triangles of all shapes and sizes danced in his imagination. He was determined to meet this challenge and prove
the theory. Albert did not tell anyone what he was working on.

By the second week of intense focus, Albert's theories
were swirling round and round in his head. Finally, on a
Friday, wild with excitement, he sat filling a sheet of paper
with cryptic drawings and numbers so furiously, the pencil lead broke. His hand twitching, he stared at the torn
paper and broken pencil. He screamed, wadded up the
paper with his shaking hands and threw it across the
room. The budding scientist put his head down on the
table and sobbed.

His mother, Pauline, rushed from the stove where she
had been stirring the stew for the evening dinner. With a
glance, she surmised what had happened. She knelt and

put a comforting arm across her son's shoulder. "Now, now, Albert. It's okay."

Albert turned and buried himself in his mother's hug. "It's not okay, Mama. There is a way to prove this theorem, but I can't find it." His face was still pinched with anger as he spoke.

Pauline thought for a moment, then brightened. "You need a break. Do something else."

"Like what, Mama?"

Pauline shrugged. "I don't know. Maybe play your violin. You know how music soothes you and clears your head."

Gently tugging at the frowning boy, Pauline urged him from his seat. "Come, Albert. Invite Johann. The two of you could practice the Mozart Sonata for the recital at school next month."

Albert didn't want to see anyone. He was stuck. He was getting nowhere. His mother's words reminded him how the family loved the recitals the two of them played during the holidays and how music lifted his spirits. And it was true that he did enjoy it when Johann joined in from time to time. Sighing in resignation, the young mathematician surrendered. "Oh, all right, I will go and get Johann."

* * *

"Wow, did your pet goldfish die or something, Albert? You look terrible!" Johann shook his head in disapproval as his friend led him through the front door.

Despite himself, Albert had to smile at Johann's cheerfulness. "Ah, I'm just stuck on a problem and don't know how to get out of it." Albert waved his arm as if to brush away his vexation. He was still hiding his mission and didn't even want his good friend to know what he was pursuing. Albert ushered Johann into the parlor. "My mother thinks taking a break will help. We need to practice for the recital, anyway."

Used to Albert's moods, Johann nodded. "Okay, I can practice for an hour. My father needs me at the alehouse to help serve the evening meal." He wiped his hands on his lederhosen and sat on the wooden piano bench, his legs stuffed under the piano, and shuffled the sheet music on the music stand. Albert had already memorized the piece, so he readied his violin as he stood next to Johann.

After fifteen minutes of stops and starts to refine their duet, the notes sparkled. The music's sweetness began to seep into Albert's troubled heart. He closed his eyes and, like fireworks, a burst of triangles within the notes flew in rhythm across his violin. His imagination blossomed and flowed with new ideas as Albert opened to new dimensions inside himself.

After another thirty minutes of playing, Albert had regained a sense of peace—as well as a new enthusiasm for his project. Albert began to fidget with his brow. He urged Johann to his feet and helped him on with his jacket. "It's good, Johann, we're ready for our recital," Albert pronounced, propelling Johann to the door.

Attempting to straighten his jacket amid the hustle, Johann said, "Well, I guess we are ready." Then Johann dug in his feet and turned to Albert, hiding a grin. "But are you sure you wouldn't like to practice a few more times? I could stay a couple more minutes..."

"No, no, I am certain we are ready. Hurry up now, I don't want you to be late for work," Albert replied, almost slamming the door shut and utterly oblivious to the fact that Johann knew precisely what Albert was up to. On the porch, Johann smiled and shook his head as he turned to walk back to the alehouse. He had grown to love Albert and, truth be told, he was happy that his friend had regained his happiness.

With the breakthrough in awareness he had gained when he and Johann had been playing the Mozart piece, Albert became more confident as he worked over the next days. And with the confidence came serenity. The boy would awaken each morning with awareness of the music of the Pythagorean theorem dancing in his imagination. It was as if he was viewing the mathematics of it in its completeness from high above. And he knew he would find its temporarily elusive proof.

Chapter 6
Spring 1894
A Miracle

*D*eep in thought, Johann watched the twilight sky all but oblivious to the cookie he was slowly munching on.

The fresh summer breeze fluttered across the azure canopy of the Bavarian Alps. It was that ethereal moment when day transformed into night. Space and time seemed to expand as the sun made its steady, stately descent. Pastel purple clouds gave way to gray against the darkening skies. Like diamonds, thousands upon thousands of tiny sparkles—planets and stars—slowly made their evening appearance, emerging with the fading light.

From the bright field of stars, Johann's eyes sought the constellations in the Milky Way. He spotted the belt of Orion overhead, and then he found the Big Dipper, which led him to the North Star. Brightest of the lights,

Polaris pointed the way to the true north. On the gas-lantern-lit porch of the inn, the dreamy young sky watcher, lost in the vast night, slowly put his cookie to his mouth and took another barely noticed bite.

Two monks walked by on their way to evening Mass at the Andechs Monastery Brewery. Summer was a favorite time for the people of Munich to visit the Hermitage. They would hike or take the hour train ride up the mountain. The tenth-century beer garden was a beautiful destination in the warm weather. A liter of beer and a lunch of roast pork with sauerkraut gave visitors an added something to talk about when they got back home.

The door of the inn slammed behind Johann, jarring him out of his reverie. Albert had an inquiring look on his face as he strode over to his friend. "Are you going to the church service with your parents?"

"Um, no... I don't know. Maybe. Do you want to go?" replied Johann, who struggled to gather his thoughts.

Albert frowned, sensing something was going on with his friend. "What's wrong, Johann?"

Johann brushed cookie crumbs from his chin. "Nothing," he said as he examined his shoes.

Albert kept his mouth shut and just stared at Johann, patiently waiting.

Johann squirmed for a moment, then sighed. "When a boy in the Thomas family reaches sixteen, he has to do a month-long apprenticeship at the brewery in this monastery. The monks have been brewing beer for centuries, so I guess the idea is that we can learn a lot." He paused and looked up at his friend. "And you know I turned sixteen last month."

Albert thought for a moment; then he got the picture. "Oh, it's like when Jewish boys turn thirteen and have a bar mitzvah. It's a rite of passage into manhood."

Johann looked away into the distance as if he was looking for his future. "Yeah, but what if I don't want to work for my father in the brewery? What if I want to do something different?" Realizing what he'd just revealed, Johann quickly turned to Albert. "You won't tell anyone, will you? I mean, I feel I have to do this apprenticeship for my family, but..."

Albert shook his head. "Of course not." He plopped himself onto the bench next to Johann. "You never said you didn't want to work in the family business before. What's changed?"

Johann turned away from his friend, searching for another cookie in his pockets. Food made him feel better when he was anxious. Food made him feel better on almost any occasion. "I don't know," he mumbled around the new cookie he was stuffing into his mouth. Albert's gaze hardened.

"It's just that... well... I've been thinking..."

Albert nodded encouragingly, and Johann blurted out his dilemma. "I think I might want to pursue religious studies." Johann waited expectantly as Albert digested the surprise revelation.

After a moment, Albert smiled. "If that's what is calling to you, I think you should talk to your parents about it."

"Really?" Johann said, visibly relieved. "You don't think it's crazy?"

Albert shook his head, a severe look on his face. "I don't know what I'd do if my parents insisted I go into the family electronics business. I mean, I know they'd like me to do that, but they are very tolerant of my curiosity."

"Well, you're sure lucky. I don't think my parents are ready to hear that I may not want to get involved with the brewery."

Albert gave Johann's arm an encouraging squeeze. "The good news is, you don't have to make a final decision now. I'd say just to go ahead with your apprenticeship, so you get an excellent taste of what being in the business will involve."

Johann considered his friend's advice as Albert continued. "You might find you learn something that captures your interest. But at least you'll know from your experience, and not just what you think it might be like."

Johann started nodding. "You're the best, Albert. That really makes sense. I'm delighted you came with us," he said, smiling for the first time in the entire day. Relieved of his worry, at least for the present, Johann perked up. "Hey, did you bring your compass?"

Albert brightened at the question. "Of course, I have my compass. Why?"

"The monks at the brewery have their annual treasure hunt tomorrow. Guys our age will be competing, and I signed us up. There'll be a lunch buffet afterward, too," he added, never one to pass up a good meal. "I bet your compass will give us an edge!"

"Could be," Albert said thoughtfully. "A treasure hunt, eh? Interesting."

* * *

A crowd gathered on the east side of the Ammer Lake Holy Mountain. The early morning sun broke over the summit. Five Benedictine monks passed out papers with instructions to the hunters. The scavenger hunt would begin at 9:00 a.m.

The dark-haired, blue-eyed, thirtyish monk, Dr. Peter Collins, stood on a step stool in his brown monk's habit. Looking out over the crowd, he cleared his throat and in a loud, enthusiastic voice shouted, "Good morning, everyone! Welcome to our annual scavenger hunt commemorating the feast day of Mary Magdalene. Today you will be seeking replicas of ancient relics in our monastery, one of which is that of the venerable saint herself!"

Johann surveyed the crowd from the middle of the pack and guessed there were about thirty or so; fifteen teams of two boys each. He, of course, was paired with Albert, who held the piece of paper they'd been given when they arrived that morning.

Johann noticed that the bully, Werner von Wiesel, was at the center of a group of his toadies—boys who sucked up to him because his father, a retired Prussian Army colonel, was considered an "important citizen" of Munich. From Johann's perspective, Werner was just a spoiled rich kid. But for some reason, he seemed to have it in for Albert. He rarely passed up an opportunity to give Albert a hard time.

As Johann reflected on Werner, the brother continued. "Each team has an instruction sheet with a map of the area. At the bottom of the map, you will see that there is a list of map coordinates and clues that relate to some of the monastery's relics." Then he looked up with a mischievous smirk. "However, to make things interesting, not all coordinates or clues apply to the relics we have placed out for this hunt."

"How many relics are there, Brother Peter?" Werner wanted to know.

The monk's smirk broadened into a grin. "Well, if we told you that, Werner, it would take away some of the fun." The boys groaned.

"When you find a relic, we want you to write what that relic is next to the clue that hints at it. Do not touch or remove what you find. We want everyone to have a chance to complete the hunt."

The monk looked down and consulted his notes, then continued his spiel. "When you have located all the relics you can find and noted their locations on your map, bring your entry form to the dining hall. One of our brothers will take it and record your time."

The abbot, looking very serious, said, "Since I'm sure you will have built up quite an appetite on your quest, you all will be treated to a hearty lunch." He smiled and nodded as the resulting cheers dissipated.

"The winner will be based on the number of relics you find, the accuracy of your notes on the relics you have identified, and the speed with which you found them."

"What will I be winning this year, Brother Peter?" Werner haughtily called out.

The monk waited for the catcalls and jeering to stop, then said, "We're not revealing the prize in advance, Werner, so you'll just have to wait to find out."

After the predictable grumbling, the monk asked, "Okay, any questions?"

"Enough talking! Let's get started!" Werner hollered impatiently. The monk held up his hands and frowned at Werner. "Hold your horses, Werner. We want to make sure everyone knows what they need to know."

Werner scowled and glared, looking threateningly around the room. Many of the boys cringed at Werner's anger, and no one dared ask a question.

The monk waited, then, hearing no questions, nodded. "Okay then. Gentlemen, you may begin!"

Most of the boys rushed off on the hunt. Werner managed to bump into Albert as he rushed by, nearly knocking him over. "Oops, *sorry*, Einstein," he sneered insincerely as Albert regained his balance.

Though they were as eager as the rest of the boys to start their search, instead of rushing off aimlessly, Albert and Johann trotted over to the green lawn next to the monastery's central walkway and sat down. Albert wanted to approach the hunt rationally. He laid the map on the grass and took out his precious compass.

"What are you going to do with the compass, Albert?" Johann wanted to know.

"I'm not sure, but I felt like it might help us focus on the clues and where we want to go," he replied as Johann settled himself next to him, watching with interest.

Albert opened the top of the gem-encrusted compass and set it on the map as he considered the layout. The morning rays were reflecting on the device's face. Looking at the map and then the topography of the surroundings, Albert tried to determine where they needed to go. He pointed to the chart and said, "The first set of coordinates is 47.58 north 11.118 east, but it's not clear exactly where that is."

As Albert spoke the coordinates, a beam of violet light suddenly shot out of the compass, extending to a point on the map. Both boys gasped in shock. They could not believe what they saw!

Johann gulped and whispered, "What was that?"

Albert could only stare as the light disappeared. Then he closed his eyes and rubbed his temples as if he was trying to ease an ache. "I have no idea. It's scientifically not possible."

Johann regained his wits and grabbed Albert's arm. "Yeah, but it happened. If it's scientifically impossible, then it must be magic!"

Albert shook his head as if to clear the thought from his mind. "I can't say it's magic..." Then Albert brightened. "But whatever it is, it's given us a destination. Let's go!" He scooped up the compass and the map and scrambled to his feet.

Spurred by their desire to win the competition, the two adventurers scampered down from the mountain church into a grove of fir trees. As they walked, Albert's gaze was drawn to a young woman dressed in a red cloak near the edge of the trees. Her dark eyes radiated pleasant warmth as she beckoned him to follow her. For a moment, Albert's eyes met hers, and Albert jerked as if he had been jolted by a bolt of electricity. The woman smiled and motioned again.

Albert could only stare for a moment, speechless. Then, gathering his wits, he pointed and said to Johann, "I... I think that woman wants us to follow her!"

"What woman?" replied Johann, looking around.

To Albert, Johann was looking right at the woman. He paused, then said, "Never mind. Just follow me," as he started off after the woman.

"Uh, right," Johann agreed, a very puzzled look on his face.

The boys hiked through a meadow of brightly colored flowers and thick wild grasses. Their mysterious guide glided ahead of them, then stopped at a whitewashed picket fence. She pointed to a cluster of white, purple, and red roses inside the enclosure. "She wants us to go in there," Albert said. His heart seemed to swell as her gaze crossed over him.

Frowning in bewilderment, Johann swung open the garden gate and stepped onto a pathway that led to the center of the rose garden. There was a red flag on a thin pole that reached over the rose bushes. Near the marker was a single gold rose laying on a mahogany bench, the sun's rays glistening off its metal petals.

Albert approached it, making sure he didn't disturb it. "Looks like we've found our first relic," he said, handing the map to Johann. "Which of the clues does the gold rose to go with?"

Johann scanned the clues. "Hmm. I've been studying the relics of the monastery, so let's see if my work was worth it." Moving his finger down the clue list, Johann suddenly stopped. "Here!" he said, poking the paper. The clue read, "The founder's prize." Johann nodded to himself. "The gold rose belonged to the founder of the monastery, Duke Albrecht," he said, writing: "Albrecht's gold rose in the rose garden" next to the clue.

"Good work, Johann!" Albert said approvingly.

Johann nodded and looked up from the map. "Thanks. But your compass sure played its part. Have you used it for directions before today?"

Albert shook his head. "I don't need a compass to get around Munich, so there's been no need. That's one of the reasons I was looking forward to this trip—to test it out. Uh, and of course, to spend some time with my best friend," he added with a grin. "This treasure hunt is a fantastic exercise—a real experiment in a controlled environment." Albert scratched his head. "But I have to say, I was as surprised as you were when I opened the compass and that beam of light shot out of it."

"So that's not what usually happens with compasses?" Johann asked, pretty sure he knew the answer.

"Not by a long shot," Albert responded, his dark eyes sparkling with delight.

"Well, let's open the map and see if the compass helps with the next clue," Johann suggested.

"Right," Albert agreed his curiosity now in high gear. This time, he was ready to observe the phenomenon, if it happened again.

Albert carefully opened the map on the opposite end of the mahogany bench from where the golden rose sat. He laid the compass on it and picked another set of coordinates at random. "How about 47.964 north, 11.202 east." For a moment, nothing happened, and Albert thought the first instance must have been a fluke. Then, the compass lit up and projected a thin beam of violet light to a point on the map.

"Oh. My. Gosh," Albert gasped.

Johann shook his head in awe. "How does it do that, Albert?"

"I have no idea! There isn't a power source, yet the light radiates out when I say the coordinates. That's... just...not...possible."

"Yeah, but it happened...again!" Johann tugged on Albert's arm. "Come on. We've got a scavenger hunt to win!"

Carefully closing the compass, Albert let his friend lead him toward where the compass had indicated the next relic would be. As the two adventurers made their way through the countryside, Albert saw the woman in red nearby. She appeared to be waiting for them. Albert closed his eyes and shook his head. He opened them to find her still smiling, inviting them to follow her. As before, Albert felt a tingling all over when the woman in red was nearby. It was hard to describe—a sort of joyfulness that overcame him upon seeing her. "Johann, there's that woman in red again. She wants us to follow her."

"Really? Where?" Johann turned left, then right, following Albert's lead.

"Over there."

"If you say so." Johann headed in the direction where Albert was pointing.

"When we get back to the hall, I'm going to ask one of the monks if there's a woman that looks like her living around here."

"Good idea," Johann nodded. "She sure seems to know about the treasure hunt and where the relics are."

Johann stuck close to Albert as they followed the woman through wheat fields and lush, green grounds. Finally, they came to a pristine, crystal pond. Tall, willowy pine trees and wild blueberry bushes lined the shore on its far side. Johann pointed to a blue flag near one of the trees. "There!"

"I see it," Albert responded, his heart racing and picking up his pace, not registering that the woman in red was now nowhere to be seen. Next, to the flag, they found a miniature pine decorated like a Christmas tree. Albert scratched his head. "A Christmas tree in July?"

Johann read the clue on the treasure map: "What did St. Nicholas add to the celebration of Christmas?" Looking at Albert with a smirk, he said, "That's easy! St. Nicholas started using a tree in the holiday festivities. There are several relics of his in the monastery."

"Hmm, interesting," Albert said clapping his partner on the back as Johann wrote the answer: "St. Nicholas's tree near the pond,'" next to the clue.

"Thanks to the compass and your invisible lady, we're two for two." Johann reached for a piece of cake he'd stuffed into the pocket of his lederhosen before they left. He unwrapped it from its cloth napkin and offered his friend a bite "So, what do you say we stop for a minute and rest?"

Albert firmly grasped Johann's wrist and shook his head. "Not until we've spotted all the relics. You can *rest*," Albert emphasized, "when we have completed the course and beaten everyone back to the hall." He placed the map atop a boulder near the sandy shore and carefully set the compass on it. Picking another set of coordinates, he said them aloud.

Nothing happened. Johann and Albert both blinked and stared at the compass. Albert spoke the coordinates again—this time more slowly and clearly. The boys waited. Nothing. The compass did nothing.

"I guess we've lost our edge," Johann shrugged.

"Wait, Johann, the abbot, told us not all the clues were useful. Let's give the compass another chance." Albert scanned the map and picked another set of coordinates. "Find 47.968 north, 11.194 east."

After only the briefest pause, the compass beamed a tiny light to a point on the map. Johann's face lit up. "You were right! Come on!" Johann yanked Albert's sleeve. It was all Albert could do to snatch up the compass and map before Johann had him hurrying off in the new direction.

As the boys marched past the tree line, Albert once again saw the woman in red a short distance away. She pointed to a farmhouse down the road, but as Albert and Johann stepped closer, she evaporated into thin air. Albert froze in his tracks, but Johann just kept walking as if nothing had happened. *Of course,* Albert realized, *Johann can't see our mysterious guide…only I can.*

The boys walked down a narrow, dusty road toward the farmhouse. It was a long, red-brick-and-timber-framed house about 15 meters long. Behind the house, several chickens scratched in the yard. A green flag stood next to the chicken coop. As the boys approached the flag, they saw a short, wooden stool. On the seat, in a woven basket trimmed with fresh moss, sat a single red egg.

Albert smiled to see the flag. "Okay, this must be it." He paused and wrinkled his brow. "But what kind of relic is a red egg?"

Johann smirked. He liked knowing things Albert did not. It was undoubtedly a rare occurrence. "The red egg was a present Mary Magdalene gave Emperor Tiberius. She brought him a white egg to signify the birth of Christ. When he saw the egg, he laughed and said, 'I will believe it represents the Christ when the egg turns red.' As Mary Magdalene extended the egg to the emperor," Johann continued, "it turned red."

"Really?" said Albert, not quite sure what to make of this story.

"Uh-huh," Johann nodded, taking the map and writing: "Mary Magdalene's red egg in farmyard" next to a clue that said, "What convinced Tiberius?"

"Well, I don't know about the story," Albert said, "but I'm sure glad your secret studies included the relics of the monastery. I would have had no idea which relic matched what clue."

Johann blushed at the praise, "Thanks for saying so, Albert. But let's keep going with the hunt."

Albert agreed and spread open the map. He placed the compass on it. Johann pointed to one of the coordinates, and Albert read the numbers aloud. Nothing emitted from the compass. Albert repeated the coordinates, and when there was no response again, he quickly learned through the few remaining coordinates. Each time, the compass remained unresponsive.

Johann frowned. "Do you think the compass is broken, Albert?"

"Could be, but I think it's more likely that we have found all the clues."

"That sort of makes more sense, I guess," Johann conceded. "If that's the case, then let's head back to the dining hall."

"Right." Albert carefully folded the map. "We did this together, and I want us to win."

Johann smiled. "We did it together."

* * *

Albert peered into the dining hall. His heart sank. The place was bustling with the boys who had been on the treasure hunt. It looked like he and Johann were the last to return. Being competitive by nature, Albert had really wanted to win. As they entered, Werner looked up from his lunch from across the hall. "About time you finally made it back, losers," he sneered.

Johann grimaced and started to respond, but Albert put his hand on Johann's shoulder. "Don't pay any attention to him, Johann. He's just a jerk."

A smiling monk near the door greeted Albert and Johann. "Congratulations for completing the hunt." He lifted a silver chain and checked his pocket watch. Nodding at the time, he recorded it next to Johann and Albert's names.

"I wonder if you could answer a question for me," Albert asked the monk,

The kind monk's hazel eyes sparkled. "Of course, my friend, what would you like to know?"

"Well, I saw a young woman in the forest." Albert's thoughts raced as he tried to make sense of what he had seen. "She had dark hair and brown eyes. She might have been in her twenties. My friend didn't see her, but I would like to thank her. It was kind of her to help us find the relics."

The brother stared straight at Albert, his eyes narrowing slightly. Albert squirmed.

"Dark hair, you say?"

"Yes. Oh, and she was wearing a red cloak."

The monk frowned. "Dark hair, brown eyes, and a red cloak. Perhaps olive skin?"

Albert nodded. "Uh, right."

The monk's brow furrowed, and he knelt to Albert's level. "Please tell me your name. The abbot will want to hear of this."

Have I done something wrong? Albert wondered. "My name is Albert Einstein. I am visiting with my friend Johann and the Thomas family." He pointed toward Johann, who was a few steps away eyeing a table generously laden with food.

"Of course, I know the Thomas family," the monk said, putting his hand on Johann's shoulder. "I understand you will be doing your internship here soon."

"Yes, sir," Johann nodded.

The gentle brother directed the boys toward the massive table at the head of the room near a podium. Nearby, two long tables with benches on either side of them were filled with the boys from the treasure hunt.

"Enjoy the lunch we've put out for you. You've earned it." Eyeing the spread, Johann began to cheer up. "In the meantime," the monk continued, "we will check each of the maps and announce the winners of the hunt in just a little while."

Johann dragged Albert to the food table, and the boys filled their plates. Albert had to admit that covering all that ground in the treasure hunt had given him an appetite. Johann ate with gusto, but Albert's enthusiasm was dampened by his disappointment at returning so late. He felt they had little chance of winning. Albert was also a bit concerned at the monk's suspicious and puzzling response to his question about the woman in red. Glancing down the length of the long table, he saw Werner holding court with many of the boys. Albert shook his head, as he watched the other boys play up to the loudmouth.

Lifting a bite of sausage to his lips, Albert considered the woman in red. He could not deny the intense feeling of connection and joy when his eyes met hers. Albert munched on his cheese and sausage, lost in thought.

Just as the boys were finishing up, a hush fell over the room. Albert and Johann saw the smiling monk and another man with an ornate necklace hanging in front of his robe. "The abbot," Johann muttered. "He doesn't usually come to these events."

The abbot stepped to the front of the hall and looked out over the room. His kind eyes briefly met Albert's as he surveyed the crowd. He smiled and addressed the group. "Well, this has been some scavenger hunt!" All the boys chuckled or murmured in agreement. The abbot raised his hands for silence.

"I'm sure you're all eager to know who won this year's prize," the abbot said. "But before we get to that, I am curious to know if any of you noticed a woman on the grounds during your hunt." The question was answered with puzzled looks. Most of the boys shook their heads or murmured no. A self-conscious Albert hesitantly raised his hand.

The abbot looked at Albert. "Young man, could you describe the woman you saw?" Albert felt beads of sweat forming on his forehead. Everyone in the room watched as he stood to respond to the abbot.

"Um, well, she had sort of dark hair. And, uh, she was wearing a red cloak."

"Anything else?" the abbot asked, stroking his jaw.

"She looked like she spent a lot of time out in the sun." Albert closed his eyes, remembering the woman. "Oh, and her eyes."

"What about her eyes, my son?"

"They were... I don't know." Albert's tone became wistful. "They were... beautiful. They were filled with this sort of... something...I don't know. I felt kind of warm when I looked at them." The abbot waited as Albert recalled the encounter. "It was really amazing. I almost felt like she was hugging me when I saw her eyes."

The young boys in the room burst out with laughter. Werner stood up from his chair with his hands on his hips in a wide stance projected his voice over the crowd, "Hey what a sissy." The abbot said in a loud tone, "Silence."

Johann was staring at Albert. "Wow, how did I miss that?" he whispered.

The abbot did not seem baffled at all. In fact, happiness radiated from him. "Gentlemen, we have been blessed." He beckoned to a monk who had just entered the room carrying a package wrapped in cloth. Holding it up for the abbot, the older monk began removing the wrapping. "This is a painting that has been in a storage room in our cellar. I don't believe anyone has looked at it in many years."

As the last of the wrapping was removed, Albert gasped and plopped back down in his seat. It was her. It was the woman in red who had led him and Johann to the relics. "This, my friends," The abbot continued, "is a painting of Mary Magdalene, whose feast day, July 22, we are celebrating today with our scavenger hunt." Albert's jaw dropped.

The abbot smiled toward Albert as he continued. "It is rare, but not unheard of, that someone with an extraordinary heart will see Mary Magdalene on the grounds here. I honestly can't remember the last time it happened, but apparently, we have been honored by her presence today." Turning to face Albert directly, the abbot continued, "You, young sir, are very fortunate. Seeing her can only bode well for you, and I congratulate you on this very great blessing you have been given."

Albert closed his mouth and nodded his head sheepishly as the other boys in the hall whispered among themselves. Werner was unusually silent, Albert noticed, watching the boy's eyes narrow as if he didn't believe what Albert had said.

The room quieted again, and the abbot spoke, this time with a chuckle in his voice. "While I'm sure you're all very pleased for young Herr Einstein, I'll bet you're just a little bit curious about who won the scavenger hunt." The room, which had become hushed, now became raucous again, with hoots and hollers and shouts of, "You're right about that!" and "Yeah, get to it!"

Gesturing for silence, the abbot said, "The team of Werner von Wiesel and Ulli Schmidt were the first to make it back to the dining hall with their map and two correct relics identified." The room erupted in chatter, and Werner made a big show of strutting around, pumping his arm in a victory salute. Albert's heart sank, but he forced a smile onto his face in support of the boys' success. Johann had a more expectant look on his face. Albert gave him a puzzled glance. Johann just held up two fingers. Albert frowned, trying to understand what his friend was telling him.

The abbot held up his hands, and the room quieted. "I commend you young men on your speed and cleverness." Werner and Ulli nodded smugly.

However, the abbot was not yet finished. "But, as you may recall, speed was only one of the criteria." Albert was listening intently. "Only one team correctly found and identified all *three* relics we placed out." A hush fell over the room as the boys all looked around. Each team knew they had found only two relics.

The abbot turned his gaze to Albert and Johann and smiled. "Apparently Mary Magdalene smiled upon these two young men," he said, pointing to Albert and Johann. "For discovering and correctly identifying all the relics in this hunt"—the abbot held up a smaller version of the red egg the boys had found in the farmyard—"this replica of Mary Magdalene's red egg, which was hand-carved and painted by one of our fine artisans here at the monastery, goes to... Johann Thomas and Albert Einstein!"

The room went quiet. Albert gulped, hoping the boys were not angry about not winning. Werner stood and glared at Albert. "How could that scrawny little Jew see Mary Magdalene?" he spat out in a whisper to the boy next to him.

With an angry wave, he summoned the half-dozen boys in his entourage and stormed out of the dining hall amidst stunned silence. As soon as Werner's posse was clear of the room, the entire hall burst into enthusiastic cheers and applause. The boys gathered around Albert and Johann thumping them on the back and shaking their hands. The two boys stood, shyly accepting all the attention.

As they sat back down, Johann leaned over and whispered, "I think it's great we won, but I don't think Werner's going to be happy about losing, especially to you."

"I know," Albert said shrugging off his concerns to enjoy the moment. "But so, what? I mean, what can he do?"

Johann shrugged in agreement. "Yeah, what can he do?"

Chapter 7
September 1894
Oktoberfest

A crisp west wind blew away the last days of September 1894 and hailed in the 16-day annual folk festival known as Oktoberfest. The first Oktoberfest was held on October 12, 1810, when all the citizens of Munich were invited to attend the wedding party of King Ludwig I as he married Princess Therese Charlotte Luise of Saxony-Hildburghausen. The event was such a success it stuck, and Oktoberfest became a favorite annual celebration.

Wearing lederhosen and his favorite emerald-green alpine wool hat, sixteen-year-old Albert strolled into the fairgrounds. He'd been saving his appetite for the afternoon feast, and his stomach was growling in anticipation. Festive, tent-like canopies dotted the grounds, and Albert inhaled the enticing scents of dumplings baking in huge pans, chickens roasting on spits, and sausages sizzling in their juices. Albert's eyes widened at the abundance of Bavarian delicacies, and his stomach rumbled again.

Twilight was slowly descending across the sea of colorful tents, which were lit with the still novel electric light bulbs. A week before, as an assistant in the family-owned electrical company Elektrotechnische Fabrik J. Einstein & Cie., Albert had mounted the light bulbs in the Schottenhamel marquee.

The excited teenager made his way past the Hippodrome, which had magically been transformed from a horse-racing track into a dance hall. The sweet smell of the fresh, bracing autumn air was filled with the screaming, hooting and shouting of the revelers, underscored by the joyous sounds of a sprightly polka band. Outside the large, ornate building, families in their festive best chatted animatedly with neighbors waiting in line with them.

The crunch of fallen red and gold leaves under his feet, Albert whistled under his breath as he made his way to the far west end of the fairground. A new exhibit hosted by Munich Brau featured a competition for the best crossbowman. Near the Munich Brau beer wagon, Albert found Johann setting up the targets. "Hey, Johann, do you need any help?" Albert shouted above the chatter and music.

Johann, in a sweaty white peasant shirt and lederhosen, turned around. "Albert! You made it!" He gave his friend a brotherly hug.

"Wouldn't miss Oktoberfest," Albert replied with mock indignation.

"Thanks for stopping by our tent. My father has invested a lot of money in the crossbow contest, so I'm just finishing up here. You go on inside. I'll catch up with you soon."

Albert waved goodbye and headed into the Munich Brau pavilion. A wooden dance floor covered the center of the pagoda-style tent that measured fifty feet square. Rows and rows of tables and benches lined the sides. On planks at the far south side of the party room, plate after plate of fresh bratwurst and mugs of frosty beer beckoned.

I'm starved, Albert said to himself and strode purposefully toward the food table. Suddenly, someone thrust their foot into the crowded aisle and sent Albert sprawling into the dirty straw that covered the floor. Albert could hear the derisive laughter, as he hoisted himself to his feet. Brushing the straw from his clothing, he found himself face-to-face with Werner von Wiesel.

"Walk much, clumsy?" the bully sneered, "and look at that stupid hat!" Werner backhanded Albert's goat-hair cap from his head.

"That's enough, Werner," shouted a stout man dressed in a white apron and balancing a large platter brimming with hot sausage. It was Johann's father, Frederick Thomas, "This is not sportsmanlike conduct. I will pull you from the crossbow competition if you continue to behave like this."

Albert glared at the bully and brushed sawdust from the cap. Werner, all innocence, looked hurt as he responded to the man. "Me? I didn't do anything." Werner glanced at a nearby table for support from his father, a retired Prussian colonel who had served in the German Army under Bismarck. But between bites of bratwurst and swallows of cold beer, the senior Von Wiesel was chatting with friends and missed his son's performance. Werner shrugged and strode off toward the food table as if Albert were beneath his notice.

Shaking his head at Werner's audacity, Herr Thomas turned to Albert and offered him a plate of sausages. "I'm sorry for that, Albert. You did an excellent job installing the electric lights. Now enjoy what *we* do best."

Albert's mouth watered as he inhaled the savory, steaming sausages. He accepted the plate gratefully and walked to a table near the six-piece band. He snagged a frosty mug of beer from the beer wagon along the way. The musicians were tuning their instruments as a group of dancers waited for the music to start. He set the platter onto the table and proceeded to pile a couple sausages onto one of the clean plates arranged along the table's edge. At a nearby table, a pretty young dark-haired girl smiled at Albert. Albert blushed a little and smiled back.

The encounter with Werner had not diminished Albert's appetite, and he turned his attention to the steaming sausages in front of him. Before long, his plate was clean and the mug empty. Sated, Albert relaxed back into his chair and closed his eyes. *Should I stay or go? There are many tents in which to enjoy the festivities. If I open my eyes, will Werner be gone?* Then, he grimaced. *If I leave, will he follow me?* The accordion wheezed into life, and the drum began beating the tempo for a lively polka. Albert felt the music, opened his eyes, and joined in singing with the enthusiastic crowd. He clapped his hands and watched the band.

Johann's mother, Christine, her ginger hair tucked under a white cap, tapped Albert's shoulder and pointed to the young *fräulein* who had smiled at Albert earlier. "Albert, please dance with Mileva. She is the daughter of a lovely family we met. They're visiting from Austro-Hungary."

Albert gazed shyly at the delicate beauty at the next table. She smiled demurely and then looked down. Albert plucked up a bit of courage from somewhere and hesitantly asked, "Um, hi. Would you like to, uh, dance?"

Mileva nodded, and the two stood so Albert could lead the dainty Fräulein to the dance floor. *What a beautiful girl*, he thought as he glanced sideways to take a surreptitious look. Taking their positions on the dance floor, Albert held Mileva like a porcelain doll. Despite his shyness, he was an accomplished dancer, handily navigating through the many couples on the floor. Mileva's bright-blue eyes twinkled with delight as Albert masterfully guided her to the strains of Strauss's "Blue Danube Waltz."

After a few dances, Albert returned his partner to her seat. As he turned to go back to his table, Mileva put her hand on his arm. "Please join me," she said, looking up into his eyes. Albert just makes the drinking age of sixteen in Germany. Albert gulped and nodded, settling into a chair next to the young girl. He motioned to a passing hostess carrying a tray with mugs of beer. "Mileva, would you like something to drink?"

"That would be lovely." Mileva smiled.

As the hostess set two mugs on the table, she knocked a cardboard coaster to the ground. As Albert bent to pick it up, an arrow streaked past her, flying through the crown of Albert's hat, and knocking it off his head. Albert flinched, jarring the table and knocking over one of the mugs of beer. The frothy brew spilled over the edge of the table right into his overturned hat.

Mileva was enraged. "Who would do something like this?"

Albert put on a brave smile as he leaned over, picked up his hat and the arrow that had embedded itself in the straw-covered dirt floor. He shook the last wisps of foam out of his hat. "I'm sure it's nothing. Just an accident." Placing his hat on the table, he looked directly into Mileva's beautiful eyes and smiled. "Or maybe Cupid has shot his arrow."

Mileva blushed and looked down at the table.

"But, seriously," Albert continued, breaking the mood, "please don't say anything to anyone about this."

"I won't, if you don't want me to," Mileva agreed.

Albert scanned the crowd for Werner, who was nowhere to be seen. With Mileva watching quietly, Albert studied the arrow. It was small, as if from a child's bow. Turning it in his fingers, he noticed a "WvW" burnished on the wood. Albert wondered how anyone could be so stupid as to pull such a prank with their *initials* carved into the arrow. *But then, Werner had never been the brightest bulb on the string*, Albert thought.

Scanning the room again, Albert spotted Herr Thomas on the far side of the tent, pouring a seemingly endless stream of frothy beer into mugs. Albert considered whether he should take the arrow to him. If he did, Werner would be expelled from the crossbow competition, and possibly suspended from school. *This is neither the time nor the place*, Albert sighed, looking at the crowds around Herr Thomas. *But it won't do to stay here, either.*

Beer-soaked hat in his left hand, Albert held out his right hand and bowed. "I'm sorry, Mileva, but I think I need to... uh, tend to something at my home."

Unable to hide her disappointment, Mileva clasped his hand. "I'm sorry you have to leave so soon."

"Me, too," Albert said, his natural shyness coming to the fore. "I... um... really enjoyed dancing with you."

Mileva brightened a little. "Me too. Maybe I'll see you again while I'm here... or sometime?" she said, tilting her head quizzically.

"I... I'd really like that," Albert turned hastily, slipped the arrow under his jacket, and made his way through the crowd and out of the tent.

Chapter 8
October 1894
Called to Task

*A*s Albert secured his bicycle at the side entrance of the Gymnasium and took his books from the basket mounted in front of the handlebars, he wondered what the Benedictine monks thought of a Jewish boy attending their prestigious boarding school.

Dressed in a stylish charcoal wool suit, Albert walked toward the front of the building. Mounting the steps, he took off his inky, short-brimmed, felt bowler hat and smoothed back his unruly chestnut hair. He was late. Again. But he didn't care.

Dwarfed by the tall Doric columns, he kept his eyes on the ground. He didn't even glance at the long wall scroll with the Bavarian monks' black-and-gold coat of arms that hung above him. Albert's pace slowed. *I am not looking forward to another day of boredom with these dullards.*

At sixteen and standing five feet nine, Albert was not an imposing figure. The mild expression on his face hid the firestorm of rage that brewed in his mind. *Day after day, the same thing.*

This rote memorizing hurts my brain. Taking a deep breath to calm himself, Albert let his thoughts drift to his mother and father. He missed his family.

Melancholy came over him as he remembered their goodbyes in early summer. His parents left him with his aunt and uncle so they could pursue work in Italy. He had loved his life before they went. Now, he was stuck in classes where the boys were studying things that he had mastered years earlier. His guardians, unfortunately, were not as understanding as his parents about Albert's boredom.

Albert stopped next to a column and leaned against it, remembering his initial discovery of the magic of mathematics. He had been only around twelve when Max Talmud, a family friend and struggling medical student, visited the Einstein's for Shabbat one Friday and gave Albert a gift that changed his life. It was a mathematics book called *Simple Algebra*, and it opened new worlds to Albert, who at the time was in Folkenshuler elementary school. Albert mastered the text by himself and would delight in surprising Max with how much he had learned since the previous Shabbat.

For Albert, *Simple Algebra* was like a prayer book. He remembered his wonderment as the book began stimulating questions in his mind. Each problem became a puzzle to solve. Life was a series of "Xs" he decided, a series of unknowns.

Albert forced himself out of his reverie and reluctantly resumed his walk to class. He entered the classroom and glanced over at his friend, Johann. The teacher, Herr von Achen, was writing on the blackboard, his back to the class. Von Achen was a rigid and disciplined man on whom forty resembled sixty. His eyes were a bleak gray behind gold-rimmed spectacles, and he wore a perpetual frown under his balding head.

"The 'late' Herr Einstein," taunted Werner von Wiesel as Albert made his way to his seat. Werner was his usual obnoxious self. The boys in the class would have laughed at the play on words, but they had heard this phrase numerous times already from Von Wiesel. His entourage did manage a weak guffaw as Albert slid into his seat.

Von Achen turned and frowned. "Enough, Herr von Wiesel," he said in a halfhearted admonishment. Albert, who often challenged Herr von Achen, was far from the teacher's favorite student. Additionally, Von Achen didn't want to antagonize the son of Colonel von Wiesel, one of Munich's substantial citizens.

With a disapproving glare at Albert, Von Achen began the lesson. "Today, we will discuss mathematical treatment of astronomy, Newton's development of celestial mechanics and the laws of gravitation. Does everyone have their textbook?" Several of the boys nodded, taking out their copies of Josef Krist's *Essentials of Natural Science.*

Albert raised his hand. "With all due respect, Herr von Achen, what does astronomy have to do with physics?"

Murmurs and grumbles rippled through the classroom. Werner rolled his eyes, moaning, "Not again... Einstein, do you have to do this?"

Albert stood his ground. "My interest is in learning physics. Astronomy is a waste of my time."

Herr von Achen turned and glared at Albert. "As part of this course, we are covering the five branches of natural science: astronomy, biology, chemistry, the Earth sciences, and physics. You are to learn a broad range of subjects here, not just one or two."

I have already covered this, Albert thought. He shook his head in resignation.

Herr von Achen challenged Albert. "Herr Einstein, please stand and explain to the class Newton's theory of celestial mechanics."

"The law of universal gravitation states that any two bodies in the universe attract each other with a force that is directly proportional to the product of their masses and inversely proportional to the square of the distance between them," Albert rattled off sitting in his seat.

Herr von Achen's face reddened. "What are you talking about? Where in your textbook did you see that?" His anger building, the older man, spat, "And when I tell you to stand young man, you will stand!"

Albert threw his hands up and stood beside his chair. "Herr von Achen, I learned Newton's theory of celestial mechanics several years ago. I read the *Peoples Books of Natural Science* when I was twelve. All twenty-one volumes." A collective gasp rippled through the classroom.

Herr von Achen could barely contain his fury. "I don't care what you read or when." He grabbed the copy of the textbook from his desk and held it up. "We are working with this textbook and the information in it. So…" he continued as his body quivered and he slammed the book down on his desk with a sharp crack, "you can shut your mouth now and sit down immediately!"

Turning from Albert to the blackboard, Herr von Achen began madly scribbling as he spoke in short staccato bursts of scientific jargon. Albert wished he were anywhere but here. As the other boys feverishly took notes, attempting to keep up with their still enraged teacher, Albert slumped into his chair and pulled his brass compass from his pocket. He found endless fascination studying his prized possession. Pushing on the twelve gemstones like buttons, he tried to turn it on again. How could he get the number 33 to flash the way it had when he first opened the compass?

He was pulled from his dream-like state by the clock striking the hour and marking the end of the class. Albert put away his compass and gathered his books, happy to be heading for the door. Just as he was about to escape, Herr von Achen motioned him over to his desk. Albert approached cautiously. Herr von Achen pointed his right index finger at Albert and through clenched teeth growled, "Just who do you think you are, Herr Einstein?"

Albert took in a deep breath. "What do you want me to say, Herr von Achen?"

With a vein throbbing just above his brow, Von Achen spat out, "You come to class late, sit in the back row with your attention elsewhere, and argue with me whenever you can. Where is your respect?"

"Sorry, sir," Albert replied, his patience at an end.

Herr von Achen leaned forward across his desk, coming only inches from Albert's face. "Well then, perhaps you would do better somewhere else." He pulled an envelope from his inside jacket pocket and smacked it against Albert's chest. "You are to meet with the Academik Committee in six weeks. The letter explains everything." He spun around to straighten some papers on his desk. "And, Herr Einstein," he said with sarcasm, his attention on the papers, "be on time."

Not knowing what to say, Albert stepped back and stared blankly at the letter in his hand. Albert's face flushed as the idea of being expelled from school and having his plans shattered took hold. His thoughts raced. His teachers at the Folkenshuler tried to force him to conform. Albert found it suffocating. Suddenly, the whole place felt like it was closing in on him.

Albert bolted from the classroom, ran through the hall and bolted out the front door. The biting, near-winter wind smacked Albert in the face as he burst out of the Gymnasium. Running and out of breath.

He inhaled the cold air into his lungs. Albert tried to calm himself and take stock. He needed to be alone. Slowly Albert calmed down, and rationality returned. He realized he needed his bicycle. Keeping his eyes down to avoid engaging with anyone, made his way back to the side entrance of the Gymnasium. No one paid any attention to Albert as he mounted his bicycle and pedaled away. His heavy wool suit barely kept him warm in the fall chill, but he hardly noticed.

Finally, on the edge of campus, he took one hand off the handlebars to wipe the tears from his eyes. Albert pedaled fast to Gasteig Park and the bridge at the end of the Prinzregentenstrasse. He slowed before a bench in the formal gardens and set his bicycle on the brittle, brown grass.

Sitting back, like a lost soul Albert closed his eyes. He felt crushed and out of control and just wanted to scream out his anger with Herr von Achen. He gazed across the terraces where the bare branches of tall birch and maples trees quivered in the wind. Rising above in the axis of the Prinzregentenstrasse was the *Angel of Peace,* a statue of the ancient Greek goddess of victory, Athena Nike. Albert stared at the towering, golden figure. "My only god is mathematics," he declared out loud. The sun began to set, and Albert shivered in the chill air. *I need to be somewhere where I can think.* He didn't want to discuss this with Johann, and his aunt and uncle would be of no assistance. Then he realized he had the perfect place.

It was fully dark by the time Albert found himself riding past candlelit houses of middle-class families. A short time later, he arrived at his destination. Quietly Albert walked his bike to the back of the house and left it under a small canopy made for the family vehicles. He opened the back door and entered a quiet house. He was alone. Since his parents had taken his younger sister, Mara, to Italy, he had the family home all to himself.

He turned on the hall light and climbed the stairs two at a time. He opened the door to find his bed, dresser, and armoire had accumulated only a light coat of dust since he'd left them in the summer. Just being back in the familiar room helped to calm him. Taking a deep breath, Albert reached under the bed and pulled out his violin case. He opened it and carefully picked up his friend, Violina. Albert stood in the middle of the living room, closed his eyes and remembered playing the Mozart lullaby "I See the Moon" with his mother accompanying him on the piano. Profoundly missing his family, he began to play the favorite tune on his violin. As the sweet notes emerged from Violina, Albert started walking, then gently waltzing, around the room. He could almost hear his mother singing the melody and laughing. The folksy love song lifted his heart. Lost in his dreams, Albert let the song fill him.

Bowing the last strains of the beautiful melody, Albert found the memory of his ordeal with Herr von Achen intruding into his awareness. The warm Violina still in his hands, he opened his eyes to a dimly lit bedroom, abandoned. He sighed and settled Violina into her case. Feeling forlorn, Albert collapsed onto his bed fully clothed and fell into a deep sleep. Tomorrow would be a new day.

Chapter 9
A Dream (Or Was It?)

*A*lbert loved to walk. It made his mind fresher, and he would snap his fingers with the fast rhythm of each step. Humming a tune to keep pace with, he breathed in the crisp, fall air. The concern he felt from the letter he had received from Herr von Achen had withdrawn into the recesses of his mind. Before long, Albert found himself in Marienplatz, the heart of Munich.

Young couples and families milled through the streets of the city's downtown. The crowds gathered to watch the glockenspiel show. Albert gazed up at the towering Gothic clock, with its thirty-two carved figurines. They seemed to touch the sky. Every day at 11:00 a.m., the Glockenspiel chimed. It reenacted the sixteenth-century marriage and celebration of the local duke, Wilhelm V, to Renata of Lorraine. The clock displayed a joust with life-sized knights on horseback, resplendent in their local colors: white and blue for the Bavarians, and red and white for the Lothringian champions. The Bavarian knight won every time. The clock's dance lasted around 12 minutes, and at the end of the show, a tiny golden bird at the top of the glockenspiel chirped three times.

As the marvelous spectacle came to an end and the people began to walk away, a small, almost hidden door at the clock tower's base opened soundlessly. The movement caught Albert's eye, and he frowned. For all the times he'd walked past the clock tower, he'd never noticed a door. Noting that no one else seemed to be paying attention to it, he turned and walked toward the opening.

Gazing into the dark entryway, Albert saw an engraved metal sign: "No Entrance." But the open door beckoned, and he stepped over the threshold. Once he was inside, the door slowly swung shut. Albert reached out and pulled the gargoyle-shaped wrought iron handle, but the door seemed firmly closed.

He began to struggle with the door, but the tick... tock... tick... tock of the clock's inner workings caught his attention, and he stopped tugging. *What could be inside this magnificent timepiece?* He wondered as the possibilities began running around in his mind.

Following the internal beating of the clock tower's heart, Albert moved toward a spiral staircase. The only light in the hallway came from high above him. Tick... tock... tick... tock.

Albert stepped to the beat of the clock and round and round he rose. Time seemed to stand still as he climbed. He stopped at the top of the steps, then the shining light drew him to a massive, carved wooden door and Albert approached it.

The door was partially open and, peering into the room, Albert's gaze landed on a large mahogany desk. Then Albert noticed the man seated at the desk. He looked to be around 50 years of age and had soft-looking, silver, shoulder-length hair. He was dressed in a white, long-sleeved peasant shirt and dark-brown leather breeches. Arrayed on the desk in front of him were quill pens with pots of ink, stacks of paper, and on the right corner of the writing table, an apple. The entire back wall of the room was lined with shelves stocked with ancient-looking volumes and several brass candlesticks holding candles that cast a soft glow about the place. In the ceiling of the room was some sort of skylight through which a beam of sunlight streamed.

The man at the desk held a triangular-shaped crystal up to the beam of light, and the refracted light of the polished glass threw a rainbow of colors onto the wall. The man smiled with satisfaction.

Albert saw the rainbow and murmured to himself, "Newton's theory is that white light is a composite of all the colors of the spectrum."

The man looked up from the rainbows and smiled at Albert. "Well said, Albert. So glad you made your way in here to visit."

Albert's jaw dropped. "How did you...?"

The man held up his hand and smiled. "All in good time, my boy." He rose from his chair and walked to Albert, holding out his hand. "My name is Isaac. Please, sit down." Speechless, Albert, managed to make his way to a chair in front of the desk as Isaac returned to his seat.

"I know who you are, Albert," Isaac said with a kind smile. "You must not concern yourself too deeply with what you are learning now. You have grasped the *Mathematical Principles of Natural Philosophy*. Let that be the foundation of your work that is to come." Isaac picked up the apple on his desk and gently tossed it to Albert. "Gravity, the universe, space, distance, and motion are your future." Catching the apple, Albert nodded as the ticking of the massive clock pulled at his awareness. Tick... tock... tick... tock...

Tick... tock... Ringgggggggg. The alarm clock next to Albert's bed screamed at him. Albert sat bolt upright and struggled to reorient himself. Vacillating between the dream and waking reality, Albert let himself fall back onto his pillow. He turned his head to see what time it was. There, on the table next to the alarm clock, sat an apple. "What the...?" Albert groaned.

Albert pulled himself from his bed and began dressing as he considered the implications of what he had dreamed. The more he thought about it, the more excited he became. Buttoning the last button of his shirt and throwing on his jacket, Albert dashed out of the house. He had to investigate the *glockenspiel.*

He jumped on his bike and pedaled as fast as he could to the clock tower. The sun met him as it rose in the early morning over the city. He raced to the scene of his dream, thinking, *I must be going crazy!* He found the center of Munich still asleep. He dismounted and walked to where he'd entered the tower in his dream. There was no door. Albert felt the cold stone with his hands, seeking a crack or a hinge; anything that would reveal the presence of an entryway. He encountered nothing but the rough stone surface. He looked up and found no windows or radiating light other than the sunlight that glistened in the early dawn.

Disappointed, he turned away from the tower, went back to his bicycle, and slowly headed back to his home. As he rode away, the tiny golden bird at the top of the glockenspiel chirped three times.

Interlude II

*T*hrough the opening in the domed ceiling of the Temple of Healing, Ezekiel scanned the salmon-pink sky, his gaze passing across the twin moons suspended in it. He observed hundreds of angels descending like diamonds falling from the heavens, a visual symphony of transcendent splendor. The iridescent guardians of Light, in robes of pastel colors, gently touched down outside the glistening white temple on the garden grounds. An aura of loving energy permeated the air. Shaded by majestic oak trees on the lofty hill near the bank of a serenely flowing river, rows of tall, fragrant, purple roses grew in profusion.

At the Temple of Healing, neophytes studied methods of energy manipulation to balance body and mind. To the right of the Healing Temple was the Temple of Teaching. In it, students learned the second level of training, which used sound and Light to raise the energy frequency of the body. To the Healing Temple's left stood the Temple of Research, where the graduates of the Healing and Teaching curricula experimented with crystals and methods of enhancing life.

Ezekiel strode to the temple's arched doorway and gazed upon the scene. As he did, Father-Mother-God called upon him and the Travelers of Light. Soundlessly, It communicated that It wanted them to intervene on behalf of Albert and Johann, though within the guidelines of Cosmic Law.

Ezekiel summoned his heart energy to levitate his body and transport him to the garden. A matrix of golden and amethyst light pulsed a telepathic call to the assembly of Lightworkers. In response, the angels and Light Travelers convened in the garden.

As the last arrivals settled in, Ezekiel brought them up to date on the situation he had been monitoring since discovering that a fragment of the Shamir Stone was not with the Ark of the Covenant. "We have discovered a fragment of the Shamir Stone is in the hands of two children on planet Earth. They do not know what they have. Neither do they know that they are in grave danger."

The assembly listened intently as he elaborated. "Raka, the dark angel, knows the stone is awake. I felt his darkness near the children. Raka will also know that the stone has become attuned to the boy who possesses it and that if the boy lives, the stone will be useless to him. We are to protect the boy and the stone at all costs—but within the boundaries of God's law of the universe."

Ezekiel paused, then smiled. "Father-Mother-God has declared Albert Einstein, a star Child of Light and peace. It may be necessary to bring him here to fulfill his numerological 33 master path destiny. We will not know until he matures whether he can hold the energy of enlightenment."

Many heads nodded in understanding. "For now, we observe. We know Raka will ruthlessly stop at nothing to apprehend the stone, but we do not know exactly how he will proceed. Most likely he will become a changeling, assuming the form of someone near the children so he can beguile those in his community and manipulate them to his ends since he cannot directly attack Albert without huge spiritual consequences. The Masters of Light in the Temple of Research will track the situation."

Looking at a group of angels, Ezekiel directed, "All of you are to be on alert for Raka and his minions on planet Earth. Meanwhile, the Light Travelers will assist young Albert with his karmic path. His friend, Johann's mission, is to be Albert's friend and confident. While this may sound simple, it will not be an easy task in this phase of humankind's progression. In fact, it could bring Johann, and even his family, into danger."

Ezekiel paused again, assessing the room to be sure all understood. Then he bowed his head and concluded, "We pray that our loving for the peace of God, the Holy Spirit, the Christ, and Light Travelers surround, fill, and protect us. We bless Albert Einstein and Johann Thomas, and we know God's will is done for the highest good of all concerned."

After a moment of reverent silence, the gathering dispersed. As often happened when he tapped into the higher energies of Spirit, Ezekiel was filled with awe and appreciation for being able to serve God's plan in this way. Even so, he brought his awareness back to what was in front of him and frowned. He would not speculate on what Raka would do to gain control of the Shamir Stone, but he knew his actions could be horrendous. Ezekiel was aware that God's plan was perfect. He also knew it would likely bring Albert great joy—and great sorrow—as it unfolded.

Chapter 10
November 1894
Hate

The room was filled with wooden desks arranged in three precisely regimented double rows facing the wall-to-wall blackboard at the front of the room. Albert made his way to a seat at the end of one of the rows. Dropping his books on the desk, he searched for Johann. He was surprised to see his friend sitting next to Werner von Wiesel. When Johann glanced up, Albert gestured for his friend to sit next to him. Johann shook his head and looked down, unable to meet Albert's eyes. Puzzled, Albert shrugged and sat as a blond boy took what was to have been Johann's seat.

His back to the class, the teacher, Herr Hamlin, spoke while he wrote on the blackboard, "What... does it... mean... to be... German?" Dressed in a simple, dark-green wool suit, the tall, white-haired gentleman stood stiffly erect. He turned to face the class. "Today we will discuss the Franco-Prussian War of 1870 and its impact on the people of Germany. Can anyone tell the class how the war of 1870 changed Germany?"

The boy next to Albert raised a hand.

Herr Hamlin gestured with chalk. "Yes, Herr Frederick?"

Ulrich Frederick stood, cleared his throat, and precisely stated his answer. "Prussian and German victory brought about the final unification of Germany. It was under King Werner I of Prussia."

Hamlin, facing the class, crossed his arms. "Who were the two military leaders who conducted the war?"

Werner von Wiesel, shouted in a bored tone from his seat, "Napoleon III for France and Bismarck for Germany."

Hamlin nodded, "Good." Then he smiled. "You know, Herr von Wiesel, I served under your father during the Franco-Prussian War."

Werner puffed himself up as he stood. "Yes, Herr Hamlin. When my father talks of the war, he often mentions you and your bravery as a soldier." All eyes on him, Werner smiled and straightened his waistcoat. "My father feels that all Germany should have helped the Prussians."

In a loud voice, Hamlin stabbed the blackboard with his index finger. "The young of our nation needs to be reminded of who we are. So, tell me, Herr von Wiesel, what does it mean to be German?"

Werner pulled his shoulders back and thrust out his chest, saying, "To be German means to be STRONG!"

Hamlin nodded approvingly, then turned to Albert's seatmate. "Herr Frederick, what do *you* say it means to be a German?"

"That one is brave and honorable," Herr Frederick said, then sat with near-military precision.

All eyes turned to Albert. He stood to answer, but before he could get a word out, Werner spat out, "You're a Jew, not a German. You're a foreigner who will disgrace the German Army when you get drafted next year."

Albert glared at Werner, putting his hands on his hips. "I only want to be a scientist. I will not serve in the army. I do not believe in war." *What an arrogant loud-mouth,* Albert thought.

Werner turned and gave Johann a wicked wink. He pointed at Albert and taunted, "As you can see by his comment, Herr Hamlin, our Jew is a coward."

Albert's face reddened as his anger rose. "To my mind, compulsory military service is the prime cause of moral decay. It threatens not just the survival of our country, but of our very civilization!"

Herr Hamlin removed his spectacles and polished them with a clean, white handkerchief. In a stern voice he warned, "Careful, Herr Einstein, you could face imprisonment if you do not serve." Holding his glasses up to the light and approving of their cleanliness, he said, "After all, the German National Army and universal military service were organized after the Franco-Prussian War. Bismarck's vision brought about the victory over Napoleon III that led to the unification of our nation. You wouldn't challenge that, now would you?"

Albert clenched his jaw but had the sense to hold his tongue as Herr Hamlin continued after a pause. "Napoleon III surrendered in January 1871, after being under siege from Sept 19, 1870. The Treaty of Frankfurt was signed on May 10, 1871. France ceded Alsace, except Belfort and eastern Lorraine, to Germany." Hamlin put his spectacles back on, saying, "The German Army could occupy northern France until we received payment of five billion Francs. Now, Germany has the strongest economy on the Continent thanks to this war." Hamlin started to turn, then turned back. "And the strongest military!"

Once again turning his gaze from Albert, Hamlin said, "I am going to end our discussion of what it means to be German and move on to other topics. However, I want each of you to attend the *Volkisch* rally this evening. It is at the Englischer Garden." Straightening the rare items on his already meticulously neat desk, he instructed, "Be prepared to give your answer to my question in our next class."

Albert frowned, thinking about the rally that was sure to be filled with anti-Semitic rhetoric. Those thoughts kept him distracted for the rest of the period. The nationalistic talk that promoted violence and hatred was becoming more prevalent by the day.

When Herr Hamlin dismissed the class, Albert gathered his books, then looked to where Johann had been sitting. His friend was no longer there. In fact, Albert did not see him anywhere in the rapidly emptying room. Leaving the classroom, he resumed his search outside the building.

He eventually found Johann huddled under a tree facing away from the Gymnasium. "Johann?" Albert saw his friend cringe at the sound of his voice. Albert carefully sat on the ground next to Johann. "What's the matter, my friend?" Johann would not look at Albert and only shook his head, nervously glancing around. Puzzled, Albert tried again. "So, why did you sit with Werner today? You and I usually sit together."

A forlorn whimper escaped Johann's lips. With pain in his eyes, he turned to his friend. "Albert, I know we have been friends for years, but..." Johann paused, then sighed, "no more." Albert gasped as if he'd been hit in the stomach. Johann was more brother than a friend. Johann looked down and said, "Things are changing in Germany. Bullies like Werner..."

"...are rising in popularity and influence. I know," Albert completed Johann's sentence.

"Yes," said Johann bleakly. "It's gotten to the point that harm will come to my family and me if I remain friends with you."

Albert's eyes began to fill with tears. "You're right. It's getting that ugly." Albert's heart filled with resolve. "We cannot let anything happen to you or your family because of me and mine." Albert gripped Johann's arm. "We will not surrender to this type of hatred... but we will go along with what must be done to keep you safe, for now."

Tears spilled onto Johann's cheeks as well. He looked into Albert's eyes. "I knew you would understand. You are a better man than I am, Albert." He squeezed Albert's arm again, as he made his way to his feet. "And... thank you, Albert. We will find a way through this. I know we will."

Albert could only nod as he watched his friend walk away. "We *will* find a way." But he sighed as he got back up. *But God only knows how long it will take and what will happen in the meantime*, he thought. Albert walked back toward the school building, a cold feeling of dread filling his stomach, and sadness weighing down his heart.

* * *

The German brass band played the national anthem "Das Deutschlandlied." The opening words called to all Germans to bond together. Tears streamed down many faces in the crowd of hundreds of the Volkisch North-German Confederation. Their voices rang out in the open-air amphitheater of the Englischer Garden.

> *Deutschland, Deutschland, Uber Alles—Germany,*
> *Germany above everything.*
> *Above everything in the world*
> *When for protection and defense,*
> *it always takes a brotherly stand together.*
> *From the Meuse to the Memel,*
> *From the Adige to the Belt,*
> *Germany, Germany above everything,*
> *Above everything in the world!*

The song ended with a roaring cheer. Standing amid the crowd, Werner von Wiesel joined with his classmates in surrendering to the frenzy. Sweat ran down his pale face.

On the bandstand sat Werner's barrel-chested father. Gunter von Wiesel, all five feet ten inches of him was vibrating with near-religious fervor. The aristocratic Prussian anti-Semite wore his blue regimental uniform. An officer in the Kaiser's Army, Colonel von Wiesel did not consider Jews to be Germans. He barely considered them to be human. He nodded to his former comrade, his son's history teacher, Dieter Hamlin. Hamlin responded with a seated bow, awe for the colonel in his eyes.

Hans Torbiger, leader of the North-German Volkisch Confederation, waved his ebony top hat. His jet-black handlebar mustache and precisely trimmed beard gleamed in the amphitheater's lights. He wore a formal waistcoat and pearled ascot. As the raucous crowd settled down, Torbiger shouted: "My friends, we face a terrible problem. We have an enemy within. That enemy is none other than the Jew!"

The crowd went wild with shouts of agreement. Torbiger gestured with his hands to quiet the crowd. "Jews are not like us!"

The crowd muttered in agreement, many heads nodding.

"Jews are not merely a different religious community, they are an altogether different race!" Torbiger stated flatly.

Murmurs of agreement could be heard throughout the crowd.

"The Jew is a stranger," Torbiger continued, "who emigrated from Asia. He is a disease eating into the flesh of Germany!"

The rumblings of the crowd grew louder.

"Exploitation of the true people is his only aim. Selfishness and a lack of personal courage are his chief characteristics. Self-sacrifice and patriotism are altogether foreign to him." Torbiger ended his speech with a warning. "Be wary of the Jew—he weakens the fatherland!"

Speaker after speaker spewed forth poisonous, inflammatory remarks and exhortations of hatred. Finally, the fervor began to cool. After the last speaker had made his anti-Semitic point, the crowd started to disperse. Werner joined his father, and they turned toward their home.

"What did you think of the rally, Werner?"

"It was wonderful! Inspiring! I could not agree more that the Jew is a scourge upon our nation," Werner said with a scowl.

The elder von Wiesel nodded. "When your mother and I were first married, I went to the Jew banker for a loan to buy a house. The Yid refused. Apparently, we did not meet his Jew standard."

Werner shook his head. "Typical."

Gunter nodded. "When we fought the Franco-Prussian War, I refused to allow a single Jew in my regiment. They are cowards all." The elder von Wiesel paused, then said, "You know, Werner, I have hoped you will be a great leader."

"I will do my very best, Father," the boy answered with resolve.

But, Gunter was not so sure. This fair-haired boy resembled his doe-eyed mother more than his stout, staunch father.

Werner gazed up in awe of his papa. He knew deep down his father would never see him as the strong German he knew himself to be. Somehow, he resolved, he would find a way to show his father just how strong he was.

Interlude III

*T*he regal Akhenaten, in a simple, knee-length, ivory shendyt, slipped off his sandals. He sat down and crossed his legs, relaxing into a lotus position under a majestic oak tree outside the Temple of Research. The distinctive oop-oop-oop call of a hoopoe bird circling above did not distract him, even as the bird's broad and rounded wings beat gracefully and carried it into a nest box mounted between two branches of the tree.

"M-master Akhenaten?" came a hesitant voice. Kendra, a young girl in the simple temple garment of a neophyte, her chestnut hair wrapped in golden threads bouncing with her stride, cautiously approached Akhenaten. Kendra was determined to possess the gift of looking through the Infinity Portal. But she had yet to test her skills. The training necessary to prepare her for the task was extremely demanding. Neophytes needed to learn to go beyond intellectual understanding and into intuition, and many did not make it through the preparation. But Kendra had worked diligently and with great devotion. She lived within a temple of seers, the home to all women who accepted the rigors of the temple as their way of life. It was a devotion she loved.

"Yes, Kendra. What can I do for you?" said Master Akhenaten, looking up at the girl.

Kendra was surprised that the master knew her name. She was not aware that her progress had come to the attention of many of the masters. "Theresa of Avila suggested you might be able to help me. Do you have a moment?"

"She did? Then, of course, I do." Akhenaten cocked his head to one side, his brow furrowing in thought. "Have you completed your training in the seer's temple, then?"

Kendra nodded solemnly, but Akhenaten could see the girl's excitement swirling in her aura. "I have. So, I was wondering if you might take me on as your student and show me how a Light Traveler sees through time." Kendra paused expectantly, but Akhenaten's face revealed nothing to her.

She took in a deep breath and pressed on, hoping to convince the master that she was worthy. "I learned that these travelers come to bring a special balancing; to help transmute the negativity of the people they serve in each period in history."

"I see," Akhenaten said. "Well, you are correct in your understanding of the role of a Light Traveler." The master paused, considering his next words. "However, In addition to bringing this balance, we teach the virtues of keeping one's word, personal integrity, unconditionally loving, as well as holding a consciousness of upliftment. These are all supportive of preparing people to know their true selves. And necessary for self-knowing, I might add."

Kendra nodded as awareness dawned within her. "Hmmm. Of course. It's clear from my studies that this is what travelers do. I just hadn't put it together until you said that."

Akhenaten's face remained serious. "Good. I see the keywords I spoke stimulated understanding in you."

Encouraged, Kendra looked down modestly. "Thank you for the awareness. I can understand that those qualities impart the strength for people to advance to even higher levels of awareness."

"You're welcome." Master Akhenaten gestured for Kendra to sit in front of him on the carpet of grass. "But before I decide whether to accept you as a student of the Infinity Portal, I think there are some things we need to discuss."

Nodding, Kendra sat and tried to prepare herself for whatever test Akhenaten might have for her. She had worked hard and felt ready to meet any challenge, but being accepted by Master Akhenaten was a huge step in her advancement, and she felt nervous. Despite the unease, her curiosity was insatiable, and she couldn't help but state, "What you just said brought some things to mind."

Akhenaten's eyebrows rose quizzically. "Oh?"

Kendra forged ahead, aware that the master's time was not to be wasted. But she was burning with a desire for knowledge. "Yes, may I ask you some questions?"

Akhenaten stroked his chin thoughtfully, then inclined his head. "If I am to evaluate your worthiness to be my student, then you also have the right to see if I am the one you want to be your teacher."

Kendra was slightly taken aback at Akhenaten's practical thinking on the matter, but quickly regained her composure and asked, "Well, first of all, how did you become a Light Traveler?"

Akhenaten laughed out loud, and Kendra cringed inwardly, fearing her question might seem frivolous to the great teacher. But he did not seem put off. "It was surely not something I set out to do," Akhenaten said, settling back against the tree. "On the Earth plane, I ruled the country of Egypt. They called me Pharaoh Amenhotep IV. In a dream, God asked me to build the city Amarna—a place comparable to a 'New Jerusalem.

"God spoke to you?" asked Kendra, awed by the concept.

"It was in a dream, as I said. That's one of the things you will be challenged with as you learn and grow; how to recognize what is given to you as you travel in your dreams."

"So, you weren't sure if it was God or not?"

Akhenaten solemnly shook his head. "The only way you can be sure of what you hear in your dreams is to test them out in the world. To become a 'spiritual scientist.'"

Kendra took in a deep breath and tried to grasp the implications of what Akhenaten had experienced. "So, you had a city built based on a dream?"

A small smile appeared on Akhenaten's lips. "Well, I was the pharaoh, so I didn't have to explain myself to anyone." Then Akhenaten became serious again. "Not only did I build a new city, but I was also inspired to introduce new teaching: monotheism; the knowledge of one God. His name was Aten. And I became Akhenaten."

"Changing a peoples' belief sounds like a daunting task," Kendra said, her brows furrowing.

Akhenaten nodded. "I would not have thought it possible. But since a radiant being had communicated this to me through Light and sound, I knew that not only could I do it, I had to do it. My knowing was that strong."

Akhenaten seemed to gaze into the far past, remembering, "As Akhenaten, I turned Egyptian tradition upside down. And those changes were not welcomed by most of my people."

Falling more in-depth into the story, Kendra asked, "So what did you do about that?"

Akhenaten shrugged. "There was little I could do but hold to the integrity of the vision I was given." He sighed. "My 'heresy' was rejected entirely. And the punishment was handled with swiftness, an efficiency I would have admired had the results not been my murder." Then Akhenaten smiled and looked at Kendra. "But the seed was planted. And the seed of Truth can grow, even when the soil is less than welcoming to it."

Kendra hesitantly smiled back. "So, you're saying that people don't choose to be Light Travelers, but the Spirit chooses them?"

"It's something like that," Akhenaten said with a chuckle. "It's more like who we are—the soul—prepares, but we may not be consciously aware of it when we reembody."

Kendra let that concept sink in, then, with a slight shake of her head, pressed on. "Well, I know that there have always been Light Travelers on the Earth, but I don't know much about them. You were a king... are all the travelers' people of high stature?"

Not unkindly, Master Akhenaten chuckled. "Not at all. Some have been poets, writers, scientists, philosophers, and teachers on the Earth plane. Others have led such ordinary lives that they went virtually unnoticed, even as they anchored this powerful energy of Light into the physical realm."

"What do you mean that they 'anchored' this Light?" Kendra immediately asked. She was fascinated and delighted that Master Akhenaten was willing to be so forthcoming. While very loving, these teachers of the Light and sound were not often this responsive to the questions of their students—possibly because once started, the issues could be endless. But Akhenaten seemed content to satisfy Kendra's curiosity at least a little further.

"The Father-Mother-God extends Its Light and sound everywhere. On the Earth plane, it is necessary for a physical body to receive and allow this energy to flow into that level. That is what Light Travelers do."

Understanding dawned in Kendra's eyes, so Akhenaten continued. "At special times in human evolution, a traveler is given the keys to soul transcendence: The practices that awaken the awareness of oneself as a soul and as more than that, knowing their oneness with God. This is not a theoretical understanding, but the actual experience of that living reality."

"Is that what you taught, Master Akhenaten?" Kendra wanted to know.

Akhenaten shook his head but smiled. "I did not teach that when I was Pharaoh because people were not at the stage of their development to be able to know that. The inner mysteries of Light and sound were mostly secret for many centuries until a Light Traveler who became known as Jesus embodied."

Once again, Kendra nodded. Jesus was known to all the neophytes. "During his lifetime," Akhenaten continued, "he made the inner wisdom available to the masses. After that, the spiritual knowledge was available to anyone who awakened to the Truth within."

As Kendra allowed the wisdom she had been receiving to settle within her, Akhenaten made a gesture while holding his consciousness on a secret, sacred thought and conjured an Infinity Portal. "Now let us consider the history of the Shamir Stone," the master said as the Portal sprang into being. Despite wanting to impress Akhenaten, Kendra gasped. She knew this was the test Akhenaten would use to evaluate her readiness to be his student. Any sense of confidence she had gained as the master had spoken so freely with her evaporated as the gateway solidified, and tension filled the girl. This was far too important to make even a single error. Just because Akhenaten had summoned the entrance did not mean she would be able to see the visions it presented. It was up to her to maintain the requisite singleness of focus for as long as the master instructed her.

The Portal itself was the size of an open book. Its surface had the appearance of a mirror cut from a large, precious stone polished to crystal smoothness. The students training to be seers would gaze within these Portals throughout their training. They would see the colors and the light and symbols of the spirit world. Their vision would deepen to the vibration and intensity of the world around them. They would feel, hear, and see in their Portal the emanations of the higher realms of spirit. Daily meditations and inner spiritual exercises would strengthen their ability. It was momentous that Akhenaten had opened a Portal for Kendra. She knew every bit of her training would be called upon to maintain her connection to it.

Master Akhenaten gestured again, and the Portal projected the holographic sacred geometric pattern of the Flower of Life. The floating flower pulsed energy all around.

Akhenaten closed his eyes and blessed the Portal. "We call forward and bless the history of the Shamir Stone for the highest good." Akhenaten touched the center of the Portal, causing the geometric pattern to spin, saying, "I will use the history of the Shamir Stone to show how we search through time. The Flower of Life Portal is only for advanced initiates; those who have demonstrated the ability to focus through time."

The master touched Kendra at the middle of her forehead, and she felt a tingling sensation. She closed her eyes briefly, then opened them as Akhenaten said, "Let's see if you can hold the energy long enough to follow the story as we go along."

Kendra gazed more closely at the Portal. Despite her anxiety, her amber eyes sparkled with excitement. She had learned that touching a Portal without a blessing would not open the door of time. Only creating a clear, heartfelt intention would bring the best results.

As the Portal surface showed scenes of events through time, Akhenaten began explaining the mysterious Shamir Stone. "The Shamir was one of ten mysterious artifacts created by God at twilight upon the sixth day of creation. It is a supernatural worm the size of a single grain of barleycorn. Its gaze is so powerful that it can cut through any material with ease; even through diamond itself, the hardest substance on Earth. Such a wondrous creature God entrusted to the hoopoe bird. It was charged with serving the Shamir whenever and wherever the time came."

Akhenaten pointed to the bird's nest above in the oak tree. "His species is to protect the Shamir from all harm. Hoopoes are not supernatural. They are widespread throughout places called Europe and Asia on the Earth plane."

Kendra's eyes narrowed as she asked in an uncertain tone, "Wait, I am confused. Why is the Shamir called a stone when it is a worm?"

Akhenaten replied, "The Shamir is called a stone to keep its identity secret. Only those who know what a Shamir is would know it's a worm. And, the tiny lead box in which it rests looks like a stone."

The Portal revealed symbols and a projection of Hermes, the high priest of Atlantis, bringing the Shamir from Atlantis to Egypt.

As Hermes appeared, Kendra frowned. "That's Hermes! I have seen him in our garden. What did he have to do with the Shamir?" Kendra was so excited, she didn't even realize that she had succeeded in maintaining the consciousness needed to view through the Portal.

"You will see," said Akhenaten wisely.

Fascinated, Kendra watched Hermes near a pyramid in Egypt. It was under construction at a site where an energy vortex extended from the Earth and aligned with the stars of the constellation Orion in the heavens.

Akhenaten continued, "Do you see Hermes carrying a tiny metal box?" Kendra nodded, caught up in the scene. "The Shamir was always wrapped in wool and stored in a container made of lead, where it rested and traveled the inner realms of Light until it was needed in the Earth realm. Any other vessel would melt and disintegrate under the Shamir's gaze."

Kendra watched Hermes as he donned a gold breast-plate. He opened the lid of the small lead box and unwrapped the wool cloth. Next, he set the Shamir over the construction plans of the Pyramid of the North. The Shamir hovered, absorbing the images. At a signal unseen by the observers, Hermes placed it back into its box, closed it, and rose.

The scene in the Portal faded, then a new view appeared. The master and hopeful initiate watched as Hermes arrived at the site where several uncut stones lay near the partly constructed pyramid. Again, Hermes, with a hoopoe bird perched nearby, opened the box. The bird, with its long bill, delicately picked up the tiny worm and placed it near the roughly hewn stones. There was a brief pause, and then a beam of light burst from the Shamir's gaze and extended to the hard stone. In moments, the light cut the rocks precisely to the measurements of the drawing it had absorbed.

The Portal revealed that day after day, the hoopoe bird moved the worm from stone to stone. Once all the massive stones were cut, Hermes stepped forward and beckoned to a group of Atlantean priests. With intensely focused concentration, they raised their hands and projected immensely *powerful energy that reversed gravity and polarity. As if weightless, the multi-ton stones rose and moved into place.*

As the final stone settled, Master Akhenaten raised his left hand over the Portal, ending the session. He glanced at Kendra to see if she was able to hold the consciousness necessary to maintain contact with the gateway. He saw beads of sweat had formed on her forehead, and her face was slightly haggard from the strain of intense concentration. But he saw from her aura that she had followed the story through to the end.

Despite her near exhaustion, at the master's glance, Kendra tensed and waited for Akhenaten's next words. She knew this would be the pronouncement that could alter the course of her entire life. Time seemed to slow as he considered his decision.

Have I demonstrated worthiness to become a student of this man? *Kendra wondered to herself.* Have I asked too many questions? Was I strong enough? Should I say something? Should I keep a respectful silence? *As these questions raced through Kendra's mind, she became more and more uncertain.* What will I do if he refuses me?

Akhenaten nodded once, coming to his conclusion. He took in a breath, almost a sigh, and said, "I think that is quite enough for your first Flower of Life Portal lesson."

Kendra paled. "I can do better!" she blurted out. "Really, I will work harder. I'm sure I can..." Near tears,

Kendra paused, and her mouth shut with a clap. "Wait, what did you say?"

Reaching forward, Akhenaten enfolded Kendra in a gentle hug. "I said, young initiate, that you have done enough for your first lesson. We will get together again soon."

"We will?" Kendra asked in a daze.

Akhenaten laughed, "Of course we will. Since you are now my student, we will see a lot of each other."

"Your st..."

Akhenaten nodded his head and laughed, shooing her away with his hands. Kendra sprang to her feet. "Oh, thank you Master Akhenaten. You will not be sorry you have made this choice."

The master nodded, still smiling as Kendra backed away. "Go, find a drink of water, celebrate with your friends..." As she turned, his face became slightly more serious. "... because your real work is only now beginning," he said too quietly for her to hear.

Kendra could barely contain her joy. It would not do at all for a brand-new initiate to be seen running through the serene garden. But there was a definite spring in her step as she went to find her friends and share with them her good fortune.

From its nest high in the oak tree, the hoopoe, with its crown of colorful feathers, took wing, then glided down to rest on Akhenaten's shoulder. "Yes, my friend," said Akhenaten to the bird, "this one will be a brilliant student and one whose future will be very bright." The bird seemed to nod its head once and appeared far wiser than a bird should be.

Chapter 11
December 1894
Hope

*T*he bracing wind of the late December afternoon gusted outside and intruded into Albert's thoughts. It was the first Thursday of the winter school break. Hoping to escape his troubles, Albert went to the Bavarian Library near the Gymnasium campus where he sat contemplating his compass. Inspiration was not forthcoming, so he put his treasure in his coat pocket and wandered over to the bookshelves. He searched half-heartedly for one of his favorite philosophers, Kant, and found *Critique of Pure Reason*. As he pulled the book from the shelf, he heard a familiar voice call his name.

"Albert?"

Albert turned, and his face lit up. "Herr Talmud, it is so good to see you!"

They embraced cordially, Max, a head taller, with a premature touch of gray in his chestnut hair and mus-

148

tache. Though only in his mid-30s, he had the air of a wise older gentleman.

Max was equally excited to see his young friend. He held Albert at arm's length and assessed the boy. "You're growing up nicely, Albert. How have you been? Are you at the Gymnasium getting your diploma?"

At the mention of the Gymnasium, Albert's body slumped. "Uh, that's kind of a long story. Say, maybe I can tell you about it over dinner. Can you join me?"

"Of course," Max responded with a smile, putting an arm around Albert's shoulders. "I would love to find out what has been going on with one of my favorite people."

For the first time in a long time, Albert felt himself relax in the company of a friend as the two walked to the coatroom. Moments later, they stepped into the cold evening air and headed down the hill to an alehouse a couple blocks away.

* * *

Not far from the Bavarian Library, Raka surreptitiously peered beneath his cloak and inspected his walking stick. Pressing the ruby eyes set in the dragon's head, he made sure the steel needle tipped with venom was ready. He knew he could not do harm to the possessor of the Shamir without paying a massive karmic price, but you never knew when it might be a useful tool for coercing someone to do his will. He was hot on the trail of the Shamir and knew it was near at hand. Satisfied that all was in readiness, he reset the needle and continued his way.

Sniffing the air, he found the Shamir scent much stronger than it had been just minutes ago. He quickened his pace, practically salivating at the thought of possessing the stone.

A few blocks from the library, Max and Albert entered the alehouse and found a quiet table. After ordering beer and sauerbraten from the plump, middle-aged waitress, they resumed their conversation.

"Do you remember when I would visit you and your family each Shabbat?" Max asked. "Your parents were so kind to me when I was a struggling medical student."

Albert nodded, a warm feeling filling him along with the memories of simpler days. "Yes, I remember. I have missed you. It was an exciting time when you were twenty-nine and I only ten, and you brought me books on philosophy and mathematics. I loved the quizzes you made up for me to test how well I'd understood my assignments."

Max grinned as he chewed a bite of beef and pointed his fork at Albert. "It wasn't very long before I could no longer follow *you*."

Albert beamed at the praise, and the two chatted amiably, recalling the many Shabbat evenings they had spent together.

Outside the alehouse, Raka approached, his pace quickening in anticipation. He took a final sniff and satisfied himself he was at the right place. His thoughts were confirmed when he saw the hoopoe bird perched above the door. The aroma of human food coming from the alehouse did not interest him. Instead, the rat that ran around the corner of the building as he approached made him remember it had been a while since he had eaten.

Raka entered and casually made his way to the table next to the one where Albert and Max were chatting. When the waitress approached, he ordered a beer to justify his presence and settled back, giving no indication that he was listening intently to the boy and the man at the nearby table. Raka wondered which of the two possessed the Shamir.

Though he had found the conversation relaxing and enjoyable, Albert decided it was time to bring up the topic he really wanted to discuss. Taking a bite of his pot roast, Albert became serious. "Max, may I confide in you?"

The smile faded from Max's face and was replaced by a look of concern. "Of course, you can tell me anything. What is it, Albert? Is something wrong with your parents?"

"No, no, my parents are fine. They are in Italy. I am staying with my aunt and uncle, who live not far from here." Albert paused and took a long drink of beer as he gathered his thoughts. He was trying to figure out just how to tell his story, but when no inspiration appeared, he just plowed ahead. "It's just that I feel I am wasting my time at the Gymnasium. I pass my math and science examinations easily because I taught myself the things we're studying in class years ago." Albert pulled the Gymnasium Direktor's letter from his pocket, saying, "But when I ask to be given more advanced work to study, I am met only with anger." He handed the letter to Max, who frowned as he read it.

Dear Herr Einstein,

You are requested to attend a meeting at 10:00 a.m. on December 15, 1894, at the Office of the Direktor to discuss your future at the Luitpold Gymnasium with the Academik Committee Council. Please be prompt.

Sincerely,
Stefan Braun,
Direktor

Max shook his head as he folded the letter and gave it back to Albert. "I'm not surprised, Albert. I suspected you would have a hard time at the Gymnasium."

"You did?"

Max nodded. "Yes. You're right in the middle of a struggle within the school system itself. The *schulkrieg*, the war over the schools, is a fight between proponents of the classical values associated with education in Latin and Greek and supporters of instruction in modern languages and natural sciences."

Albert leaned back in his chair, surprised at this revelation. "I had no idea."

"How could you know?" Max sighed, "But, you see, I struggled too as I went through school to become a doctor."

"Really?" Albert was taken aback.

"Mmm hmm. Believe it or not, the Luitpold Gymnasium has had a reputation as an enlightened school. All of Germany celebrates its 'institutes of learning' because of how prosperous it has become in the last three decades. Germany leads the world in what people are calling the industrial revolution."

Albert waved his hand as if brushing away Max's statement. "Institutes of learning? Bah! They are just factories of rote instruction."

153

Max did not argue. "Be that as it may, Germany boasts of its schools." As Albert scowled, Max continued. "But, my friend, I can tell you that there are schools in Switzerland that may be of interest to you. I attended one of them before I went to the University of Munich."

Albert raised his eyebrows. "Switzerland?"

Max nodded. "The Polytechnic in Zurich, where I studied. And I have an uncle who lives in Zurich. He was instrumental in having me attend the Polytechnic, and I believe he would be willing to assist you as well. It would give you the education I think you are looking for."

Albert's face brightened. "That would be wonderful... if it would not be too much trouble, I mean."

Max touched Albert's arm, reassuring him, and said, "As far as I'm concerned, you're family, Albert. I would be glad to help you. No trouble at all. It is the least I can do for people who treated me with such kindness."

Albert sat back in his chair. For the first time in months, he felt like he could breathe.

Albert and Max went back to reminiscing as they finished their supper together. Feeling a refreshing wind in his sails blowing him in a new direction, Albert was now more than ready to meet the direktor and his lieutenants. When the two finished the last of their beer, Albert prepared to pay the check.

Raka was deep in thought, speculating on what he had heard when he saw the younger man reach into his pocket and pull out his money clip along with a round, brass device. Raka held his breath. There it was, his treasure! He wanted to jump up and grab it but had enough presence of mind to know that was not the way to achieve his objective. In the excitement of seeing the Shamir, Raka's concentration weakened, and the illusion of his human form began to fade. Scales began to appear on his face. He rubbed his hands over his cheeks quickly, and his soft, human complexion returned. Shaking with anticipation, Raka was overwhelmed by his proximity to the prize he had sought for millennia. As Albert and Max stood up and made their way to the front door, neither noticed the blond gentleman at the table behind them.

Raka waited until Max and Albert had left the alehouse before he tossed a few coins on the table and followed. As he exited the building, he saw Max walking to the left and Albert going right to fetch his bicycle at the library. Raka grinned and moved along the cobblestone street toward Albert, melting into the pitch-black night. Albert rounded the corner of the now-dark library and walked to where he had parked his bike. Lost in thoughts of his future, he was unaware of Raka approaching him from behind. Panting in anticipation, Raka prepared to strike, cosmic law be damned. He readied his weapon by pressing the dragon's ruby eyes and exposing the toxic steel needle. Just as he began to aim, out of nowhere, the hoopoe bird flew straight into the evil lizard, its pointed bill piercing his left eye. Raka stifled a cry and crouched to the ground in pain as the swift bird flew away.

Pulled from his musing by the muffled sound, Albert looked around. But the night was dark, and he saw neither Raka nor the weapon, which fell from his grasp as the lizard covered his wounded eye. The walking stick tumbled to the cobblestone pavement, and the poisoned needle tip broke with a snap, bouncing onto a squirrel nearby, causing it to chatter angrily. As he was placing his leg over his bicycle, Albert heard the noise and saw the little rodent scurry past him. Because it was so dark, Albert did not believe his eyes as the creature's fur began to smoke and the animal appeared to disintegrate into a puddle of ooze. Albert shook his head, chiding himself for the way his eyes deceived him. He pulled the collar of his coat tighter around him to protect himself from the cutting wind.

Muttering soundless curses at the hoopoe bird, Raka skulked in the darkness, attempting to tend his wound. Far from fatal for the changeling, it was painful enough to demand his attention. He cursed himself soundly for his over-eagerness and realized what he had nearly done. The price he would have paid, he realized, would have been too high, even for the Shamir. He would not make that mistake again.

Walking in the dark, cold night, Raka vowed to lay a far more foolproof plan. Yes, it would take time. Yes, he would have to be patient. But he would not let the Shamir slip through his clutches again. A plan began to form in his mind—one that involved other humans. Like a precious seed, he would nurture it until it blossomed and bore fruit.

Astride his bicycle, Albert pedaled toward his aunt's house, his mind filled with thoughts of a much brighter future. Not far behind, the hoopoe flew, ever vigilant, watching for the potential dangers of which Albert was blissfully unaware.

Chapter 12
December 1894
Twist of Fate

*B*right umbrellas dotted the farmer's market in central Munich, creating a rainbow of slightly faded but still festive colors. The shouts of buyers haggling for fresh fruits, vegetables, and meats on the cold December Saturday filled the air. By mid-morning, tired patrons of the market, having been up since before dawn, began to shuffle into Munich Brau Biergarten for sandwiches and beer. Rows of people sat family style on long picnic tables taking a well-earned break and enjoying their repast.

Johann was wiping down the bar with a damp rag when he saw Albert walk through the doorway. His immediate reaction was happiness, which was quickly replaced with fear. Johann frantically looked around to see if any of the boys, who often hung out at the Biergarten on Saturdays after a tough week at school, had noticed

Albert's arrival. Since their critical discussion the day of the Volkisch rally, Albert had been staying away from his friend—in fact, the whole Thomas family—to avoid causing them problems for associating with a Jew.

Even so, Albert couldn't keep a smile from his face as he pulled up a barstool at the far end of the bar. Johann continued polishing the bar as he slowly made his way to where Albert sat. Glancing furtively around, Johann hissed at Albert in a whisper, "What are you doing here, Albert? You know it's dangerous for us if you're seen talking to me."

Albert waved away his friend's concern and leaned toward him. "My 'problem' looks to have been solved! And with it, *our* problem will go away as well."

Johann frowned, appearing to rub at a particularly stubborn stain on the bar. "Are you crazy? What do you mean?"

With a grin, Albert gave Johann a quick recap of his dinner with Herr Talmud and his hopes of going to Switzerland—which would effectively remove Albert from the local scene and keep him safely away from Johann and his family. As Albert laid out the situation, Johann wiped in slower and slower circles, and his frown began to change into a smile. By the time Albert finished his narrative, Johann had all but forgotten his concerns. "Albert, that would be wonderful!" he exclaimed, then clapped his hand over his mouth and looked around to see if anyone had heard.

Albert was grinning and nodding when a thought hit Johann, and he deflated like a punctured balloon. "But... Switzerland?"

Albert put his hand on his friend's arm. "I know. But it's not so far away. Since I will no longer be the center of attention, I think we will be able to see each other when I come home to visit my family."

"Yes. Maybe so," Johann said, not entirely convinced as he went back to polishing the bar.

Behind Albert, the senior class boys were toasting each other. They were filled with the optimism and hope of young men preparing to make their way into the world in a few months. Johann drew Albert a beer, then excused himself from taking the overflowing garbage pail to the trash bin outside. As he was emptying the last scraps out of the bucket, Werner von Wiesel rode up on his bicycle.

Hoping to avoid his classmate, Johann turned to walk away. But Werner called out to him. "Wait just a minute, Johann!" His back to Werner, Johann grimaced. He wanted nothing to do with the bully who had threatened him if he stayed friends with Albert. But the boy was becoming increasingly influential at school. There was no way Johann could ignore him without reprisals.

Walking up to Johann, Werner put his hand on Johann's shoulder. "Johann, I want to apologize for what I said about you and Albert."

Johann turned, his eyes widening with incredulity. "What?"

"No, really. I've been thinking about it. There's no reason you and I can't be friends." Werner smiled and laughed nervously as he extended his hand to shake.

Johann wasn't buying it. "What do you want, Werner?" he asked, ignoring the proffered hand and being as brusque as he dared to be.

Werner looked at Johann for a moment, and Johann could practically see the wheels turning in the boy's head. Then Werner leaned toward Johann. "Okay, look," he said conspiratorially. "I remember hearing you and Albert talking about this compass of his. I want to get a look at it."

Johann frowned, thinking hard. "Compass? Uh, I don't know what you're talking about, Werner."

Werner expression turned serious, his patience evaporating. He grabbed Johann by the front of his shirt and pulled him close. Through clenched teeth, he said, "Don't play dumb, Johann. I want to see the compass, and I *will* see it." Then he pushed Johann away roughly, so the boy fell to one knee. Werner turned his back on Johann and strode into the *Biergarten* while Johann dusted off his trousers and straightened his clothing. When he was satisfied with his appearance, he reclaimed his empty garbage pail and followed Werner back inside.

Meanwhile, Raka, astride a bicycle, had been tracking the smell of the Shamir. Attracted by a sudden spike in negative energy, he paused his quest to investigate. The negativity of any sort pleased him. Dismounting, he walked his bicycle toward the source of power at the back of the *Biergarten* and cautiously peered around the corner of the building. He was just in time to overhear most of Johann and Werner's exchange about the compass.

The hatred in Werner's consciousness tasted pleasant, almost sweet, on Raka's tongue as he considered this development. A human boy with the same objective—though certainly not the same motive—as himself. And a boy in whom fear and hatred simmered, just waiting for something to bring it to a boil. This was just too good to be true. Raka relished the thought of turning the boy into a minion who would do his bidding. He would have to come up with a plan to pull Werner to his cause.

A dormant blackthorn bush at the side of the *Biergarten* gave him an idea. He broke off a short twig that held a hard, long spike. From a gland in his throat, he secreted a toxic venom, then spit it onto the thorn. Looking furtively left, then right, he affixed the lethal barb onto the outside of the handle on the right side of Werner's bicycle. He knew that to some this secretion could be deadly. But to those who were steeped in hatred and negativity, it would have a different effect.

His plan set in motion, Raka left his own bicycle leaning against the wall and walked to the front of the building, where he entered and found a place to watch his target. He spotted Werner with his friends at the end of one of the large family tables.

Johann stood unhappily in the kitchen area. He didn't much like the idea of Albert going to Switzerland, even though he could see it was probably a good thing. And he didn't want that Werner was interested in Albert's compass. But there was nothing he could do about either situation now. With a heavy sigh, he placed several paper-wrapped ham sandwiches and bottles of beer into a sack to take to his father who was working nearby.

As he walked past Albert, he said, "I'll be back in a few minutes. I want to talk more about your news."

From his table, Werner was preparing to approach Johann once again. But seeing he was about to leave, he waited and tracked Johann's movements with interest. As Johann made his way out of the *Biergarten,* Werner went to the back of the building where he had left his bicycle.

Out front, Johann put the sack into the wicker basket on his bicycle. He shivered in the December chill as he mounted his bike and began the short ride to deliver lunch to his father and the clerks.

In the back of the *Biergarten*, Werner wrapped his scarf around his neck and face to protect himself from the chill air as he rushed to mount his bike. He grabbed the handlebars, then yelped with pain. The bully stared at his hand and saw a thorn sticking in the palm of his hand. He plucked the barb out and angrily threw it to the ground as he began pedaling to catch up with Johann. He'd give the boy one more chance to get Albert to show him his compass.

As he pedaled, the venom from the thorn began coursing through his body. The effect was immediate. His face turned crimson. Nostrils flared, and his eyes bulged. His muscles and veins strained against his skin.

He felt a rush of hatred and anger toward Johann. "Who was he to say no?" he asked himself. Werner gripped the handlebars harder as he raced to catch up with Johann.

Wanting to see how Werner would react to his venom, Raka also had slipped out of the *Biergarten*. He laughed in satisfaction when saw the boy grasp his handlebars, then flinch. As Werner rode away, Raka mounted his bicycle and followed a small distance behind. He smiled to see the boy's aura become suffused with red; a sure sign the venom had the desired result.

Johann pedaled his way down the uneven cobble-stones, crossing Thal and turning onto the Marienplatz. Riding parallel to the streetcar tracks, Johann began to apply his brakes as he saw a streetcar speeding toward him in the distance. He knew they went at a good clip along this stretch of their route. Suddenly, Johann heard a sound behind him. He glanced over his shoulder to see a bicycle rider rapidly gaining on him, his face obscured by a fluffy scarf, overtaking him. He recognized Werner shaking his fist. "You Jew-lover, this is what you get when you defy me!"

Before Johann could react, Werner pulled alongside Johann and struck him with all the force he could muster, then rapidly veered out of sight down an intersecting street. Johann's bike swerved from the power of the blow, and the hapless rider tumbled with it onto the track in front of the speeding streetcar. The boy and bike disap-peared under the onrushing vehicle with a sickening crunch of metal and bone. Though the car was already braking, its momentum carried it for half a block before coming to a stop.

The conductor ran from the streetcar to the mangled bicycle and Johann's lifeless body. He looked down the side street where Werner had fled, but there was no sign of bike or rider. As the onlookers began to converge on the conductor, he could only shake his head. He had no idea who the mystery rider had been. Raka, now standing near the scene next to his bicycle, had seen the whole thing. A wave of satisfaction came over him; he knew he had found someone who could help him further his dark purpose.

Back at the *Biergarten*, Albert sat happily humming, awaiting Johann's return. He sorely missed his best friend. He smiled, thinking that was all going to change now that fortune was smiling on him.

Chapter 13
December 1894
Farewell

*M*unich Times – Monday, December 17, 1894 – *Sixteen-year-old Johann Thomas was struck and killed by a southbound electric Städtische Straßenbahnen train on Thursday, December 12, at 11:45 a.m. The accident occurred in central Munich near the town hall. Young Thomas, of Obergiesing, lost control of his bicycle and fell onto the tracks in front of the train. According to Munich County Coroner Hans Gottlieb, he would have died instantly from his wounds. Foul play is suspected, according to the Munich Police Department and Munich County Coroner, though there is no ascertainable motive.*

The new bells of St. Luke's Lutheran Church rang out mournfully, announcing the passing of Johann Thomas. The gray winter skies felt heavy over Munich; all the drearier since Johann had been in the springtime of his life. His stoic father, Frederick, comforted his wife, Christine, who seemed unable to stop wailing. Friends and family from all over Munich came to the Gothic cathedral to pay their respects to the son of this upstanding family.

Dark circles lay under Albert's empty eyes. He longed for an embrace from his best friend. Albert had not slept since the day Johann died. The few days that had passed felt like years as the memory of that fateful morning kept playing over and over in Albert's mind.

He had struck out on his bicycle when Johann did not return from his delivery of sandwiches and beer. As he approached the Marienplatz, his concern grew when he saw the crowd of people surrounding the plaza. Albert jumped off his bicycle and pushed his way through the crowd. He screamed in horror to find his friend's battered and lifeless body sprawled over the streetcar tracks. The police forced him back when he tried to reach the limp body of his beloved friend.

Standing over Johann had been Johann's father, Frederick, his face crimson with ire. He had witnessed the event from the window above in a nearby building. Frederick had smiled when he saw Johann on his ride delivering his basket of refreshments. He was proud of his son. Suddenly, from behind Johann, a youth on a bicycle pushed his son in the way of the streetcar. He sprang to his feet; he could not believe what he had seen. He had cried out, "Oh my God, no!" and rushed down to the street.

White lilies draped the closed oak casket. The congregation of mourners dressed for the season filled the enormous nave of the church. The pipe organ bellowed "Amazing Grace." Albert pushed his grief aside. Holding onto the carved doves on the four corners, he and three of his school friends raised the casket from the pedestal on which it sat. They stepped to the rhythm of the sacred music, carrying Johann to the waiting black-lacquered hearse carriage outside the church.

Snowflakes were falling. Albert joined the Thomas family in their ebony carriage. A majestic sable Friesian horse-drawn hearse led the parade of mourners to the Ostfriedhof Cemetery. Albert huddled next to Christine and Frederick as Christine tucked a woolen blanket around them. His heart breaking, Albert wanted to reach out to Johann's parents. He was about to speak when the equine carriage halted at the cemetery entrance.

Johann's final journey took them through the cemetery maze to the Thomas burial plot. Behind the towering angel protectorate statue near the burial site huddled Werner von Wiesel. Wringing his hands, he cringed further into the shadows, his eyes darting around to see if anyone he knew saw him.

At a nearby headstone stood a lean, tall, blond stranger. He was looking straight at Werner. He smiled, though it was less than a cheerful one, and tipped his hand to his hat as if to say hello. Werner's face went white with fear as he froze in place. His thoughts raced: *he knows what I have done.* Werner wanted to run, but his feet would not move. Raka, calm as a warm summer breeze, saw the terror in Werner's face when their eyes met. His smile widened. Werner tried to breathe as he rubbed his eyes, trying to determine if what he had seen was a ghost or a real person. When Werner opened his eyes, he found himself standing alone.

Chapter 14
Garden of Remembrance

*T*he glockenspiel chimed twelve times. The rhythm of time seemed to slow with each beat as Johann tumbled into the path of the streetcar. The last thing he heard was Werner's loud, angry cry. Out of control, his bicycle swerved wildly, the basket of sandwiches flying into the air. Still trying to regain control of his bike, Johann plunged onto the tracks and under the unforgiving steel wheels of the oncoming train. His last thought was of his father, Frederick. Johann had glanced up and found him watching from the second-story window. Then his head hit the ground and that, mercifully, was the last thing in the world he saw as the cold iron undercarriage of the train mangled his body.

* * *

There was light. Johann wondered about that. Whatever its origin, a bright vortex of light seemed to be pulling him up. He felt oddly at peace. In fact, he felt terrific. As Johann transcended his body, a veil lifted, and it seemed to him as if he floated in space. He closed his eyes and drifted in his consciousness.

After an indeterminate amount of time, he awoke and found himself laying in a garden. Lush, green lawns with paths of iridescent stone that formed gentle rambling arcs through the greenery surrounded a glistening white building. A river with calm, blue waters flowed past where Johann lay. Sitting up, Johann saw that lush beds of giant purple roses and red-and-white tulips dotted a nearby hillside. On the far side of the building lay a valley where he could see people dressed in white walking. As he stared at the scene, Johann realized their legs were not moving; they were gliding just above the ground toward the building.

Johann's mind rebelled as he tried to make sense of what he was seeing. In confusion, he wondered what had happened and how had he gotten here—and where "here" was. He closed his eyes and rubbed his temples. Receiving no inspiration, he opened his eyes to see a radiant young woman dressed in white approaching him.

The Light Initiate, Kendra, smiled, inwardly hearing Johann's questions. "You are safe now, Johann," she said, reassuring him.

Johann shook his head in disbelief. "Safe? I've been run over by a train!" To prove it, he looked down, and his eyes grew wide as he saw his body was whole and well. "What...? How...? Who are you?" Johann tried to stand but stumbled.

With a quick step, Kendra caught Johann's arm and eased him back to the soft ground. "It's all right. I know you have a million questions." Placing her hand on her chest, she said, "My name is Kendra, and I am an agent of God sent to help you." As Johann's jaw dropped, Kendra squeezed his arm and sat. "Here, let me see if I can explain this to you." Johann nodded blankly.

With warmth and caring, Kendra asked, "What is the last thing you remember?"

Johann gazed down and blinked several times, trying to capture his last moments. "I... I was on my bicycle, and the streetcar came along... and, I... fell." As he said that, awareness hit Johann. "Oh my God! Am I, ah, am I... dead?"

With a compassionate smile, Kendra leaned in and took Johann's hand. "Well, Johann, you are no longer living as you once did. Your body has been damaged beyond repair. It is, indeed, dead." Johann gulped as Kendra continued. "But *you*, my dear friend, are far from dead as people on Earth imagine that state."

Johann pinched himself. It felt like a pinch always had. "Um, I guess I see what you mean." He looked around. "Yeah, no one with wings and harps that I can see, heh-heh," he said, reaching for a joke.

Kendra kissed Johann's hand. "Excellent, Johann. Some people take a lot longer to accept what has happened to them."

Relaxing in the love that was the essence of this plane of existence, he asked, "But where am I. *What* am I?"

"Those are exactly the right questions," Kendra said encouragingly. "You are in God's Garden of Remembrance. Some call it Summerland and consider it Heaven. You will see people here whom you know, those who have passed on. You are what some people might call an angel—but not what people traditionally think angels are."

"But what does that mean, Kendra?"

With another bright smile, she said, "It means that soon you will have a new role in which to serve the people on Earth. And some people very specifically," she said with a wink.

Johann's mind was reeling; he shook his head in disbelief. "But if I am dead, why do I have a body?"

Kendra laughed, her eyes sparkling with delight. "You have a body here because you are on the astral plane, which makes you appear as if you have a body. Many realms of beingness exist.

People are aware of the physical realm and can identify it. It is evident: You have a physical body, so you exist on that physical realm. The astral body is a replica of the physical body, but subtler. It is a sheath of energy that most people inhabit immediately after death. When we are alive, the astral body remains attached to the physical body via a stream or ribbon of energy. You can leave the physical body during sleep, coma, meditation, or when you're in a kind of trance. Sometimes people extend out of the body under the influence of drugs, or as you experienced, in an accident."

Then Kendra furrowed her brow and asked, "Can you recall what you felt when you left the Earth plane?"

Johann sighed and thought about it. "I was falling. Then I felt lifted in bright, white light."

He held his hand to his heart and closed his eyes. "Loving filled and surrounded me. It was so beautiful. I was floating. I think I might have fallen asleep. When I opened my eyes, I was here."

With a gentle smile still radiating from her eyes, Kendra nodded and reached out toward Johann. "Excellent. Sometimes when people are in an accident or experience a violent death, they don't recognize what happened and stay tied to their physical body. They wander around on Earth, not knowing they need to move on until someone of an elevated consciousness can guide them to their next level."

"Really?" Johann asked, fascinated.

Kendra nodded solemnly. "Uh-huh. But you didn't resist, and allowed yourself to follow the love and the Light here," she said approvingly. "So, are you ready to discover what is in store for you? There is much for me to show you."

For some reason, Johann was not feeling scared or sad or worried. In fact, he was amazingly calm and relaxed. This Summerland garden seemed somehow almost familiar, and all Johann really felt was... loved.

He reached out, took Kendra's hand, and rose to his feet. He sensed the rightness of it all. "I'm ready."

"I'm glad to hear that," said a man's voice from behind them.

As they turned, Kendra broke into a great smile. Two men stood there, both radiating peace. A sense of joy filled Johann as Kendra said, "Johann, I would like you to meet—"

Johann gulped, then tears filled his eyes. He fell to his knees, and the taller of the two men reached down and gently lifted him to his feet. "Now, now, Johann. No need for that."

Johann wiped his eyes and smiled sheepishly. "Sorry, uh..." Johann blinked and shook his head, trying to gather his thoughts. "You're, um, Jesus, right?"

The man's smile radiated from his eyes as he nodded and pointed to his companion. "Mm-hmm. And this is my friend, Moses."

Moses nodded. "We have some special training for you in addition to what Kendra will be teaching you."

"Training? For me? But why?"

Jesus put his arm around Johann's shoulder. "Well, it has to do with a friend of yours. A boy named Albert Einstein."

Chapter 15
Raka Recruits

Johann's funeral came to an end, and the weary mourners began to drift away. Johann's mother thought Albert should have one last goodbye, so Albert followed his friend's parents to their motor carriage.

After the evening of mourning at the Thomas home, he planned to spend the night in Johann's bedroom. Raka, on the other hand, was in no hurry to depart the cemetery. He had some business to attend to there. After the crowd had left, he made his way over to the angel protectorate statue where a young boy lurked. Approaching from behind, Raka reached out and grasped the boy's shoulder. A gasp escaped Werner von Wiesel's lips as Raka turned the boy to face him.

Werner looked pale and haggard. Filled with self-loathing, he wished he could go back and change what he'd done to Johann. Everyone must know he was the one who had murdered his schoolmate. Why did he do it?

What made him so enraged? He thought of confessing but could bear neither his father's disappointment nor the consequences of his act.

Raka glanced left, then right, to make certain no one was nearby. He leaned in close to Werner. The boy recoiled from the man's foul breath, but Raka's grip was too tight. The dark lord's steely blue eyes captured Werner's gaze, as the boy squirmed. When Werner finally submitted, Raka said, "That's better. Now then, I found it... interesting... what you did to your friend."

Werner sucked in a deep breath. "I... I didn't d-do anything. I don't know what you're talking about!"

"Oh, come now, dear boy. I saw you push your friend in front of the streetcar." Raka enjoyed watching Werner's distress.

Werner's hopes of escaping retribution disintegrated as he realized he'd been discovered. Then, in a flash, anger replaced his fear. He looked back up at Raka with a sneer. "Oh, all right, so what? It was his fault. He wouldn't tell Albert to let me see his compass."

Raka nodded. "And that made you angry, did it?"

Werner face contorted as he grew more furious. "You bet it did. I had to show him I wasn't going to stand for his insolence." Werner paused, realizing what he had just admitted, and thought to dial it back just a bit. "I didn't exactly mean to kill him, though. I just wanted to scare him is all."

Raka's brow furrowed as if he was considering Werner's story. "Hmmm, I see."

Before Werner could react, Raka reached out and covered Werner's head with his hands. Hot energy coursed through his palms and into Werner's head. Suddenly, Werner found himself back on the street where Johann's murder had occurred. His actions began to replay before his eyes. Werner gasped as he saw how angry he had been and that he most definitely wanted to harm Johann. As the scene completed, he found himself back in the cemetery. Satisfied, Raka dropped his hands.

"I don't know how you did that, mister, but okay, you got me. Are you going to turn me into the police now?"

Raka seemed to consider that suggestion for a moment, allowing the boy to squirm in distress. "Hmm, that would seem to be the right thing to do... however..."

Werner scowled. Deciding he had little to lose, he took a gamble. "Look, I don't know who you are or what you're up to, but, like I said, it was all the Jew-lovers fault."

"You don't have to explain it to me. I understand what you did. You had to show Johann you were a man to respect."

"Exactly," Werner agreed, starting to relax just a bit. This was not going at all like he thought being caught would be.

Raka's eyes narrowed, and he tapped his lip with his index finger as if an idea had just occurred to him. "What is your name, young man? I think you have potential, and I want you to meet some friends of mine."

"Werner. Werner von Wiesel. Friends, you say?" Werner was intrigued.

"Yes," Raka said, smiling. He leaned closer to Werner. "There is a meeting of a secret society tonight." Raka's face became grave. "But it is a secret—just for you and me to know. Do you understand, Werner von Wiesel?"

Werner's face brightened. Maybe this would be a chance to show his father that he was stronger than he was given credit for. "Yes, of course. Secret. I will tell no one."

Raka nodded, satisfied. "All right then. Meet me at the Bavarian State Library tonight at ten—near the rear entrance."

Werner stood tall. "I will be there."

Raka looked at Werner with a piercing gaze, nodded, then turned and walked away.

Werner watched the mysterious man recede into the distance. He had an excellent feeling about all of this.

* * *

The pitch-black of the night and the gusting winds of the winter rainstorm gave Werner the shivers. He passed four scholars scurrying toward an alehouse as he rode his bicycle down the Ludwigstrasse. He was having second thoughts.

I don't know what I'm doing out on a night like this. It's cold, and I'm getting wet. He grimaced, and his hands clutched tighter on the damp bicycle handlebars. *On the other hand, that man seems to see me; the real me. This just might be a golden opportunity.* He felt tightness in his chest as his mind raced with what-ifs on both sides of the ledger. In the end, Werner's ego and desire for respect won out.

Raka waited for his young potential protégé by the stairs leading down to the rotunda door of the Temple of Satan. He shuddered in the damp night air. *I hate the cold,* he mused to himself bitterly. His mind drifted to warm summer days lying naked in the sun.

The sound of Werner's approach snapped him back to the present, and he smiled to himself. He loved teaching young boys—they were so malleable. Werner, like many of his students, would be eager to please. His mind was fresh, like a clean slate on which to write. He just needed to train the boy.

Werner's heart began pounding in anticipation as he parked his bike behind the library and strode over to meet Raka. He smiled as he shook the water off his arms and extended his right hand.

Raka frowned and ignored Werner's gesture. "You're almost late," he said disapprovingly. "Did you tell anyone where you were going?"

"No. No, of course not," Werner replied, a little crestfallen. "You said—"

Raka cut off Werner's reply by turning his back on him and walking toward the stairs. With a swipe of his newly repaired golden dragon head cane, he motioned for the boy to follow. They descended the curving staircase of twenty narrow cobblestone steps to the dungeon-like entry of the church. The teacher tapped his walking stick two, then three times on the ancient, arched oak door. Werner felt a shudder as he noticed the goat-like gargoyle at the apex of the arch.

The massive door creaked open, revealing an old, cavernous, torch-lit fire-temple with a freshly painted blood pentagram in the middle. Raka motioned for Werner to enter and a statuesque, redheaded woman dressed in a tight-fitting, low-cut black leather riding habit greeted them. Werner heard a subtle hum, and his body began to vibrate as if a force of energy were penetrating it. Raka acknowledged the woman with a kiss on the back of her right hand. Then he motioned to Werner, who was trying to look everywhere at once. "Countess Victoria von Baden, I want you to meet my guest, Herr Werner von Wiesel."

Not knowing what to do, and feeling out of his depth, Werner made a short bow and nodded.

The Countess moistened her crimson lips as she regarded the boy. Several thoughts of what she could do with a young man like him flitted through her mind.

"Countess, would you kindly show my guest around?"

The thirtyish noble smiled as she fondled her waist-length ginger French braid. "Of course, Herr Raka. I had heard you were bringing someone of interest to the initiation this evening." The Countess took Werner by the arm and urged him to walk with her, her five-inch leather stiletto heels clicking on the stone floor. Unused to attention from women of any sort, and certainly not from one as sleek and svelte as the Countess, Werner thrilled at her touch.

Raka slipped away to the far corner of the room to watch Werner with the Countess.

The couple made their way through the clusters of men and women chatting in the dark, shadowy, medieval Gothic Dungeon. A torch illuminated each of the five corners of the pentagon-shaped house of dark worship. For some reason, Werner again shuddered when he noticed the goat-headed gargoyles holding the torches on the walls.

The Countess smiled and nodded at several of the members, all of them dressed in black. Werner noted with interest that each carried an ornate walking stick topped with a ruby embedded into a gold pentagram.

Sensing Werner's nervousness, the Countess grinned to herself. It gave her a feeling of even more control than she usually commanded from men. Her amber eyes sized him up. She saw potential in him and someone who would be unable to resist her will. Better than an ally, he could become a servant of her ambitions. The corners of her mouth turned up with pleasure at the thought, and she asked, "Do you know anyone here, Herr von Wiesel?"

Werner looked around, then swallowed hard, his forehead and palms sweating. "No, I don't think so," he managed to say. "Who are these people? And, why am I here?" He paused, then his eyes narrowed. "And what is that sound?"

Cautiously glancing right, then left, the Countess guided the boy to a quiet corner of the room. Turning her back to the wall, she faced Werner.

"This is the Society of Truth. There on the floor in the middle of the room is their symbol, the lightning bolt Black Sun." Werner's eyes grew wide as he recognized the image. The Countess pointed to a muscular, blond man in his fifties. "And that is Herr von Hofer, the leader of the Makers of Darkness."

The Knight of the Black Sun saw her gesture and ended his conversation with a young man. With a questioning look, he strode over to join the Countess and Werner. The well-tanned, formidable von Hofer took the right hand of the Countess and kissed it. The Countess closed her eyes for a moment to experience the feeling.

After the briefest pause, she opened her eyes and smiled, saying, "Herr von Hofer, please allow me to introduce Werner von Wiesel. He is a guest of Herr Raka."

Von Hofer smiled and turned to Werner. "Von Wiesel? Are you related to Prussian General von Wiesel?"

Werner puffed himself up. "Yes, Herr von Hofer. I am proud to say that the general is my father."

Von Hofer nodded, and his smile grew even more extensive. "Well then, it's even more of a pleasure to meet you. I hope you will enjoy the evening."

"I'm sure I will," Werner said, basking in von Hofer's apparent approval and beginning to feel more relaxed.

Von Hofer hesitated, considering how much he should reveal to this stranger. With a probing gaze, and being careful with his words, he continued, "Tell me, Herr von Wiesel, do you feel anything? Hear anything?"

Werner thought it odd to ask such questions but replied, "Why, actually, I hear a soft hum, and I feel... I don't know... uh, lighter, perhaps." He wrinkled his brow, remembering. "It felt as if a force took hold of me when I entered the room."

The Knight of Darkness narrowed his eyes, considering the response, then decided to reveal a bit of the arcane nature of the location. "Very good. There is a large ruby crystal under the floor of the temple. Its capacity generates a power that elevates our mind and abilities. That you can feel it certainly bodes well for you."

Werner smiled at the compliment as von Hofer continued. "You know Herr Raka. What you may not know is that his formidable mastery originates from this energy. His family line of Atlantean Aryans came here from an alien planet to perfect humans."

"His what?" Werner blurted out.

Von Hofer did not pause. "They brought many crystals of power with them. People of nobility are of the pure blood of this ancient line. Isn't that right, Countess?"

The Countess smiled and tilted her head in acknowledgment.

Werner was staggered by what he'd heard and took in a deep breath to calm himself. He closed his eyes and allowed himself to feel the energy for a few seconds. The vibration seemed to soothe him, and his mind became calmer. He would get more answers about Herr Raka later. But for now, he was more interested in what he was feeling and how he might use it to his advantage. "Hmmm. How do you use these powers?"

The Countess gave a quick false smile. "I'm sure you have many questions, Herr von Wiesel, and there will be time for them later." She looked once again to von Hofer. "But I believe it is getting close to time for the initiation of our newest member."

Von Hofer looked at his wristwatch and nodded. "Indeed. Thank you, Countess." He nodded goodbye to Werner, then strode toward the center of the large room. As he passed, one of his underlings handed him a rod that matched the one he already carried. When he neared the center of the room, the pentagram of lightning bolts of the Black Sun in the floor began to rise. Raka, the Countess, and three others of the Black Sun gathered around the circle, their initiates crowding behind as the large disk stopped at the height of about two feet, forming a stage.

Von Hofer stepped up onto the platform and walked to the center of the circle. All eyes were upon him. "We recognize darkness, light, creation, and destruction. The creative and the destructive principles determine our technical means. Everything destructive is of satanic origin. Everything creative is of Vril divine energy."

There were nods and murmurs of agreement among those gathered. "Now, I want each of you to extend your rod toward the center of the Black Sun. Feel the power of the Vril charge your lightning rods!"

As each member of the order pointed the head of his walking stick toward the center of the platform, von Hofer looked out into the gathering. "We welcome into our new world order... Hans von Schrader!"

The faithful raised their staves and shouted, "Hail! Hail, Dark Prince!"

A strapping, blue-eyed, flaxen-haired youth emerged from the crowd and strode purposefully to the center of the circle. As von Schrader reached von Hofer and the others surrounding him, he stopped and stood at rigid attention. The leader gave the initiate a welcoming smile and handed him his lightning rod, saying, "Herr von Schrader has proved himself worthy by eliminating a Jew banker for the greater good." The gathered members gave a cheer of approval, and von Hofer's eyes sparkled. "Thus, we award you the almighty rod of power. Please recite for us from Revelation 6:12, the prayer of the Black Sun and Temple of Satan."

Von Schrader stood with his prize in his right hand and raised his arms. From memory, he recited the prayer.

Revelation 6:12-17: When he opened the sixth seal, I looked and behold, there was a great Earthquake, and the sun became black as sackcloth. The full moon became like blood. And the stars of the sky fell to the Earth as the fig tree sheds its winter fruit when shaken by a gale. The sky vanished like a scroll, and every mountain and island removed from its place. Kings, princes, generals, rich, every slave and every free man, hid in caves among the rocks of the mountains. They called to the mountains and the rocks. Fall on us and hide us from the face of him who sits on the throne and from the wrath of the Lamb! For the great day of their wrath has come, and who can stand?

Werner, awed and shaken, could not believe what he was seeing. The walking staves were glowing. A wave of loud shouting came from the crowd.

Von Hofer said, "We bless you in the name of Samael, the serpent in the Garden of Eden." He handed the initiate a skull-shaped, golden cup. "Now drink this cup of blood from the Jew banker and join your spirit with the Angel of Death."

Werner stood outside the circle, his eyes fixed on the new initiate. Now he knew why he was here. It had to do with Jews. He despised them. His thoughts went wild. *I killed Johann because he was a Jew-lover. One night, I will be honored like this!*

He turned and found Raka smiling down at him, then his gaze fell to the man's hand. Raka saw Werner stare at his hand and looked down. He frowned at the black, scaled claw he saw and casually moved his hand into his pocket.

Raka's body had been unstable all day. Taking over a human and shape-shifting to that form was not permanent. It required energy and focus.

Werner could not contain himself. "What happened to your hand?"

The dragon frowned and said, "It's nothing. An injury."

Before Werner could question him further, Raka asked, "What did you think of the ceremony?"

Werner immediately became serious. "It, it was..." He searched for the right word. "Very powerful," he finally exclaimed.

Raka nodded with a smile. "Yes, I thought so too." As if it were a novel thought, he asked, "Say, Herr von Wiesel, would you like to become a member of our society?"

Werner felt a warmness fill him and he replied, "I think I would like that very much." Then, remembering what Herr von Shrader had done to earn his membership, his heart began to race with excitement. "So, what would I have to do?"

Standing nearby, von Hofer responded to Raka's subtle summons and walked over to the two. Raka said, "Herr von Hofer, would you tell Herr von Wiesel what it takes to become a member of the Black Sun?"

Von Hofer nodded. "Of course." He looked down at Werner and became very serious. "It is no small thing to take this step, Herr von Wiesel. And once you step upon this path, there is no turning back."

Werner realized he stood on the threshold of something momentous, and for a moment, he had second thoughts. But they did not last. "I understand," he said with resolve.

Von Hofer nodded. "Of course, first you must prove yourself worthy."

Werner nodded solemnly. "I assumed as much from what I've seen tonight, Herr von Hofer." Then, with a sidelong glance at Raka, Werner said with a sly grin, "I think I have proved that I am capable of dealing with... the Jewish problem."

Von Hofer also glanced at Raka, who nodded very slightly for him to continue. "Well, that may be; however, we have an extraordinary task for you." He pointed to the very lifelike stuffed black panther near the entrance and said, "One that will require you to be as stealthy and as ruthless as a panther."

"I'm sure I can do it if it will lead to the extermination of the"—Werner's mouth curled down into a frown—"Jews," he spat.

Both Von Hofer and Raka smiled at the boy's vehemence. Raka put a hand on Werner's shoulder. "In a way, it will lead to the destruction of the Jews—and many others who are inferior," he said, his eyes glowing with enthusiasm.

Von Hofer nodded. "You see, Herr von Wiesel, your task is to steal a very special compass for us."

Werner could not believe what he heard. "What? You just want me to steal Albert Einstein's Compass" he said with disappointment. Then his eyes and his lips curled up into a smile. "Do you want me to kill him to get it?"

Raka smiled, "That would be part of the task, yes."

Werner nodded in satisfaction. "So, what's so important about this compass?" he asked, feeling as if he had moved up a notch in the esteem of these two men.

Raka's eyes turned red as he reacted to the boy's impudence. "That is not your concern. Just get it."

Werner recoiled, but Raka's grip tightened on his shoulder. He leaned down and whispered, "We wouldn't want the authorities to know what really happened to the Thomas boy, would we?" Werner paled and shook his head.

Raka stood. "I thought not. That is your task.

Let us know when you have accomplished it." Then he and von Hofer turned back to the crowd, leaving Werner standing alone. He was excited about joining the Black Sun, but he felt let down by such a trivial task. Beating up on a Jew he could handle. Enjoy, even. Stealing a stupid compass was a task below his importance. He glanced around, wanting to leave as he muttered half to himself, "I don't know what to do. How do I go about stealing a stupid compass?"

Suddenly, Werner felt something in his hand. Looking down, he saw someone had slipped him a note. He turned to look behind him and found the Countess casually standing there, her body turned partly away from him. Puzzled, Werner surreptitiously opened the slip of paper. His eyes grew wide as he read. Along with an address, it just said, "I will help you."

Chapter 16
The Spider Spins Her Web

*T*he midday sun was finally breaking through the heavy snow clouds. Werner grasped the crumpled note he had gotten at the Dark Sun initiation a few nights back; a hastily written invitation from Countess von Baden to visit her home, Altes Schloss Castle. As he hiked up the steep trail, Werner could hear waves breaking against the craggy cliff behind the castle, which sat on a rocky promontory overlooking Lake Constance.

Werner was more than a little nervous about his meeting with this woman. He did not know anyone like her. He rolled his shoulders in a vain attempt to relax. The nearly three-hour train ride from Munich had left him tired and restless. He was getting in deeper and deeper with these people he hardly knew, and he wondered why the Countess wanted to help him with his initiation task. Despite the cold, his hands were warm and sweaty in the knit gloves he wore.

The smell of wood burning in a fireplace of the nearby castle made him melancholy. He really wanted to be in the familiar comfort of his family home, with the Christmas decorations around the tall spruce tree in the parlor. Instead, he was trudging in God knows where to find out how to do a stupid task that somehow would get him closer to the respect he so rightly deserved.

He finally reached the bridge that led to the castle's entrance. He made his way across it and walked through the open wrought iron gate. He found himself in a snow-covered courtyard, and he passed a statue of a knight from the Crusades sitting astride a horse, his sword drawn as if in salute. Looking around for the castle door, Werner saw a torch lit on the western side of the courtyard. He walked over to it and found a massive iron key in the lock waiting for him. He took in a breath, stuffed the invitation into his pocket, and tugged on his clothes to straighten them.

Satisfied that he was presentable, he turned the giant key. A loud clunk shattered the quiet. A slight chill shivered up his spine as he strained to push the massive door open. Time seemed to stand still as he peered around into the grand hall. His heart raced when he gazed up at the soaring Gothic architecture.

His gaze was attracted by movement inside the room. As his eyes adjusted to the gloom, Werner saw the Countess.

She was walking toward him, cat-like, in her floor-length maroon silk robes, their black mink trimming shimmering in the dim light. Smiling, she crossed the black-and-white checkerboard tile floor and extended her hand. "Welcome, Herr von Wiesel. How was your journey?"

Her voice was sultry, and she ran her hands through her waist-length ginger locks, then flipped her cascading hair back over her shoulder. Her mesmerizing, amber, cat-like eyes seemed to glow, and they mesmerized the boy. Then his gaze was captured by a red ruby embedded in a gold spider hanging on a gold chain necklace nestled in her amply displayed cleavage. Werner sucked in a breath as he became more firmly enmeshed in her web.

He managed to tear his gaze away from the spider and licked his lips. "Uh, it was good. I was glad to leave Munich for a while. And please call me Werner." Fighting to regain his composure, he smoothed back his hair, then crossed his arms.

The temptress said, "You must be cold from your journey." She took Werner's hand and led him toward the fireplace. "Come, sit with me on the sofa near the fire."

As they sat, Werner was grateful to see that the knee-high rosewood table in front of the couch held a polished silver tray with a lavish spread of fresh fruit, cheese, meat, bread, and cakes. A silver teapot with a monogrammed "B" adorned the china.

Werner had last eaten at breakfast and did not pack anything for the train ride. That and the trudge from the station up to the castle had built up a monster hunger. The Countess noticed his glance and said, "Forgive me, you must be famished." She gestured to the tray. "I had had my servants prepare a snack for you before I dismissed them for the remainder of the day. Please, help yourself." He needed no more invitation than that and began piling cheese and sausages on a thick slice of still-warm homemade bread. He closed his eyes, inhaled in delight, and his mouth opened wide for a big bite.

The sorceress teased Werner by smiling and pushing his hand with the sandwich away from his mouth. "Not so fast. I invited you here so we could talk privately. Have you told anyone about your visit?"

"No, of course not. You were quite clear I was to tell no one."

The Countess narrowed her eyes. "Not even Raka? Especially him."

Werner shook his head firmly. "No, I told no one. Not even my parents. I just said I had to do some school stuff for the day and I might be back late." His puppy dog eyes pleaded with the Countess to allow him to take a bite from his sandwich.

The Countess paused just a moment longer, letting Werner know who held power here, then, with a smile, motioned with her inch-long, blood-red fingernails for Werner to eat. The hungry young man turned his attention to the food and in just a few brief minutes had sated his hunger. Heaving a deep sigh of satisfaction, he slouched back into the depths of the plush couch and turned once again to the Countess. She had a half-amused smirk on her face as his eyes were once again drawn to the gold necklace... and what it rested upon.

"Do you like it?" she asked coyly.

With an effort, Werner brought his eyes to her face, and he turned quite red. "Um, what?" he asked sheepishly.

"The necklace," the Countess said, leaning toward Werner and revealing even more of her ample cleavage. "Do you like it?"

"Oh, yes," he stammered. "It's very... I mean..."

The Countess laughed and sat back as Werner struggled to bring his thoughts to the reason for his visit. He was very distracted and was experiencing feelings that were unfamiliar to him. The Countess, for her part, found his discomfort amusing. Finally, Werner gathered his wits. "Countess, you said you would help me. Why am I here?"

Victoria was thrilled with Werner's naiveté. It had been a long time since she'd felt young and vulnerable like him. From childhood, her father held her as a pawn in a chess game of power and influence. Her beauty, plus the fact that she was a von Baden, made her the focus of attention of the rich and mighty. As she grew into puberty and beyond, she learned the effect she had on men. She also learned she could bend them toward her will, but she also had to be very careful and not cross the line with them. Her father's command that she be demure and please men was alien to her character. When he demanded she be the weak little maiden, it made her want to scream.

The Countess's mother had died in childbirth. Her older brother was cruel and domineering while her father was controlling and, at the same time, overprotective. Like a lioness in a cage, she had felt trapped for most of her life.

As a teen, she had loved to explore the vast castle. It was her favorite way to escape when life threatened to close in on her, perhaps because they were so isolated from the rest of the world. She loved the cellars and dungeons that seemed to extend into the bowels of the Earth. Even as she grew into young adulthood, she would retreat to these subterranean chambers.

One day she went down into them, hoping to escape the trials of her life. She opened the door to her favorite hiding place to find a terrifying creature sitting on a bench. She froze, unable to move, let alone flee. The sense of a human presence awakened Raka, and he saw a frightened young woman staring at him. The dragon creature in a warm, soft voice said, "Do not be afraid, Victoria, I have been waiting for you. I will not harm you."

Victoria was mesmerized. Transforming to his human shape, Raka smiled, "I can see that you are a brave and a smart young woman. But you are being stifled by your father's controlling agenda for you."

Her jaw dropped in amazement. How did this stranger know her? In an instant, she felt as if he could see right through her. Raka smiled to himself.

Raka sensed her vulnerability and knew she needed him to find her real power—which was considerable. "Believe me, I can help you achieve the things of which you dream." This was too strange. But it was also intriguing. She did not know what to do. At first. But she had stayed to listen.

Over the next several years, Raka had guided her development, building on her frustrations and displeasure with her father's plans and step by step, corrupting her to his dark ways.

Then her father died, and it was just her and her brother. For a while. Her father had wanted her to fulfill his vision of having a husband to rescue her; a concept she did not share in the slightest. The lord of the manor would have been aghast to learn how she applied the skill she had acquired thanks to his shooting lessons. Such a pity that her brother had died in a freak hunting accident. Even odder that the bullet that killed him had gone through his back and straight to his heart. Following his funeral, the Countess declared herself a lady of the castle.

The Countess brought herself back to the present. She saw a similar conflict within Werner. She smiled and replied to his question, "I invited you here to help me steal back what is mine."

At Werner's puzzled look, she continued. "Raka told me your friend has my compass. My father traded it and other jewels some years ago when he needed money to install electric lighting in our home."

Her porcelain face reddened, and her nostrils flared. "My father had no right to take it from me. It is mine!

I found it in a chest of relics from the Crusades. My many-times-great grandfather acquired it long ago. My father said the story, told down through generations, was that the knights were searching for the Ark of the Covenant." She closed her cat-like eyes, reminiscing the pleasure. "The jewels sparkled in the light and always made me feel good. I miss having it. I must have it back."

Werner hesitated, knowing that Raka wanted the compass. Seeing his hesitation, the Countess intensified her appeal. She grasped Werner's hand in both of hers and clutched it to her chest, just under her throat, her lips trembling and tears starting to spill onto her cheeks. "Oh, please Herr von Wiesel—Werner—you are my only hope of reclaiming my beloved treasure."

Werner's glance vacillated between the woman's tears and his hand, which was inches away from her cleavage. "Uh, well, um..." Just then, a log in the fireplace popped, sounding for all the world like a gunshot.

Werner jerked back, startled, then realized what had happened. He struggled to regain his composure and drew the Countess's hands away from her chest. He patted them and looked her in the eyes. "I understand your distress, Countess. But Herr Raka—"

The Countess smiled, sniffing back her tears. "I know Herr Raka has asked you to steal it for him. But it is mine in the first place."

Werner hesitated, so the Countess leaned toward him. "Besides, I know how to handle Herr Raka."

"You do?" asked Werner, once again falling under her spell. *She is so beautiful,* he thought. *And she obviously cares for me.* The Countess could see the boy was faltering. She nodded and smiled. "Yes."

Werner wanted nothing more in the world than to please this woman, but there was one more concern. "Uh, Herr Raka has some... information... about me, that could get me in trouble with the authorities. He threatened to expose me if I fail to secure the compass."

The girls at school think I'm still a boy. What do they know? This beautiful woman sees me as a man who knows how to take care of her.

Watching Werner, the Countess assessed that the time was right. She suddenly brightened. "I have it! I know what we can do."

The Countess retook Werner's hand. "Yes. I will explain to Herr Raka that you understand the compass is mine and that I assured you that once I have it, I would be glad to share it with him."

Hearing her words, Werner felt fantastic. The heaviness that had been suppressing him lifted. "Yes! That's the perfect solution," he said, squeezing her hand affectionately.

"Yes, perfect. You are my hero," said the Countess as she leaned toward Werner and kissed him on the cheek. Werner's spirits soared.

That evening, on the train home, Werner tried to plan for how he would steal Albert's compass. But his thoughts kept going back to that kiss.

Chapter 17
Werner's Attempt

*W*erner twitched his shoulders. It felt like someone was watching him.

He furtively glanced around and, seeing no one suspicious, shook his head as he walked toward the Gymnasium. Maybe he was just paranoid. Since Johann's murder, he felt like everyone around him was watching him with accusatory stares. Because of the stress, he had lost weight and retreated more and more inside of himself. Sleep was an erratic visitor. It had come to him last night but did not stay long.

To take his mind off his concerns, he replayed in his mind the meeting he had had at Altes Schloss Castle. He felt a thrill at the thought of the Countess. In hindsight, he was more convinced than ever that it was the right move to help her recover the compass. It was hers, after all. The thought of the sensuous woman filled Werner with an unfamiliar warmth, a welcome distraction from the angst that had become his almost constant companion.

Thanks to his father being on the Gymnasium Academik Committee, Werner had learned that Albert was to appear today at 10:00 a.m. to discuss his future at the school. Werner figured that would provide an excellent opportunity for him to secure the compass.

Earlier, after the patriarch had left for work, Werner stole his way into his father's study. Herr von Wiesel was an avid collector of firearms, and Werner knew just what he wanted. He carefully took his father's new Borchardt C93—the first modern "automatic" pistol—from its display case.

The first time he had been allowed to handle it was when he and his father had been target shooting. The handgun had felt like a toy in Werner's hand. The spring-loaded mechanism was in the grip, and all you had to do was pull the trigger. No more black powder to leave clouds of messy smoke. Werner had smiled when he had tucked the weapon and bullets behind his back into his flannel trousers under his coat. With this little beauty, it would be a clean kill.

Werner again brought his thoughts to the present as he stood near the bicycle rack in the rear of the Gymnasium. He tapped his foot impatiently and checked his silver pocket watch. It was 9:45 a.m. He paced and muttered under his breath, "Come on, Albert. Where are you?" He knew Albert would park his bicycle here before entering the building. It was Saturday, and the area was mostly deserted.

He went over in his mind exactly how he was going to take the compass. When Albert arrived, he would greet him as he parked his bike. Then he would take out his pistol and demand the compass. Albert was such a coward, he probably would surrender it without a fuss. Once it was in his hands and the Jew had relaxed, Werner would pull the trigger. He smiled at that thought and took an-other sip of the elixir.

Moments later, he saw Albert round the corner of a building and head toward him. He straightened and waved, reaching his other hand behind his back to make sure the gun was easily accessible. But as the rider came closer, he saw it wasn't Albert. The figure riding toward him was Johann on the bicycle that had been crushed under a streetcar.

Werner staggered back, his knees going weak. He blinked, but still, he saw Johann. Had the dead come back to life? He felt dizzy and grabbed for the bicycle rack as he lost control of himself and began to vomit.

Johann, in his radiant spirit, stopped in front of Werner. "I know what you are doing here, Werner. I have come to warn you not to harm Albert."

Werner straightened and wiped his mouth on the back of his hand. At first, he could not speak. Beads of sweat popped out on his forehead, and in a shaky voice he managed to stammer, "I... I thought you were dead? I mean, how can you be dead and be here?"

Johann parked his bicycle and stepped closer to the stunned Werner. "Never mind what you did to me, I am warning you; leave Albert alone. Forget about the compass. It is not what you think it is, and what it truly is, is not for you to know."

With that, the ghost turned and strode to the Gymnasium. When he opened the door to enter, it was Albert that Werner saw walking into the building.

Shaking, Werner hastily turned and ran back the way he had come.

Chapter 18
Dragon Disappointed

The dull glow of the incandescent light bulb dimly illuminated the dragon's lair. It was barely better than a torch, Countess Victoria von Baden thought as she paced the stone floor, impatiently waiting for her mentor. Hands clenching and unclenching, she wanted to hurt someone, to see blood. She let out a loud, guttural roar of frustration and threw her black, hooded cape onto the crushed red velvet sofa. Raka slipped in through his private entrance to find his protégé enraged. They had enlisted Werner von Wiesel to steal the compass and kill Einstein, but the boy had failed, despite the Countess's implied rewards.

Raka's presence did nothing to calm the woman. She glared at him.

"Don't be angry at me, Victoria. It was not I who failed to get the compass."

The Countess threw herself onto the plush sofa with a sigh. "I know. It's just that..."

Raka raised his hands in a placating manner. "Oh, please, my pet, patience. I share your frustration. Let's consider what happened."

Though remaining petulant, the Countess nodded.

"So, do you think Werner was ready for the task?" asked Raka.

"I thought he was. Apparently, I was mistaken." She rubbed her forehead, trying to massage away the tension. "We went over about the pistol and the need to kill Albert. He knew what to do and seemed... eager... to do it." She paused and shook her head. "I was watching him from across the street with my long-lens telescope." Her eyes narrowed. "Something... strange happened."

That caught Raka's attention. "Strange?" he said suspiciously.

"Yes. When Albert rode up, a... a bright cloud appeared. I have no other words to describe it. Werner seemed... I don't know... freaked-out."

Raka started pacing and became angrier with each step. "Then what happened?" he said through clenched teeth.

"Werner became very pale and distraught. He staggered, then threw up," she said with a resigned sigh.

Raka shook his head. "You saw a bright cloud? What time did that happen?"

"Just before ten this morning. Why?" Victoria asked, looking up from the sofa.

"Because I felt the presence of the Light break the time continuum at that time," he replied angrily.

"What do you mean 'the Light'?" Victoria asked, surprised. Though she had been working with Raka for some time, he had not mentioned this Light before.

Raka clenched his jaw, then took a deep breath. He closed his eyes. "How do I explain a power that has vexed me for millennia?" Raka appeared to go deeply into his thoughts, then abruptly opened his eyes and pulled himself back to the present. "Never mind that for now," he said, shaking his head as if to expel the troubling ideas. "Before I can even begin discussing the Light with you, we have more pressing work to do."

The presence of the light of the Holy of Holies reminded the fallen dark angel of his twin brother Arka who had become a high priest in Atlantis. Instead of learning how to become responsible like his brother, Raka chose to rebel and turn from the light of the Holy of Holies and walk the path of darkness. He was on the warpath to show the world his power. Revenge filled his heart and mind, not just on his youthful nemesis Albert Einstein, but also on Arka, his brother.

Victoria began to protest, but at the sight of his narrowing eyes, she thought better of it. "You're right. We need to focus on getting the compass—at any cost."

Raka hissed his agreement and beckoned her closer to formulate a plan.

Chapter 19
The Spiritual Compass

ohann jerked back into awareness in the Garden of Remembrance and gasped, "I was there, at school. With Werner!" He shook his head as if to clear it, then frowned, puzzled. "He was holding a... a gun. I think I scared him."

Standing next to the bewildered journeyer, Moses smiled. He reached his arm around the boy's shoulder and drew him closer to his side. The brown-eyed sage gazed down at Johann.

"You did well. Your appearance prevented Werner from making an unwise choice." Moses glanced at the crystal viewing Portal that sat on the grass nearby. "What was it like for you, traversing through time?" he asked.

Johann's eyes misted. "It was a lot like you and Jesus told me it would be. The HU sound surrounded me, and I was filled with... joy. I floated on purple light through what felt like a door. It was like moving to another room."

Johann furrowed his brow as he worked to remember. "Suddenly, I found myself back in Germany. I was riding a bicycle." Johann's gaze took on a faraway look as he reflected. "It seemed like a dream, and I told Werner to forget the compass and leave Albert alone." The boy snapped himself back and looked at the master. "The next moment, I was here."

Moses smiled, "Excellent. Sounds like your first return to the physical world was reasonably pleasant for you."

Johann flushed with the praise. Then his face became serious. "Why is Albert's compass so important, Moses?" Though a relative newcomer to the astral realm, Johann had acclimated quickly. He no longer stared wide-eyed at the celestial beings who visited this place often, and he had come into acceptance of his new life with remarkable ease thanks to the compassion and abundance of love accorded him by all he met.

Moses directed him to the bench next to the oak tree and gestured for him to sit. "What do you know about the compass, Johann?"

The novice sat and considered the question. Johann tapped his lips with one finger, then, after a brief pause, said, "Usually a compass is used to find your way. It points to the magnetic north of the Earth so you can get your bearings." He paused again. "But I have seen Albert's compass do magical things. So, I'm guessing this is no ordinary device."

Moses smiled and nodded. "It is indeed quite unique. Albert's compass, when used with love, can create supernatural occurrences." Moses smiled again at Johann and said, "Think back to when Albert first showed you the compass and you saw the number thirty-three projected from it into the air before you."

Johann's eyes glimmered at the memory. "We were just young children when that happened. In fact, we had just met. How did you know about the number?"

Moses smiled, "Let's just say that I have been aware of you and Albert for a long time. Now think of what Albert did that caused the number to appear."

Johann's face lit up as the memory returned. "I think Albert put the compass to his chest. He said he loved his papa for giving him the compass. Then it happened."

"Yes, yes that's it," Moses said approvingly.

Johann became quiet. He thought back to when they used the compass at the monastery on Mary Magdalene's feast day. "We won a relic scavenger hunt at a monastery once, too. Albert saw Saint Mary Magdalene, and she helped us find our way. Was that the compass too?"

Moses nodded. "Albert's compass is for finding true spiritual north, for showing the direction in the realm of the spirit as a physical compass does in the natural world."

As they were talking, Jesus approached, and Moses motioned for him to join them. "Young Johann had some questions about the compass, my Friend. Perhaps you can add some explanation."

Jesus smiled as he eased himself down on Johann's other side. "Ah, an interesting topic, indeed." He stroked his beard as he considered what to say. Arriving at the angle he wanted, he asked Johann, "Do you know the story of the Ten Commandments that Moses received from God?"

Johann nodded. "Of course. Moses went up onto a mountain, and God delivered to him a stone tablet upon which were written ten rules to guide people's lives. Things like not to steal, or murder. Not to lie. Things like that."

"Right, the Ten Commandments were rules to guide men. You might say they were like a compass for men to use to make good choices."

"So, Albert is learning to find his way, and his compass will help him."

Jesus and Moses smiled at each other. "Yes... that's exactly right. And it has other powers as well—almost incredible powers—which we will discuss at another time. But for now, you have the basic idea."

Then Moses became serious. "But some forces would use these powers to set humankind on a different course. They have made it their mission to acquire the compass."

As the impact of what Jesus said sunk in, Johann jumped to his feet. "I have to tell Albert. I have to help him!"

Great loving radiated from Jesus' eyes, and he reached out and gently grasped Johann's arm. "Easy, Johann. We were hoping you would want to help Albert, and we will assist you in doing just that. Albert has an important mission for the world—and you are destined to play a part in it as well."

Moses nodded. "However, there is more you must learn before you can help your friend. There are rules and boundaries—for both sides—that must not be crossed."

Jesus nodded. "And so, you can see, my friend, we have work to do."

Chapter 20
December 1894
Confronting Authority

*A*lbert's leaden footsteps echoed through the deserted halls of the Luitpold Gymnasium as he trudged to the direktor's office. He was most definitely not looking forward to this meeting. He had little respect for the teachers who insisted he waste his time going over elementary rote information. Of course, if things went as he hoped, he wouldn't have to be here much longer. But for now, he had to put up with the formalities.

Arriving at the office, he was greeted by Miss Schmidt, a pleasant forty-something woman dressed in tweed, with dark hair plaited tightly to her head. Sitting at her small desk in the anteroom outside the direktor's office, she welcomed Albert with a sympathetic smile. "Good morning, Herr Einstein. Please sit down," she said, indicating the small settee across from her desk. "The direktor will call you after he has reviewed your situation with the Academik Committee." She looked at Albert, her expression not unkind. "We know your parents are not in Munich, so the direktor requested that Colonel von Wiesel and Frau Thomas serve in their stead. Your instructors, Herr von Achen, and Herr Hamlin are also in with them."

Like a helpless animal caught in a snare, Albert felt trapped by the situation. But putting a good face on a bad situation, Albert mustered a smile and made a slight bow. "Thank you, Miss Schmidt, for your kindness."

Inside, he was not smiling. *Why is Johann's mother here? She is fragile and has been through so much.* Albert remembered her compassion.

After the funeral, she had taken him aside and, despite her loss, had offered words of advice about his school situation. "You must treat your teachers with respect, even if you know more than they do. I know it must be hard for you, Albert, but doing otherwise will only get you in trouble." That scene faded from his mind as he thought about the other adult who was supposed to advocate for him at this meeting. *That anti-Semite von Wiesel is supposed to take my father's place? What did they think when they chose him?*

Albert stared at the tall mahogany doors to the direktor's inner office, wishing the ordeal was over, and he was walking back out through them heading home.

On the other side of the doors, Albert's future at the school was being decided by the direktor and the group he had assembled.

Frau Thomas was once happy and vivacious, but the loss of her son, Johann, had shattered her life into a million pieces. She looked frail and lifeless. It was as if the light of living had been extinguished in her. Still, she had come to the meeting to support Albert. Johann would have wanted her to be there for his best friend. But it had taken all the determination she could summon merely to get out of bed in the morning. Nonetheless, Christine had bathed and washed her ginger hair with pleasantly scented castile soap, then wrapped it in a soft, graceful knot secured with a Spanish comb. Declaring herself presentable, she made her way to the Gymnasium.

She sat at the table, clutching a monogrammed handkerchief in her hand, a birthday gift from her son. The soft cotton made her feel as if he were somehow there to give her comfort. She prayed for strength to get her through this. She hoped Albert would comport himself with respect.

Earlier, Headmaster Braun had welcomed her and sincerely thanked her for standing in support of Albert. He had said that he knew she would be an excellent advocate for the boy. Her spirits lifted slightly at his compliment.

Then he had commented about how remarkable her son had been and how much he regretted what had happened. His well-meaning condolences only reminded her of her loss, and the gray fog of depression, her constant companion since the funeral, settled once again around her.

The headmaster, Stefan Braun, had a reputation for being fair. Personable and intelligent, the fifty-ish man had plenty of experience, and could himself have made the decision regarding young Einstein. But he wanted the views of the teachers and other adults who knew Albert in hopes that he could find something that would be more in Albert's favor. He thought Albert was basically a decent boy, though perhaps a bit too smart for his own good. So far, he didn't see how he could resolve the instructors' complaints in a way that would allow Albert to continue at the Gymnasium. And that troubled him.

The five-person panel sat around a circular table. Colonel von Wiesel sat on the direktor's right side and Frau Thomas on his left. Von Achen, the physics teacher, sat next to Frau Thomas and Hamlin, who taught history, sat next to the colonel. An empty chair for Albert sat across from the direktor.

"I want to thank you all for coming," Direktor Braun had said, opening the meeting. His quiet gaze touched each person. "I have invited you here to determine whether Herr Einstein is to continue as a student in our school." Hands clasped on the table, nodding to the two teachers, he continued. "Our teachers have brought to my attention the issues surrounding the boy in the classroom. And I have heard gossip of behavior that has me concerned. So, I would appreciate each of you sharing your experience."

Von Achen jumped right in, his feeling clearly expressed in his frown. "The boy is insufferable. He's arrogant. He thinks he knows more about mathematics than I do." The man's anger grew, and his volume increased with each word. "I ask him to repeat what he has read in the textbook, and he goes off on a tangent not only unrelated to the topic but making no sense to anyone." His chest heaving, the instructor, paused. Then, as if his words had spewed all the anger he held, the balding man seemed to deflate into his chair.

Colonel von Wiesel shook his head. "Insufferable is a good description." His face turned bitter. "Those Jews think they are better than anybody else!" he spat. The man's piggish eyes swept the assemblage as if daring anyone to contradict him.

Herr Hamlin responded calmly in contrast to the colonel's vitriol. "Excuse me, Colonel, but I am Jewish. I think it's more accurate to say we of think of ourselves as determined, not better."

He cleared his throat. "Be that as it may, it's true that young Einstein doesn't follow the rules. He thinks he can do whatever he pleases. He stares out the window and will not cooperate with the plan we have established for the class. I have tried all the techniques I know, and I'm afraid I just don't know what to do to keep his attitude from disrupting my class."

Frau Thomas came to Albert's defense. "I know it must be upsetting for you when you are just trying to teach our children. But remember, Albert becomes frustrated and doesn't understand why other people are not as smart as he is. He doesn't follow the rules because he doesn't understand their value or why they have been imposed."

Von Achen pounded his fist on the table, and Frau Thomas flinched, nearly bursting into tears. Red in the face, the teacher shouted, "The rules were not established for him to understand! They were put in place by those who know better, and he must follow them whether he comprehends them or not!"

Direktor Braun raised his hands in a placating gesture. "Please, let's stay calm." He looked to each participant as he spoke. "I agree with Herr Hamlin that being Jewish is not the issue. And Frau Thomas makes a good point that Albert's conduct is founded on his not understanding." He turned his gaze to the two teachers.

"However, your comments are also valid, gentlemen. Perhaps Herr Einstein himself can give us some sense of a solution." The colonel sighed, surrendering to the necessity of being in the same room as the boy, and von Achen frowned.

The headmaster rose from the table. He strode to the office door and turned the brass knob. Looking into the adjoining room, he nodded to Albert. "Please, Herr Einstein, would you come in?" Albert stood stiffly and straightened his clothing. With as much dignity as he could summon, he walked into the direktor's office. The animosity in the room was palpable to him.

The Advisory Council members kept their silence as Albert entered the room. Frau Thomas smiled in vague encouragement at the boy, and Hamlin maintained a neutral expression. Von Wiesel and von Achen openly scowled. The headmaster gestured to a chair for Albert, but instead of taking his seat, Albert remained standing and pulled an envelope from his coat pocket. He extended it toward the headmaster. "If you would, Herr Direktor, please consider this in your discussion." With a puzzled look, the direktor took the proffered envelope.

Frau Thomas shook her head and held her breath as Direktor Braun opened the envelope and read the letter aloud.

Dear Direktor Braun,

I have examined Herr Albert Einstein and have concluded that he is suffering from nervous exhaustion, exacerbated by the death of his friend Johann Thomas. It is my professional recommendation that he be given a leave of absence from his classes at the Gymnasium for an unspecified period.

Thank you for your kind consideration in this matter.
Dr. Joshua Talmud, MD
Munich University Clinic

Thoughtfully, the headmaster neatly folded the letter and placed it back in the envelope, relief clear on his face. He turned to Albert and said, "We will undoubtedly factor this into our deliberations, Herr Einstein. Do you have anything else to say?

Albert shook his head. "I do not."

The direktor took in a breath and slowly exhaled. "Well then, thank you for coming in today. We will let you know what we decide."

Albert nodded to the direktor and then to the others seated at the table. He spared Frau Thomas a brief smile, then walked from the room.

As the door closed, the direktor eased himself back onto his chair. "Well, this changes things a bit." He read the letter to the group again and then said, "With your agreement, I will write a letter to Albert and his parents confirming that it is in the best interest of the school and Herr Einstein for him to be excused from his studies. I will suggest that during his time of recovery, they find a school that better suits his educational needs." At the nods of the others, he said, "Then it is settled. Since we have a doctor's diagnosis of nervous exhaustion, I can make sure his school record does not indicate any misconduct so it will be easier for him to find acceptance in another school."

There were more nods around the table, though Colonel von Wiesel did not look happy. He had been expecting a more severe punishment for the Jew but decided to hold his tongue. At least for the time being.

As Albert made his way home, all he felt was a relief. He was confident that he would never return to the Gymnasium. Max's letter gave the direktor the out he was no doubt looking for, and it released Albert from the stifling insipidness of the classes he had been forced to endure.

For the first time since Johann's death, he began to hope that there might be some brightness in his future. Despite the gray day and biting cold, as he considered Switzerland and what the school there might be like, Albert slowly began to smile.

Chapter 21
December 1894
New Beginnings

Albert collapsed wearily into the train seat and let out a long, heavy sigh. He was relieved to find that he was the only passenger in the compartment. Sinking into a daydream, he wondered what it would be like to see his parents again. Albert had no idea how they would receive the news about his leaving the Gymnasium.

A gray-haired porter shuffled into the compartment and said, "Tickets please." Lost in thought, Albert didn't respond. The porter tapped the troubled teen on the shoulder. "Sir, ticket please." Albert started, then smiled sheepishly. "Sorry." He reached into his pocket, then handed the clerk his voucher, which the porter punched, shaking his head, and ambled on to the next compartment.

As the train rumbled along, Albert closed his eyes and fell back into his reverie. He began composing his story so he could tell his mother all that had happened since she and his father had left. Absently the runaway tugged on the silver chain of his shiny, brass compass, then pulled it from his tweed coat pocket. Still lost in his thoughts, he smiled as he thought of his childhood companion Johann. The last time he saw him was at the farmer's market. Well, physically, at least. The last time he had "seen" him was after the funeral in his friend's bedroom.

Albert had been laying on Johann's bed after dinner, grieving for his friend. He had pulled out his compass, finding a vague comfort gazing at the jewels on its lid. From out of nowhere, a shimmering light appeared above the compass and Johann had materialized, his form shining and translucent. He was smiling, and Albert sensed a warmth and love emanating from his friend's eyes. The ethereal form just held, and a sense of peace had descended over Albert. Somehow, in his heart, he knew all was well with his friend. As that awareness presented itself to Albert, Johann had nodded, then slowly faded. From that time on, the pain of Johann's loss had become manageable, and there was even a sense of joy, knowing Johann was somehow just fine.

Morning sunlight shined through the train compartment's window and glinted in the twelve brilliant jewels as Albert swung his treasure back and forth, then lowered it to his lap. The stones shimmered like stars in a rainbow of light. A spiral of light seemed to project from the compass, and Albert floated up into it and into another dimension of time. Mesmerized, Albert drifted off.

The smell of frankincense woke him. He saw enormous flying buttresses and realized he must be in a Gothic cathedral. Seated next to him in the pew was a bearded, balding gentleman. He stared at the man, watching the swings of a bronze chandelier that hung from the ceiling on a long metal chain and swung back and forth at regular intervals.

After a moment, the man spoke. It was not a language Albert knew, but he somehow understood. "Most interesting, don't you think?"

"Uh, I'm not quite sure what I'm looking at, sir," Albert responded respectfully.

The man nodded, then said, "Put your hand over your heart for a moment, then touch your wrist with your fingers."

Albert complied. "Your heart goes bump, bump, yes?" Albert nodded. "And your pulse does the same."

"It does," Albert confirmed.

With his arm, the man mirrored the swing of the lamp. "You see, young man? I have observed that no matter how large or small the arc, the chandelier will complete its back and forth in the same amount of time."

"Really?" Albert asked, suddenly fully engaged in the

conversation.

The man nodded solemnly.

As the subject matter of the discussion began to sink in, Albert suddenly had a sense of whom he was speaking to. Awed, he hesitantly asked, "Would you be, uh, Galileo, sir?"

With a twinkle in his eye, the man affirmed it. "I must admit, I am he." Galileo leaned forward. "Now, we have established that we can measure time, correct?" Albert nodded. "Then remember that and come with me," he said, setting down a prayer book and motioning for Albert to follow.

As they strolled outside to a leaning tower nearby, Galileo picked up two rocks, one twice the size of the other. With Albert in tow, he climbed the stairs to the top of the tower. Leaning over the edge, Galileo said, "Watch. I drop them at the same time."

The rocks fell, and both landed together with a distant thump. "See, gravity! You must use gravity with time."

Albert nodded thoughtfully, leaning further over the ledge to stare again at the rocks. Suddenly he was falling over the crowning ridge of the tower... He came back to awareness in the train car compartment with a jerk.

I have been with the father of physics! Albert thought with awe as he put the compass back into his pocket and absently gazed out the compartment window, considering what Galileo had said.

His thoughts were nearly enough to distract him from his worry about how he would be received by his family.

* * *

Daylight was surrendering to dusk in the bustling town of Pavia, Italy, as the exhausted Albert dropped his bags on the doorstep of his parents' garden apartment. While it seemed as if things were about to take a turn for the better, Albert still couldn't quite shake off the stress of recent events in his life. Concern weighed heavily on him, and he hesitated before knocking on the door. On the train ride from Munich that had consumed most of the day, Albert had worried that he had disappointed his family by leaving the Gymnasium. Now, standing in front of the door, he wrung his hands, stared down at his feet, breathed in a last bit of courage and knocked.

Pauline, in a plain cotton gown, opened the door and, seeing who it was, delightedly blurted out, "Albert! Oh my God!" With a wan smile, the lost boy greeted his mother.

"Please, Mama, I must come home," Albert said, sinking into the comfort of her arms. He accepted her warm embrace and, when he inhaled her familiar fresh soap scent, he burst into tears.

Concerned with the unexpected emotion, Pauline quickly drew him into the parlor. "Albert! Of course, you will stay here. Come, sit. Tell me what has happened."

For what seemed like a long time, Albert poured out his heart.

Pauline listened without interrupting as Albert unburdened himself. When he reached the end of his tale, she smiled, and Albert could see the compassion and understanding in her eyes. It was that, as much as the catharsis of telling his story, which cleansed Albert's soul.

Nodding wisely, Pauline simply said, "That is the past, my beautiful son. Let us now look to the future."

* * *

In the three months that had elapsed since Albert materialized unannounced at his parents' home, he had settled into a new and comfortable routine. Uncle Jakob had engaged the seventeen-year-old in lending a hand in their electric lighting business, and his father, Hermann, the salesman for the family business, was happy to have him back in the fold.

One day when Albert collected the mail as he generally did, he spotted a letter addressed to him. Seeing that it was from his uncle Caesar Koch, a merchant in Belgium, his pulse quickened. He excitedly tore the envelope open and, as he read, his eyes widened. At the end of the letter, he let out a squeal of joy and raced outside to the company workshop behind the house.

"Father, Uncle Jakob!" shouted Albert, waving the letter in the air.

Jakob and Hermann reluctantly looked up from amid the blizzard of crumpled papers strewn around them. They were deep into trying to solve an electrical installation problem.

Albert slowed, and a frown replaced the happy grin he had been sporting. "What's wrong?"

Jakob shook his head, his face pinched with tension. "We have an installation of one hundred lights at a factory. It is the most complicated job we have ever had, and I just can't solve the math. We have been at it since yesterday."

Albert stuffed the letter in his shirt pocket. His news could wait. He flopped down on a bench next to his uncle. "Let me see."

Jakob handed his nephew the papers with a sigh. He closed his eyes and massaged his head. "I have such a headache."

"Give me a few minutes alone with this puzzle," Albert said as he turned his attention to the task. Since he had been working with his uncle, his knowledge of electricity had increased, and he had found the study of magnetism fascinating.

His father and uncle welcomed the break. "You can find us in the house when you've got it figured out," Hermann said with a wry grin. He knew the seventeen-year-old didn't have the experience to figure out the solution—if there was one—but he and Jakob weren't getting anywhere, and the pause might clear their heads.

As the two men left, Albert reviewed the specifications of the job, then picked up a pencil from the table and withdrew his compass from his pants pocket, setting it alongside the papers. He took a breath and prepared to get started on the math, but the sparkling jewels on top of the brass direction finder captured his attention. With the details of the problem in mind, he let himself relax, gazing absently at the compass. Minutes passed, then Albert began writing feverishly.

Albert was beaming as he walked into the kitchen. His father and uncle looked up from the table where they sat. "Solved it already?" his uncle said with a hint of joking sarcasm.

"Actually, I think I did," Albert replied, holding out some papers.

Skeptical, Jakob snatched the papers from Albert's hand. He studied what the boy had written and, slowly, his frown was replaced by a relieved if almost unbelieving smile.

As Albert's father looked over Jakob's shoulder, he read and nodded, read some more and nodded some more. Then he looked at his son. "How did you do this, Albert? We've been at it for nearly two days and come up with nothing."

Albert grinned and said, "I have been experimenting. I have new ideas based on Voile's advanced theory of physics. As I was thinking about your problem, some ideas came to me. I think the suggestions I have proposed will work."

Uncle Jakob looked at the papers again and nodded. "I believe they will. Albert, I don't know what to say."

Albert's father stood and hugged his son. "I... I can't begin to tell you how proud I am of you, Albert." Albert hugged his father back and the letter he had received earlier crinkled in his pocket.

"What's tha... oh, I remember, you had something to tell us."

Albert pulled out the now wrinkled letter from his pocket. "I do!" As he unfolded the piece of paper Albert said, "You know I have been studying on my own to hopefully qualify to attend the Zurich Polytechnic." The two men nodded. "I sent Uncle Koch an essay, 'The Investigation of the State of the Ether in a Magnetic Field.'

He knew some people in the administration at the college and got them to look at it."

"I take it they approved of your essay?" Jakob asked.

"Better," Albert said, his grin now threatening to split his face. "I have been invited to take the entrance exam in October!"

Interlude IV

*O*n the mystery school established in Summerland in the astral realm, Johann had been deeply immersed in his process of enlightenment and evolvement. Now, though, he was wandering through the lush gardens and allowing what he was learning to sink in. Lost in thought, he sensed a presence and looked up and found a smiling Jesus approaching him.

"How are you adjusting to being here, Johann?" Jesus asked.

"I'm doing fine, I think."

Jesus smiled and put his hand on the boy's shoulder. "So, no questions then?" he asked, barely hiding a grin.

The love radiating from Jesus' presence filled Johann. "I wouldn't say that," he smiled back at the Master.

"So," Jesus said, "what new insights are puzzling you?"

Johann became thoughtful. "When I died on Earth, my soul traveled here to the astral realm."

Jesus nodded. "Yes, the soul can traverse the realms with ease. Some people who have become aware of this movement have called it an out-of-body experience. You might better label it soul travel, depending upon through which chakra or portal the consciousness left the body."

Johann asked, "Well, how do we travel in our soul? Does it happen when we want it to?"

Jesus smiled, though his tone was solemn. He knew the importance of these teachings and wanted to make sure they were presented with clarity to the young seeker. "Soul travel happens all the time. The soul leaves the body to go to different mystery schools in many universes. A person cannot exactly control how or when the soul flies, but you can learn to be conscious of it. And when you drop the body after death, the soul—who we really are—leaves and goes to different realms of Light, depending on the lessons it has learned and the experience it has gained."

Johann considered that then asked, "How do we know if we have had an experience of soul travel?"

Jesus nodded. "Good question. How about we go on a field trip? There is a teacher on Earth speaking of just this topic now."

"Wow, that would be great!" Johann replied, eager for the adventure.

Jesus took Johann's hand, and in an instant, both were transported to a room in a modest building in a compound in the Punjab region of India. Johann couldn't believe his eyes. He had never seen anything so exotic, nor such a gathering of people so different from the Germans and Europeans he knew. The room was filled, but not terribly crowded, and gaslights lit the place.

As Johann took this all in, he looked up at Jesus and whispered, "Why has no one noticed us, Jesus?"

Jesus laughed out loud, and Johann cringed, looking around, concerned that those gathered would object. But still, no one seemed to notice them. Jesus, always smiling, said, "I'm sorry, Johann, I wasn't laughing at you. I forgot how new this all must be to you."

Johann continued looking around uncomfortably, and Jesus guided him to a place off to the side. "We are not in physical bodies here, Johann, we are in a subtler body. So most in here cannot see us."

Johann frowned, considering this. "I... I guess that must be so, Jesus, since no one has looked our way since we got here."

He looked to a nearby group of men who were paying rapt attention to the bearded man in a turban at the front of the room speaking in a calm, almost quiet voice. As he spoke, the man looked toward Johann and Jesus and his eyes filled with love as he nodded slightly in Jesus' direction. Johann glanced up at Jesus with a puzzled look on his face. With a twinkle in his eye, Jesus looked down at Johann. "I said most could not see us. Now, are you ready for your answer about how we can know if we're soul traveling?"

Johann remained puzzled. "Yes. Do I raise my hand or something?"

Jesus shook his head. "Not necessary. Just hold the question in your mind and see what happens."

"But we are in a strange country, and this man is obviously speaking a foreign language. How will he understand me?" Johann asked.

Jesus raised his eyebrows. "We're in a foreign land, that's true. So, are you having trouble understanding this man?"

Johann paused for a moment and realized he understood perfectly everything that was being said. He shook his head and, though it made no sense, just did as Jesus suggested, thinking of his question.

In a moment, the man at the front of the room said, "You may be wondering if we can know when we are traveling in our soul body. That is when the soul leaves the body through a higher center, the top of the third eye or the crown chakra. The answer is yes, we can. Often, the experience of soul travel will be a flash of knowing through your intuition. When you are going about your daily routine, you will feel or have a sense of the revelation. Other times, you may experience it as you practice your spiritual exercises, the chanting of the sacred names of God. Maybe most of all you will notice it accompanied with a sense of love."

Johann's eye grew wide, and he looked again to Jesus, who was smiling peacefully. "Wow, that was... I don't know... amazing. But what about people like the boy I knew named Werner? He didn't seem very in tune with love. Just the opposite; he promoted hate for the Jews and went out of his way to bully them."

Johann paused as the thought struck him. "Why, he even killed me! Can he soul travel?"

The teacher at the front of the room continued, "Soul consciousness is an active state of being, as is soul travel. But if a man turns his attention to the darkness of power and control, that can block awareness of the higher Light, and he has to find his way back into the Light."

With that, Jesus bowed slightly to the man at the front of the room, then again took Johann's hand and they were transported back to the garden. Johann struggled to collect his thoughts and absorb what had just happened. "You mean people are teaching about this soul travel? I never knew that."

"A lot is happening on Earth and in the spiritual realms that most people are not aware of," Jesus affirmed.

"When souls incarnate on Earth, they have a destiny they have prearranged before being born. For some that destiny includes connecting with a teacher or a Mystical Traveler, such as the man we just visited."

Johann took in all that Jesus was telling him as the master continued. "But back to the boy, Werner. In his quest for power—which is really seeking recognition from his peers, and especially from his father—Werner is learning how the darkness does not give him what he wants. As an emissary of Light, in your soul body, you became a teacher to him so he can learn the consequences of his choices."

Johann nodded, and Jesus continued. "Acceptance and recognition are illusions. Werner has allowed himself to be lured into the influence of an agent of darkness named Raka. Raka lusts for the power of Albert's compass."

Johann gasped. "Is that why Werner kept asking me about Albert's compass?"

Jesus nodded solemnly. "Raka tried using Werner to get the compass. When you refused to cooperate, Raka became infuriated and psychically influenced Werner to become blinded with rage. That was when Werner pushed you in front of the streetcar."

Johann was filled with empathy for Werner and his eyes filled with tears. "I had no idea..."

Jesus held quiet in loving as Johann processed this new knowledge. After a moment, Johann became peaceful and looked up at Jesus. "What's so important about the compass Albert has?"

Jesus took in a breath. "It contains a fragment of a stone that has been around for millennia. Its power is unimaginable, and Raka wants it so he can again destroy civilization on Earth like he did when he destroyed Atlantis."

Johann asked, "Oh my. Does working with this Raka affect Werner's ability to soul travel?"

Jesus replied, "Not directly. But to soul travel, Werner would have to surrender his fear and allow his wisdom to guide him. He may or may not be able to do that in his current lifetime if he succumbs to the negative influences he has begun to associate with." Then Jesus smiled, and his radiance was dazzling. "But not one soul is ever lost. So, if he doesn't accept that now, he will have many other lifetimes in which to learn."

Johann sat bathed in Jesus' warm presence for a while. Both seemed perfectly content to just be there together. Then a new thought occurred to Johann. "What about Albert? If this Raka person is after his compass, can we help him? I mean, is there something I can do?"

Jesus smiled and the ancient name and sound of God, "HU," streamed through the realms of Light. On this sound, Jesus placed forth an invitation. In a moment, the Mystical Travelers Moses, Akhenaten, and Ezekiel appeared.

Jesus nodded to the three. "Thank you for responding to my call. Johann is concerned about our Albert and the compass. Can you show him the path we hope Albert will take?"

Ezekiel nodded as he sat on the alabaster bench and opened his viewing Portal. He beckoned to Johann. "Step closer, Johann, and see one of the possible paths in God's plan." The Mystical Travelers and Johann stood around the ambassador of Light and saw that the hologram was spinning a vision of Albert in Atlantis.

Ezekiel said, "Albert was a high priest-scientist of Atlantis. His name was Arka. Albert needs to soul travel to Atlantis in his soul body, where he will meet Arka."

Johann looked up at Ezekiel. "Can he do that?" he asked in awe.

Ezekiel nodded. "He can if he chooses. We will assist and protect Albert with his mission of Light and energy. His work will affect the evolution of planet Earth."

Johann could only stare into the Portal at the image of Arka. He was staggered to think that his friend could play such a pivotal role in the planet's destiny. And he vowed to himself that he would learn about this soul travel and do all he could to help his friend and keep him safe.

Chapter 22
Spring 1895
Thought Experiment

*S*ix male students in their mid-teens dressed in wool suits, starched white shirts, and blue-and-yellow neckties sat two by two in a single row, anxiously awaiting the start of class. Albert had enrolled in Aarau High School after his unsuccessful attempt to enter the Polytechnic. Of course, he had passed the math and science section of the exam with flying colors. Yet the test showed Albert needed more study in languages, biology, literature, political science, and botany. While somewhat disappointed with the test results, he saw it would only take a year at Aarau before he could get to the Polytechnic, and he was okay with that.

The smell of fresh white chalk stimulated Albert's mind. He focused on the three *H*s the headmaster, Professor Winteler, wrote on the blackboard; the principles of teaching the school followed.

Heart – to explore what students want to learn. To develop their moral qualities, such as helping others.

Head – to understand objects, concepts, and experiences.

Hand – to learn the craft of doing good work and develop their physical skills.

Completing his writing with a flourish, the teacher turned to face his class. His brown eyes twinkled, and there was genuine warmth and enthusiasm in his voice as he said, "I have found that people learn more easily accessing their intuition, their inner powers than they do through their minds."

In the front row, Albert relaxed. For the first time in his school life, the reject from the Gymnasium in Germany felt connected.

The wise professor put down the chalk and rubbed his hands together. He adjusted his spectacles and said, "Our first exercise will be a thought experiment. It will assist us when we want to consider a hypothesis or theory when the purpose is to think through by steps to its consequences. This practice will increase your personal power of thought and imagination. What's more," he said with a smile, "by going inward, you begin to trust your-self."

A sandy-haired student raised his hand, and the professor acknowledged him. "Yes, Gregory, you have a question?"

"I do, sir," the boy said as he stood.

The professor smiled. "Good. Questions are encouraged. What do you have?"

"In this mind experiment, do we have our eyes open or closed?"

"For the purposes of our first experiment, you will have your eyes closed. Though I am sure sometimes during the day, you find yourself in a daydream where your mind is drifting in space even with your eyes open." Gregory nodded as the professor continued. "We are going to use a what-if, dreamy kind of imagination to allow you to let go and create possibilities."

As Gregory sat down, the professor instructed, "Now I want you to remove your jackets, loosen your ties, and sit up straight with your arms and legs uncrossed. Place your hands on your thighs, palms up."

The students did so and waited for the next direction.

"Close your eyes and take a slow, deep breath," Winteler said. "Inhale, then slowly let go of all the air in your lungs." He paused for a few seconds. "Again, this time breathe in more slowly." As the students did this, he paused, then said, "Hold the air inside." He paused again. "Let go of all the air, slowly. Allow your body to relax. Keep your eyes closed and focus on your breath going in and out. If your mind starts to chatter, just acknowledge that then bring your focus back to your breathing."

Albert sat with his back straight though he was relaxed, surrendering his mind. Lost in the experience, the dreamer did not even hear what the teacher said next because he found himself enveloped in a warm glow, and he felt like he was rising above the Earth. A motion caught his awareness, and he glanced to the side. Next to him flew a graceful, towering, luminous being with flowing, golden hair. Somehow, Albert sensed it was an angel. The angel's violet eyes gave the dreamer a loving smile, and Albert surrendered more fully to his experience. Archangel Michael offered Albert his hand, and Albert gently grasped it. The sound of angels singing "Glory to God in the highest" rang out over the universe.

The veil of time opened, and Albert found himself floating down onto the emerald-green grass in the Garden of Remembrance. As he attempted to take it all in, Albert saw a figure standing nearby. It slowly turned, and Albert was filled with joy to recognize his friend Johann. Somehow it all seemed perfectly right, though unreal at the same time.

The two friends embraced, then Albert pulled away. "Johann, how... how..."

Johann smiled. "Don't try to figure it all out at once, Albert. Just let the reality reveal itself to you."

"But is it a reality, Johann? Or am I just in a wishful-thinking dream?"

With a mischievous smile, Johann reached out and pinched Albert on the arm.

"Ow!" said Albert with a frown, rubbing the spot where Johann had pinched. Then his eyes grew wide. "Okay, I get it. It's real."

Johann nodded, still smiling. "It's real all right. Just not the reality you're used to." In the months since his death, Johann had become more confident about what he knew about the realm in which he found himself.

"Okay, I believe you... but why am I here?"

Johann became more serious. He took Albert's arm and guided him along the shore of a nearby pond. "We have to talk, Albert.

There is much to tell you. Things are going on you won't believe. But this visit is just to let you know that you can come here anytime you want. The thought experiment technique Herr Winteler is teaching you will help you come back."

Albert listened with rapt attention as his friend explained some of what he had been learning. Before he could digest what, he was hearing, Johann continued. "But for now, you must return to your body." Johann hugged Albert and kissed him on the cheek. "Remember this, and I'll see you later."

"But—" Albert started to protest. In the next moment, Albert felt like he was falling from a great height. Just before the dreamer hit the ground, his eyes flew open. He had returned to his body as Professor Winteler was asking the class, "What was your experience of your first thought experiment? Does anyone want to share?"

Albert did not know how to respond. He wondered who would believe him if he told them what happened. He kept his mouth shut and barely heard the answers from his classmates. He was lost in his thoughts about seeing Johann and wondering just what could be so important that he would be called to that place... wherever—or whatever—it was.

Chapter 23
September 1896
Raka's Progress

*L*urking in the steam tunnels of the Polytechnic Institute, Raka observed the classes undetected through the heating grills. He sniffed the vapors, seeking the aromatic scent of the Shamir through the ducts. The seductive perfume tantalized, but the prize remained elusive. On the fourth day of prowling the school, however, the smell became intense. Raka's heart quickened as he sensed the closeness of the Shamir.

Peering through the heating grate, he saw Albert cradling his compass in the palm of his hand as Professor Meiss expounded on the principles of physics. It was all Raka could do to keep from squealing with delight to see what he desired so near.

The dragon's plan to acquire the compass involved his accomplice, Countess Victoria von Baden. The high-born seductress had initially resisted accompanying him to Zurich, but the possibility of obtaining the Shamir was too tempting to pass up. Satisfied that he had located his prize, the reptile quietly backed away from the heating grate and went to his rendezvous with the Countess. He was eager to set his plan in motion.

* * *

The dining salon of the Hotel Rigiblick was located on the ground level of the favorite lodge where famous actors stayed when they were performing at the Theatre Zurich. It was also a favorite restaurant of Professor Meiss, who, being a man of habit, dined there most nights. Posing as a visiting actress, Countess von Baden wore a crimson velvet tea-length gown, as if she were a character from the opera *Carmen*. Wearing a wig to complete her new role, her raven hair hung down her back, a striking contrast to her well-exposed ivory shoulders. She lounged comfortably near the bar waiting for her victim to arrive.

Around eight o'clock, the lonely bachelor professor walked into the supper club and headed toward his customary table. As he approached where she sat, Victoria nudged her small evening clutch, so it fell on the floor in front of him. Ever the gentleman, the professor stooped to pick it up.

"How clumsy of me," she chided herself as he handed the purse to her.

"Not at all," he said, his eyes widening at her beauty. He could not ignore the ample décolletage the woman displayed.

"You are too kind, monsieur." She smiled and batted her eyelashes coquettishly.

The professor nodded and turned toward his table. Victoria rolled her eyes. The idiot was too dim to see she was flirting with him. "Uh, monsieur..." The professor turned back to her. "I was wondering... that is..." She paused for effect. "Well, the truth of it is, my dinner date has stood me up."

"I find that hard to believe, young lady. What man in his right mind would miss an evening with someone such as you?"

"Again, you are too kind, monsieur. I do so hate eating alone."

Struck by an idea, the professor said, "That would be a crime of major proportions. Please, you must join me at my table."

"I really couldn't impose," Victoria said, turning her head so he could not see the satisfied smile on her face as he took the bait.

"It is not an imposition at all. Please, I insist," Meiss said, gesturing toward his table.

"Well, if you insist, I will not be rude," she said, rising and allowing the professor to guide her to a plush seat.

When they were comfortably seated, the professor gestured for the waiter to bring them a bottle of wine, then turned to Victoria. "I am Tomas Meiss. I teach physics at the Swiss Polytechnic School."

"Oh, my, a scholar. And of physics. I am sure I am out of my league," she said.

The professor blushed at the compliment as Victoria smiled and said, "I am Victoria von Baden. Please, call me Victoria."

The professor nodded and smiled back at her as the waiter approached and presented the wine for him to taste. After approving the vintage, the professor turned again to Victoria as the waiter filled both their glasses.

Pointing to a painting of a hunting scene on the wall behind the professor, Victoria asked, "What a delightful picture. Do you know who painted it?"

As the professor turned to look at the painting, Victoria flicked open the gem-encrusted dome of her ring and sprinkled a dusting of a powerful opiate into his glass.

"I'm not entirely certain," the professor admitted. "Shall I ask the waiter?"

"It's not important," Victoria said, raising the professor's glass and swirling the wine, so the powder fully dissolved before she handed it to him. "Let us toast my good fortune of finding such a handsome and charming dinner partner."

The professor blushed again and took a long drink from his glass to cover his embarrassment. Dabbing his lips with a napkin, he said, "I've not been called either handsome or charming in a long time... Victoria."

She smiled back as they continued to sip and chat. After a moment, a puzzled look crossed the professor's face. His complexion going pale, he lifted the white linen napkin and patted his brow. A fleeting grin crossed Victoria's face but was quickly replaced with a concerned frown. "Is something wrong, Tomas?"

The professor shook his head, then mopped his brow once again. "No... I don't know... I'm not feeling..." Then he slumped over, unconscious.

Feigning alarm, Victoria gestured for the maître d'. "Something's wrong with Tomas," she said as he strode to the table. "Help me get him to my coach so I can take him to a doctor."

"Very good, madame," he replied, waving over the waiter. Putting the groggy professor's arms over their shoulders, the two men followed Victoria as she led them out the front door to the waiting carriage she had hired. In moments, the coachman was driving at a hurried pace through the town and came to a stop in front of an abandoned four-story clothing warehouse in Escher Wyss District across the inlet from the Polytechnic. Paddle steamboats laden with tourists dotted the waterfront.

The coachman helped the Countess and the dazed and groggy professor out of the carriage and into the recessed doorway of the warehouse. The coachman, who had been selected for his less than savory character, was happy to receive a sizeable tip to assure he would conveniently forget the entire evening.

As the sound of the horse and carriage receded, Victoria dragged the professor into the warehouse. She closed and locked the door as a moan escaped the professor's lips. "Don't worry, Tomas," she said over her shoulder, "you'll be out of your discomfort very soon."

Turning, she lifted the professor's arm over her shoulder and guided him up a dark, narrow staircase, dodging around the litter strewn on the steps. At the second landing, she opened a massive metal door and half-pushed the slowly reviving professor through it. As he staggered into the room, he was met with a scene that did not match the decrepit state of the rest of the building.

For all intents and purposes, he could have been in any of the most beautiful castles in Europe. Exquisite Oriental tapestries adorned the walls, and a matched set of velvet sofas and armchairs created an intimate conversation area. A bookcase covered half a wall, filled with the favored books of the day in fine leather bindings. At the far end of the room, the Countess had designed a sleeping chamber; a vast ornately carved four-poster bed with richly embroidered curtains that created a private space within the bed's confines. Off to the side was a fully functional kitchen and beyond that, a lady's vanity and water closet. Unfortunately, the professor was in no condition to appreciate the opulence.

Locking the door, the Countess turned, and her lips curled into a predatory smile. Grabbing the professor by the shoulders of his coat, she steered him along to the bed at the end of the room and pushed him onto it. As the professor struggled to turn over, she pulled off his overcoat and then his jacket.

"Wha... what are you doing?" he slurred.

"Never you mind, Tomas," she said, roughly turning him over and removing his cravat, then unbuttoning his shirt. The professor tried to resist, but his limbs were like rubber. In minutes, he was completely naked under the covers the Countess had thrown over his frail body and propped into a sitting position amidst plush down pillows.

Then a sound off to the side of the room drew his attention. The professor blinked uncomprehendingly at the sight of a twelve-foot reptile standing erect and making its way toward him.

The professor's bewildered gaze whipsawed between the Countess and the creature. "Wha...?"

The Countess laughed as the lizard reached under the blankets, grabbed the professor by the leg and tugged. The professor struggled, but the drug had him dazed and confused still. It would have been futile in any case, as no human would have been a match for the powerful reptile. Raka began dragging him across the floor. "Enjoy your... repast, Herr Raka," the Countess called after the retreating form.

As a metal door at the end of the room closed with a slam, Victoria stepped over to a well-stocked liquor cabinet and poured a splash of fine cognac into a crystal snifter. She inhaled the intoxicating fumes, oblivious to the muffled screams that began to emerge from behind the metal door. A smile touched her lips. She was a step closer to gaining the Shamir. Raka thought she was his tool. Well, he would learn who was using whom.

The room Raka had designed was a far cry from that of the Countess. He had no use for expensive baubles, but he had acquiesced to her foolish requests to keep her happy and compliant. His lair was more utilitarian. Its main feature was a metal table with grooves that resembled nothing so much as a trencher board. And with good reason, since its sole purpose was to contain bloody meat—which was precisely what now rested on its surface.

It had taken little time for Raka to consume the professor's body and blood. The elderly human hadn't even put up much of a struggle. His terrified screams had been somewhat satisfying, adding a special savor to this otherwise rather bland meal.

With the corpse almost entirely consumed, Raka paused. He could sense the transformation beginning; he could feel his claws retracting and his leathery skin gaining suppleness. Shaking his head, he tore back into the now lifeless professor. He would have to hurry to finish this before his lovely, sharp fangs became puny and blunt teeth. He sighed, knowing that getting rid of whatever he didn't consume would be an odious task. He decided to eat as much as he could to minimize the cleanup. He knew the Countess would never stoop to something like that.

The next morning at dawn, Raka awoke from a deep slumber in the Countess's living area, his transformation complete. Naked and curled into a fetal position, he straightened and examined his new body, disgusted by the weak limbs and lack of wings. As he stood, he nearly fell, lightheaded from the transformation. He propped himself on a nearby table, then grasped a bench and sat with a thump.

By the hearth, the Countess muttered resentfully, "I did not sign up to be a chambermaid," as she pointed to the schoolmaster's clothing that had been drying in front of the fire. When she did not rise to bring them to him, Raka hissed, "Fetch them, Victoria. You know I will not approach open flames!"

Rolling her eyes, she set down her drink and took the garments to the newly human dragon, thrusting them into his arms. "Cover that pathetic body. It's making me nauseous," she said with disgust.

Raka took the clothing and pierced Victoria with a withering stare. "Mind your tone, Countess. Despite this form that I am forced to use to accomplish my purpose, I am still your master." He allowed his anger to transform his right hand into a set of digits with wickedly sharp claws.

Cowed by the reminder of Raka's power and stung by the rebuke, she winced and said, "Forgive me, Herr Raka. I have let this frail outer form cloud my vision." She paused, then meekly added, "The previous human whose body you occupied was strong and handsome. I rather... enjoyed... you in it." Disdain crossed her face as she looked up and down the professor's form.

"I am no happier with it than you are," he spat. "But since I may not directly interfere with the boy, I must be able to observe him more closely and watch for openings to take advantage of." His nostrils flared, and heat flushed throughout his body. As Victoria stepped back in fear, he struggled to regain control of this despicable human emotion. He knew it could take up to two days to settle fully into this form, and any intense mental or emotional shock could turn him back into his reptilian self. With a grimace of exertion, he regulated his breathing and forcefully took control of his racing heartbeat. "We sometimes must make sacrifices to accomplish our goals. So, leave me for now. I need to stay quiet. I will meet you tomorrow night."

"Yes, Herr Raka," Victoria mumbled, as she rushed out the door.

Raka sat on the armchair and resumed assessing his new body. As a changeling, he appreciated the reptile glands that were still a part of his throat. They increased his body's adrenaline output and made him stronger than a human would usually be. He spat into his palms and inhaled with pleasure the acrid, viscous reptilian liquid. To a human, the odor would smell like rotting flesh.

The Dragon savored his essence. Victoria might not choose the body he currently occupied or the modest house he would be living in until he had accomplished his goals, but she would cooperate. He chuckled, reminding himself that he still retained the supreme authority of the dragon. He picked up a silver candlestick from the table and held it in one hand, considering it. *I might appear to be the meek Professor Meiss.* He thought, *but I am far from weak.* He quickly crushed the stout silver piece into a twisted mass of metal.

Chapter 24
Mileva

rofessor Henrik Martin Weber was pacing in front of the chalkboard expounding on the principles of physics when the worn brass doorknob rattled. The heads of the five young men in his class turned as one toward the door. It opened to reveal a tiny girl in her middle-twenties dressed in a starched white shirtwaist and dark-blue trumpet skirt standing in the doorway looking very nervous. A collective gasp rippled through the classroom. What was a girl doing in the hallowed halls of the Swiss Federal Polytechnic?

When the girl was not forthcoming, the professor cleared his throat. "Can I help you?"

With a faint, shaky voice the girl responded, "Oh, uh, yes. I am Mileva Maric, sir."

"How very nice for you," the professor responded haughtily. A snicker escaped from one of the boys but was quickly stifled.

The girl blushed a bright red but stood her ground. "I am sorry I was not clear, Herr Professor. I am Mileva Maric, and I am enrolled in your class."

The large-nosed, heavy-browed, bearded scholar raised his eyebrows, then went to his desk and sorted through a stack of papers. In a moment he identified the class roster, then frowned. "Hmm.

You are Maric from Serbia?" He could not hide his disdain of her Slavic heritage. To him, the Slavs were a mediocre people at best. He couldn't imagine how she'd passed the entrance examinations; something must be amiss. If this were somehow correct, she would be only the fifth woman to attend this school.

"Yes, sir," replied Mileva.

"All right, come, come," he said, motioning impatiently toward a writing table at the back of the room. "Sit there, and try to keep up. You are already fifteen minutes behind in today's lecture."

Relieved that the professor was not raising a fuss about her being in his class, Mileva nodded and stepped into the room. "Thank you, Herr Professor. I will try not to disrupt your class," she said, no longer quite so shy.

The stares of the eighteen-year-old boys followed the brave girl as she limped past them to the unoccupied seat in the corner of the room. As she sat, they all turned their attention back to the front of the room, except for Albert. He could not tear his eyes away from her. He squinted as if trying to recall something. For a moment, his eyes met Mileva's, and her face became flushed again. He smiled. The professor cleared his throat, and Albert turned with the rest toward the blackboard.

Harrumphing, he said, "I will have the focus of the whole classroom, Herr Einstein."

"Of course, Professor Weber," Albert replied, but couldn't help turning his head quickly for one more glance at the young girl. There was something about her. Then Albert forced his full attention back toward the front of the classroom and physics.

* * *

The packs on their backs filled with hiking equipment and lunch were starting to get heavy. Albert had been trudging behind Mileva for nearly two hours. He was ready to eat. Pine needles crunched underfoot, and the breeze whistled through the woods fragrant with the scent of pine. The sound of squirrels chittering and scurrying through the trees caught his attention. He smiled, "See, Dollie, the tree rats are playing the mating game." Dollie was Albert's affectionate nickname for Mileva because her small stature reminded him of a delicate figurine. The racy reference brought a flush to Mileva's face but her deep-set, dark-brown eyes twinkled as she twirled around and shot back, "Oh, my wicked sweetheart, do you fancy he will catch her?"

"Well, that depends. If little Miss Squirrel is as Bohemian as you are, then perhaps," Albert teased as he snatched a crimson wildflower and proffered it to her.

While their passion for math and physics had initially drawn them together, something else—a mysterious sense of familiarity—propelled them into a romantic relationship that had grown and flourished in just six months. This morning, the couple had taken the early morning express train to explore the Sihl virgin forest on the slopes of the Albis hills together; a last carefree time together before parting for the summer vacation. With each stride along the trail, Mileva's limp became less troublesome. Tuberculosis in her pelvis as a youngster had caused one leg to become shorter than the other. While she had never let that hold her back, climbing up the slope of the spinner's pathway made her disability seem less pronounced since equal-length legs were not an asset here. The higher they went, the wilder the flora and more peaceful the feeling became.

They aimed to arrive at the summit of the Albishorn Mountain by mid-afternoon, where they could enjoy a picnic overlooking the picturesque panorama of Zurich and the lake. The sunlight shone through the leaves, creating flickering shadows on the earth. The cry *hoopoe, hoopoe* of the hoopoe bird, trailed in the wind.

Their final outing was bittersweet. On the one hand, it was the celebration of the end of a long school term. On the other, Albert had decided to visit with his family in Italy, while Mileva would go to be with her parents in Serbia. They would be separated from each other and the other friends they had made at the school.

Mileva laughed off Albert's Bohemian remark, then changed the topic to divert her sweetheart from his current train of thought. "You know, when I think of physics, I imagine Almighty God in the hidden forces of the natural laws of the universe. Do you suppose there are secret rules about him waiting for us to discover? Sometimes I hear him whispering when I read Newton or Descartes. What do you think, Johnnie?"

Albert, who had been dubbed Johnnie one evening months ago when the two were being playful with each other, walked up to Mileva, a thoughtful look on his face. He took off his Bavarian hat and spread his fingers through his wavy brown hair, collecting his thoughts. Albert was not one to respond frivolously to such a weighty question. "I am not positive if Providence is speaking—

though I remain convinced that there is more to the world than what we see."

"Me too. It's going to be fascinating," Mileva said, her eyes glowing brightly. She was as entranced by science as Albert was—and she was quite brilliant.

As if stirred up by the conversation about forces beyond man's perception, a surge of wind swirled through the trees around the couple. Butterflies came out of nowhere, and Albert felt something brush against him. A warm glow broke over his body, and the hair on the back of his neck stood up. Beads of sweat gathered on his forehead.

"What was that?" he asked, recoiling from the mysterious energy.

"What was what, Johnnie?" Mileva asked, puzzled by his behavior.

"I don't know. It seemed like something... someone... brushed up against me."

"I'm sure it was nothing, Albert, just your imagination or something caused by the wind."

"Yes, I'm sure you're right," he smiled, calming down, "nothing at all." He kissed Mileva's hand and took a step forward up the inclined path. "Come on, let's get up this mountain before I starve to death."

The temperature dipped as the climbers ascended in silence, still pondering the questions of science they had been discussing. The gurgle of water flowing downhill filled their ears as they crossed over a footbridge. In less than an hour, they reached the edge of the woods. In the distance, the hikers saw mountains, their tops shrouded in mist. A pebble path led to the vista of a landscape dotted with rocks and boulders. The two stood for several moments gazing upon the majesty of the scene. On the crest of Albishorn, they looked down upon the town of Zurich and the pristine lake with tiny sailboats, their sails billowing in the breeze.

Free from care, Albert dropped his gear. With outstretched arms, he breathed in and shouted into the lapis-blue sky, "Oh, how I love the pure air!" Then he dropped his arms and with a smile declared, "I'm famished. Are you hungry, Dollie?"

Mileva nodded happily and tugged Albert's arm, urging him off the path toward the crumbling remains of a stone building long abandoned. Mileva threw open a patchwork quilt and began unwrapping the meal she had prepared. As Mileva busied herself setting up the picnic, Albert ambled to the edge of a nearby cliff. Humming a melody, he stepped down onto a five-inch-wide ledge that rimmed the cliff's edge. Like a tightrope walker, he stepped foot to heel along the narrow ridge, a drop of several thousand feet just a misstep away.

"Luncheon is almost ready, Johnnie!" Mileva called out.

Turning to look back at her, Albert missed his footing and stumbled. Unable to regain his balance, Albert's body pitched off the ledge and plummeted, twisting toward the rocky ground far, far below. He screamed in terror, "HELP ME."

The sound of his voice echoed off the cliff. As he plunged, his arms flailing, the compass tumbled out of his pocket. Then, out of nowhere, a hoopoe bird swooped in and snatched the compass out of the air.

As the hoopoe circled him, Albert closed his eyes, let go and waited for the impact. Time seemed to stand still. *I don't want my life to end like this at the bottom of a rocky ravine.* Within twenty feet of the ground, he felt pressure under his back. His descent stopped and like magic his body suspended in midair, then slowly floated up. In the next moment, as he tried to gain control of his breathing, he began rising toward the ledge from which he had fallen.

As Albert was deposited gently onto the grass near the picnic site, Mileva turned back from the picnic basket. "Where have you been Joh—" She paused in mid-sentence, astonished as she watched the hoopoe bird swoop gracefully to the ground, drop his prize onto the grass next to Albert, and fly away. Her eyes widened even further as Albert, in a daze, began addressing a bright cloud that hovered near him. His lips were moving, but Mileva could hear no sound. Transfixed, she could only stare in silence.

"Johann, what are you doing here?" Albert blurted out.

His friend smiled and answered, "I am your Guardian Light Being. Well, technically, guardian in training. Did you notice my spirit in the forest earlier?"

Albert shook his head. "No, I... wait, was that pressure I felt you?"

Johann nodded eagerly. "Yes, I wanted you to know I was near."

Albert blinked, trying to make sense of what he was hearing and seeing. "Do you remember when Pater Benjamin told you I was going to help protect you?" Albert looked blank, and Johann's eyes suddenly grew wide as he realized he had made a mistake. "Um, never mind. That hasn't happened yet."

"What in the world are you talking about, Johann?"

"Uh, nothing. Forget about it," Johann stuttered as he reached down and picked up the compass the hoopoe bird had dropped nearby. "Just trust that I'm looking out for you."

Before Albert could question him further, Johann's face became stern. "But what were you thinking, walking on that ledge? You could have died!"

Albert shrugged, "I guess I wasn't thinking. I'm happy, and I wanted to look over the edge."

"Well, please be more careful. That's not like you."

Albert nodded. "I will, Johann."

"Good." Johann took a deep breath. "Now, I have some information for you. It's not good news."

"You actually came to tell me something?" Albert was surprised.

Johann put his hand on Albert's arm. "Yes, I can tell you some things, and I am here to warn you about Professor Meiss."

"What do you mean?" Albert said, with a scowl. "He's a kind old man and I like his class."

Now Johann shook his head. "He *was* a kind, old man. But his body has been taken over by a... a malevolent force. He is not what he seems."

"Malevolent force? Johann, whatever do you mean?"

"I know this is a lot to swallow," Johann patted Albert's arm, "but trust me, Albert, the man you see in the classroom now is not the man you knew before. He is a deadly threat to you—and to your compass."

Albert rubbed his forehead. "What—" Albert started to ask, but Johann held up a hand.

"We're not allowed to interfere, Albert. I'm sorry, but I can only give you clues." Albert started to glare. "I'm telling you all I can. You will discover the rest of the details in due course, Albert. Trust me. He is dangerous. Be on guard around him. Never be anywhere alone with him."

"Yeah, okay. But—"

"I've told you all that's permitted, Albert. Now I must leave."

"Wait!" Albert cried, but Johann's image was already fading.

Albert blinked, refocusing on his surroundings. As his vision cleared, he saw Mileva staring at him in disbelief.

"Johnnie, what just happened? It was like you were in another world... and you were talking to a... a... cloud or something."

"I honestly can't say what is going on," Albert said, shaking his head to clear it. "I had a friend who was killed and—" Albert stopped. He took Mileva's hand in his and kissed it, then looked in her eyes. "Do you trust me, Mileva?"

Mileva paused and became thoughtful. After a moment, she nodded once. "I do, Albert. More than almost anyone in the world."

Albert released a breath he hadn't been aware he was holding. He smiled and squeezed Mileva's hand. "I am so glad you do."

I have a story to tell you. But I am going to ask you to be patient with me. I need to figure it out myself before I can say it to you. Will that be okay with you?"

Mileva hesitated but nodded again.

"Good, because now I am really starved," Albert said, grinning as he turned toward the food Mileva had set out.

Mileva shook her head, then joined him in their picnic lunch. She tried not to overthink about Albert talking to a cloud, or what a bird might have dropped in the grass near where they sat.

Chapter 25
Grasping at a Straw

The town of Zurich was beginning to stir in the raw daylight. A skinny mare with steam billowing out of its nostrils clomped along the bumpy cobblestone alley pulling a tinker's wagon. The metal cups and pans hanging from the wagon's sides clanged and rattled a wakeup call to the slowly rousing city.

In his dingy bachelor flat, Albert lay huddled under a comforter as the frigid winter air whistled through the poorly shuttered window. A tiny gas lantern cast its scant glow into the room, fighting a losing battle against the gloom. The harsh but not entirely unpleasant scent of burnt firewood pervaded, despite the cracks in the plaster that ventilated the room. Newspapers and books were strewn around with no discernible organization. The place was a mess. On the dirty, bare wood floor near the foot of the bed lay a half-empty cup of espresso. A small stack of stoneware plates with picked-over sausages sat forlornly on a battered dining table.

Plagued with inexplicable dreams, Albert had not slept in days. To compound his malaise, he missed Mileva, who had stayed with her parents. He took in a deep breath, then reluctantly pushed himself out of his warm cocoon. As the covers fell aside, a tattered flyer landed on the floor. "Discover the Secrets of The Mystical Travelers" it proclaimed. An illustration of a dignified-looking man of indeterminate age with a hint of a mischievous smile bore the inscription, "Pater Benjamin, A Great Spiritual Master."

Albert negotiated the books and the litter-strewn path to the washstand where he cringed as he poked a hole in the crust of ice that had formed overnight in the pitcher by the washbasin. With a vacant gaze and bloodshot eyes, Albert frowned into the oval gilt mirror above the coarse, soap-scrummed porcelain. He patted down his unkempt hair that was currently standing up at odd angles, and he stroked the wiry growth under his nose.

Why am I having these nightmares? He took in a ragged breath and tried to reason with himself. *When I attempt to do thought experiments, I discover myself in another universe with Johann. Am I going insane? I cannot concentrate on my studies.* Albert poured some cold water into the basin, splashed it on his face to clear his head, and prepared to shave.

* * *

Nearly every oak seat in the teaching hall at Polytechnic was filled. Albert had arrived early and positioned himself in the middle of the second row. On stage, only a chair and a square table with a pitcher of water and a glass awaited the speaker.

Just before the appointed time, a pleasant, silver-haired gentleman in his forties, dressed in a black woolen suit, walked out from a door at the back of the platform and surveyed the audience. His cerulean-blue eyes swept the crowd. When Pater Benjamin's gaze found Albert's eyes, the young student's body jolted as if he had received an electric shock. He stifled a small gasp and sat straighter in his seat. Pater Benjamin lingered on Albert a moment longer, then with an enigmatic smile, he made his way to the table.

Albert had been drawn to this lecture because of the dreams. From occasional disturbances, they had grown into nightly ordeals from which he awoke in a cold sweat. They had become more vivid. He dreamt of flying or visiting with his long-dead friend Johann. In other dreams, he interacted and discussed esoteric concepts with famous men from history—people like Galileo and Isaac Newton. It all felt so real.

Albert finally had to admit that he needed help. He felt compelled to look beyond what the rational world could explain. It was then, he'd come across the flyer for Pater Benjamin's lecture. Born in Eastern Europe, Pater Benjamin was a mystic and a visionary, who lectured about what he called the "true reality," worlds beyond the physical senses. He talked about concepts like karma— the law of cause and effect; what you sow, so shall you reap—and the idea of re-embodiment, in which humans live many lifetimes through which their souls may gain experience and progress spiritually. Had Albert known the topic of his talks, he might not have come. But he was at his wits' end and was ready to try almost anything to be able to sleep through the night again.

Reaching his chair on stage, Pater Benjamin sat and cleared his throat. The murmuring in the auditorium stilled. "What I am about to tell you may be unfamiliar to you, but I assure you it is true," he said in a calm, quiet voice. "However, I do not ask you to believe me. I ask instead that you simply listen and then check out these things for yourself."

Albert felt a warmth begin to permeate him. He felt... comfortable. He took in a deep breath and nearly sighed as he let it out.

There was something about the speaker's voice that reassured Albert. For the first time in days, Albert felt relaxed. He let Pater Benjamin's words fill him, taking them in without overanalyzing or resisting.

"The Mystical Traveler Moses taught the commandments of Almighty God," he was saying. "Don't steal, murder, or covet. When people could not adhere to the Father-Mother-God's commands, the traveler Jesus appeared to transform the laws of Moses into grace with his instructions of forgiveness and love."

Forgiveness and love, Albert thought. *Yes, forgiveness and love.* Albert relaxed even further into his chair. The next thing he knew, his eyes were fluttering open. The auditorium was empty, except for him and Pater Benjamin, who sat contentedly in the next seat. Albert sat bolt upright in his chair. "Wha... what happened?"

"My talk put you to sleep, I fear," Pater Benjamin said with a smile that lit up his face and his eyes.

"Oh, no... how rude... I—"

Pater Benjamin patted Albert on the arm. "Not at all, Albert. You needed to get some information on the other side. Since you don't know how to accept that yet, you needed to be taken out for a little while."

"Out? Out where?" Albert asked in confusion.

"Why, out of your body, of course," said Pater Benjamin matter-of-factly.

Albert's eyes grew wide. "What in the world do you mean? Wait, how did you know my name?" Albert was beginning to feel anxious. Something was going on here that he didn't understand.

Pater Benjamin smiled patiently and with such compassion and love that Albert could not help but relax again. "Let's start at the beginning, shall we?"

"Uh, yes, let's do that," Albert agreed.

"Good. So, let's see…" Pater Benjamin seemed to go off in his thoughts for a moment. "Ah, got it. Okay." He turned to Albert. "You've been dreaming about your friend Johann lately, and it's been bothering you, right? And then you also have been dreaming about scientists and philosophers."

Albert looked at Pater Benjamin dumbly and nodded.

"And these dreams have seemed so vivid that they have disturbed you, and you haven't been able to eat well or sleep much."

Albert nodded again. "I…" Albert paused. Pater Benjamin waited patiently. "…I think I am going mad," Albert said in a small voice, looking down into his lap.

Pater Benjamin put a hand on Albert's shoulder. "You are far from mad, Albert."

Albert lifted his gaze to Pater Benjamin's eyes and felt overcome with the man's compassion and love. "I am?" Pater Benjamin nodded, and Albert burst into tears. "It seems so real."

Pater Benjamin handed Albert a handkerchief. "There is a line of spiritual beings, Mystical Travelers, for lack of a better name, who have embodied throughout history. You heard me speak of two of them tonight before you were taken out for some other lessons."

"Moses and Jesus," said Albert.

"Yes, but there are many others. You have been receiving instruction from them in your dreams."

"But why me?"

Pater Benjamin smiled. "You are in possession of something very sacred and powerful, Albert, and because of that, your karma has taken a very... interesting, shall we say... turn."

"I don't know what you mean."

"Your papa gave you something unusual when you were a child, am I correct?"

"A compass."

"Yes, it is a compass," Pater Benjamin smiled, "but it is so much more, Albert."

"I suppose I knew that." Albert began to reflect. "It revealed clues on a scavenger hunt, and when I was just a boy visiting my friend Johann, it lit up with a number." Albert's speech was becoming more and more rapid.

"Thirty-three?" Pater Benjamin asked calmly.

Albert abruptly stopped. "Yes. How did you know?"

A warm light filled Pater Benjamin's eyes. "Let me ask you a question before I answer that. Albert, do you know the significance of the number thirty-three to you?"

Albert shook his head. "How can numbers have significance to people?" The skepticism was apparent in his voice.

If he was concerned that Albert was skeptical, Pater Benjamin did not show it. Calmly he explained, "Certain numbers can reveal things about a person. One of those is their birth number."

"What's a birth number?"

"It's the sum of the numerals in the person's birth date. You were born on the fourteenth day of the third month in 1879."

Albert did a quick calculation in his head. "Three plus one, plus four, plus... The numbers of my birthday add up to thirty-three."

"Correct," noted Pater Benjamin.

"So, what does that mean?"

"Ah," said the master. "That's the question." He sat back in his chair. "Well, double numerals like that signify a master path. Those with double numerals, eleven, twenty-two, and so on, tend to be leaders. Thirty-three is a very rare number. Those with this birth path want to lift the loving energy of mankind. In short, they want to do good in the world."

Pater Benjamin paused to allow Albert to reflect on his words.

"The thirty-three-life path will call you to leadership. People with this plan often achieve recognition through acts of compassion, love, and benevolence that lift up the world's awareness."

"This sounds like too great a responsibility," Albert said. "I just want to learn about light and energy and science."

The old man patted Albert's arm. "Your boundless curiosity will certainly take you into discoveries of energy and light, Albert. In fact, that is why you have been meeting with other Mystical Travelers who can assist you in understanding these things."

The enormity of what Albert was hearing began to overwhelm him. "You mean those dreams—"

"Yes, Albert," Pater Benjamin said gently. "They were actual conversations with men who understand the essence of these phenomena. Your destiny is much like theirs, and has beckoned them to assist you."

Albert struggled to take in the implications of what he was hearing, but Pater Benjamin was not quite done. "Never lose sight of thirty-three, Albert. This number is not simply your life plan. If you see it, be on the alert. It may be a portend danger."

"What kind of danger?" Albert wanted to know.

"I am not permitted to reveal everything to you right now, Albert. However, I can tell you this much: your destiny has become aligned with that of a sacred component of your compass. That component is so powerful that dark forces will do anything to secure it."

Albert held up a hand. "Wait. I have something that an evil force is after, and I am left on my own?"

"Well, not exactly on your own," Pater Benjamin smiled. "Your friend Johann has been assigned to assist you."

"Johann? What? Is he supposed to be my guardian angel or something?"

"Not exactly a guardian angel—angels have never been human. Johann is what is called a guardian of Light. He is undergoing instruction with the hosts of Heaven and Mystical Travelers. He will come to you from time to time to offer assistance like he did that time in the mountains when you were hiking with your girlfriend."

Albert's jaw dropped. He took a breath and tried to pull himself together. "I'm sorry, Pater Benjamin, but this is really a lot to take in. I mean, I'm incredibly relieved to hear that I am not going crazy, but meeting with the likes of Galileo or Newton and guardians of Light, and invisible realms of existence..." Albert shook his head.

"Take your time with this. Go home, have something to eat. Get some real sleep."

"Yes, I could use some sleep." Albert rose to leave but turned back to Pater Benjamin. "Is there some way I can contact you if I have more questions?"

"We may not see each other again in this life," Pater Benjamin said warmly, "but I'll be closer than you know, my friend."

Albert thanked Pater Benjamin and turned to leave. He had taken only a step when another question crossed his mind. Albert turned back, but Pater Benjamin was gone.

Chapter 26
Raka's Discovery

W hat a nuisance, Raka thought as the gold-filled pince-nez spectacles fell off his nose yet again. He cursed the defective eyesight of this latest body—that of the old physics teacher Professor Meiss. He sorely missed his razor-sharp dragon vision.

The ungraded papers of Meiss's students were stacked on the professor's desk. Raka knew he had to keep up appearances, and grading papers were one of a professor's tasks. He considered them for a moment, then grunted in resignation, picking up the stack. He shuffled through the papers, searching for Albert's work. Finding it among the others, he scanned it, shaking his head in disapproval. The upstart's report had insufficient validation, just scrawled notes with no proof.

As the dragon pondered Albert's lack of thoroughness, students began drifting into the classroom. At the very last moment, Marcel Grossman scurried in with Albert at his side. Bored with the old textbooks used in the class, the duo often took themselves to the Café Metropole on the banks of the Limmat River where they drank iced cappuccino. It was their favorite place to meet and debate the latest discoveries in physics. They only attended class often enough to avoid being kicked out of the university. They found the discussions at the café far more interesting.

As he entered the classroom, Albert looked around. He missed Mileva. He sorely regretted that she had been spooked by the mysterious events that had transpired during their outing in the Sihl Forest. While Albert had dismissed the incident as nothing, he had yet to calm her fears.

Resigned to another class that would be less than fulfilling, and thinking what a waste of time the next period's chemistry class would be, Albert drew nearer to Raka's desk. Professor Meiss glanced up and watched the young man with interest. As he stared at him, Raka's perception of Albert seemed to blur. The professor took off his glasses, rubbed his eyes, and blinked several times.

With his spectacles off and not being distracted by the real scene around him, Raka found his intuitive vision suddenly asserting itself. This had happened to him from time to time, and he had not ever discovered a way to control it. No longer looking with his physical eyes, Raka's vision sharpened and he stifled a gasp at what was revealed to him. Raka knew past life existences could superimpose themselves over a physical body in intuitive sight, but he was not prepared for what Albert's features had transformed into. It was a face that was sickeningly familiar; it was none other than his twin brother, Arka, from their lifetime on Atlantis! The dragon reached out to his desk to steady himself as remembered scenes of that lifetime overwhelmed his awareness. He whirled away to hide his reaction. *NO, NO, NO, this cannot be!* He shouted silently.

As his past life memories awakened, so did his rage toward his twin. His breathing quickened, and he glanced down to see his nails growing into dragon claws. He quickly sucked in two deep breaths to contain himself. Slowly, his temper calmed, and his dragon claws returned to human fingernails. Taking in another calming breath, he tucked away his hatred for the moment and turned back to face the class. Raka looked around and noticed the students hard at work. He cleared his throat. "Gentlemen open your books to page 136." The murmuring in the class fell silent as the students sought the assigned page in their books. With a sigh, Albert leafed through his writing and settled himself in for a long, boring lecture.

Feeling particularly distracted, he tuned out the talk and lost himself in his thoughts. He was jarred from his daydreaming when the boy at the desk next to him nudged him as he was packing up his books. Shaking his head, Albert packed up his own study materials and headed to his next class, Chemistry. He had little use for the subject but needed it to graduate, so he did his best to get through it.

* * *

In the lab, Albert settled himself at his assigned station and glanced at the bottles of chemicals arrayed before him. He had little interest in them and the experiment he was preparing to replicate. *What's the point of doing what others have done before?* He thought. *I want to break new ground.* He sighed and resigned to the inevitable boredom ahead. He barely noticed the redheaded woman in the white lab coat who hurriedly left the room.

"Today we will perform experiment seventeen, Transmission of Pressure." Professor Heilmann pointed to the blackboard. "The components of the experiment have been placed on your desks."

There was more muttering as the students compared the supplies on their lab benches with the list that had been written on the blackboard. After a brief pause, the professor continued, "Gentlemen, you may proceed with the experiment."

Albert poured the clear liquid into the test tube that stood upright, supported on the wooden stand. Then he began emptying the mercury on top of it. As he poured, the number 33 suddenly appeared to Albert in holographic form, blinking rapidly just above the test tube. Albert's eyes narrowed. "That's odd," he muttered to himself. He recalled Pater Benjamin's warning, but how could a mere experiment with water and stable mercury be a danger to him?

Before his eyes, the two liquids began to sizzle and bubble. Albert threw his right arm up to shield himself and ducked under the sturdy, wooden lab desk, and shouted, "Duck, everyone!" No sooner had the words escaped his lips than the experiment on the lab desk exploded with a fiery flash. Albert's sleeve was spattered with burning liquid and burst into flames. He frantically pounded his burning jacket with his left hand, trying to extinguish it. All around, his classmates were screaming and rushing out of the classroom.

Down the hall, Countess von Baden stood smiling, satisfied with the result of having substituted water and stable mercury in Albert's experiment with clear sodium nitrate and unstable mercury—a lethal combination. Composing herself and pasting an appropriately concerned look on her face, she rushed toward the classroom. As she neared the room, Professor Meiss joined her, offering an approving nod before they entered the lab. Instead of finding Albert's fatally burned corpse, they were both dismayed to see the young man clutching his arm where the blackened and charred remains of his jacket and shirt still clung. Albert's lab station was aflame, but he was fine.

Raka was furious. How could his plan have failed? The thought. "Get out of here before someone wonders about your presence," he hissed quietly at the Countess. Then, pulling himself together, he surveyed the destruction. "What have you done?" he exclaimed angrily to Albert. Pointing to the doorway, he said, "Get out of here before you burn down the building!"

Professor Heilmann rushed over and cast a cautioning glance at Meiss and said a bit more calmly, "Yes, Herr Einstein, you must get that arm looked at."

Dazed and in shock from the trauma, Albert staggered out of the classroom and into the hallway where the rest of his class milled around. His friend Marcel rushed over to him, "Albert! What happened? Are you okay?"

Albert looked at his friend. He could see he was talking, but he could only hear the ringing in his ears. "I...

I..." was all he managed to get out before he collapsed into his friend's arms.

* * *

Dazed and groggy Albert struggled back to consciousness. Through blurry eyes, he saw that he was in the university clinic. A young physician and his friend Marcel were at the side of his bed. An antiseptic odor pervaded the room, but he also detected the faint smell of burnt flesh. Albert glanced to the doctor working on his hand and saw his blackened, swollen fingers. He could see the doctor's grave expression, but the ringing in his ears from the explosion still made it hard for him to hear anything.

The thirtyish, bearded physician in his white coat was bending over Albert's burned limb applying salve to it. When Albert twitched his hand, the doctor looked up at him. "Ah, you're back, Herr Einstein. Good." Albert nodded weakly at him. The doctor glanced at Albert's hand, then leaned in toward the boy. "What in the world happened? You're lucky you weren't killed."

With the doctor closer now, Albert heard the question. He managed to respond in a weak voice, "It was a simple experiment. I don't know what could have gone wrong. Water and mercury," he said.

"I combined the elements as directed, and..." Albert shrugged, then cringed in pain. He tried to flex his hand. It was stiff and excruciating, but his fingers moved slightly. Satisfied for the moment, he looked up at the doctor. "My hand... am I going to be all right?"

The doctor sighed. "It could have been much worse. Your burns are bad, but they will heal. It will take time, though. I'll keep you here overnight, and then I think you'll be okay to go home." Albert nodded, then went into his own thoughts. The doctor turned to Marcel. "He's going to need some care until he can use his hand again."

Marcel nodded. "Albert has no family here, but I'll look in on him as long as he needs help."

"Good. I want the patient to rest now. I am giving him laudanum for the pain." The doctor poured some liquid into a small glass and urged Albert to drink it. Within minutes, Albert drifted off to sleep.

Satisfied, the doctor turned to continue his clinic rounds. "I'll leave you instructions on how to care for the burn until it's fully healed." Marcel nodded in thanks and turned back to his friend, now peacefully dozing on the cot.

Back in his classroom, Professor Meiss sat at his desk, pondering. During the confusion in the lab, he had surreptitiously gathered up the bottles containing the falsely labeled volatile ingredients that Victoria had substituted for the benign ones at Albert's station. Now, he considered next steps.

On the one hand, Meiss was disappointed that his plan to kill Albert and recover the compass with the Shamir Stone had failed. But now that he fully understood Albert's connection to his brother Arka, he looked forward to the opportunity to make sure his brother suffered before he died. It was better that his plan had not worked right away. He hadn't anticipated being able to exact re-venge on his brother for the indignities he had suffered at his and his uncle's hands. He hadn't expected this poten-tial for retaliation to the horrors that he had been subjected to when his brother's genetic experiments had gone so terribly wrong. Yet, through some twist of fate, Arka had revealed himself in this classroom.

For the first time in centuries, Raka began to hum.

Chapter 27

Intervention

*K*endra leaned back on her alabaster armchair in the Temple of Research and inhaled deeply. Garbed in a simple mauve robe, the Light Seer felt well-connected to life after a sweet morning of spiritual exercises. With a swipe of her palm over the glass tablet in her hand, she whispered a prayer for the highest good and opened the Flower of Life Infinity Portal. With the power to see the future, it was time to watch the star child Albert Einstein in the nineteenth century on Earth.

The Portal revealed a scene in Albert's chemistry class. A gasp of horror escaped Kendra's lips when Albert's beaker violently exploded, the force of the blast hurling glass, hardware, and wood across the laboratory. The view from the Portal revealed Albert's limp form sprawled on the floor, one arm of his jacket smoldering. Hastily scanning forward through time, she found Albert once again, this time asleep in a clinic bed, bandages on his arm and hand. Kendra closed the Portal and scrambled to locate the Mystical Travelers.

* * *

Three Mystical Travelers—Jesus, Akhenaten, and Moses—were seated around a marble table in the Temple of Light, listening attentively as Johann reported the newest update on Albert's mission.

"Albert is avoiding his classes because they bore him. His professors teach old science and will not entertain new concepts like Maxwell's electromagnetic theory. So, Albert's missed several days at school, and professors Weber and Pernat have admonished him on several occasions to concentrate on his studies."

The three masters shared knowing glances.

The young light worker went on, "Albert is obsessed with solving the space-time theorems, and he's missing meals and not sleeping much." Johann paused and looked at the masters. "I know how Albert can be. He is oblivious to how his behavior upsets his teachers. Even if he knew, I don't think he'd care."

A holographic image appeared on the table near Jesus. It revealed Kendra, standing in the hallway. Jesus glanced at Moses and Akhenaten, who nodded. Jesus passed his hand over a light beam, and a doorway opened, admitting Kendra into the chamber.

Wasting no time, she nodded respectfully, then began to speak in urgent tones. "I apologize for interrupting you, but Albert has been in an accident. I believe it was an attempt to take his life."

Johann's eyes widened in concern. "I left his side for just a few minutes, and—"

"Be still, Johann, this is not your fault." Jesus motioned for Kendra to sit. "Now, exactly what happened?"

Kendra quickly opened the Infinity Portal and pointed at the unfolding scene.

Johann and the travelers watched as Countess von Baden planted the volatile elements. Johann shook his head. "I've warned Albert that his life was in danger."

Moses narrowed his eyes, and Johann hastily added, "Of course, I did not reveal more than the Cosmic Law allows."

The travelers sat back in their chairs as Johann looked to each of them. "I realize we can only do so much, and we must respect the Laws of Karma and Time, but I'm worried that Albert will be tricked by Raka."

Akhenaten smiled kindly at Johann. "I know it's hard to watch your friend tread so close to such danger, but this must play out according to the Divine Plan. There is only so much influence we can exert."

Johann nodded, accepting the truth of what Akhenaten said. "But—"

Akhenaten raised his hand. "Have faith, Johann. The balance of Light and Darkness must be maintained. God's grace is stunningly powerful. Things always are perfect— if we're unhappy, it's because we don't like them that way."

The others nodded with knowing smiles as Johann's protests died on his lips.

"But is there anything we can do?" asked Johann hopefully.

"Increase our vigilance so if God's grace allows us to step in, we are ready," Jesus suggested.

"Nothing else? Albert is in real danger!" Johann complained.

Moses replied, "Once Albert completes his mission, the compass will go dormant. Raka will no longer be a threat. We need to keep Albert safe from him until then."

"There is one thing we can do," Akhenaten said. Kendra and Johann both looked at him, hoping to lift their spirits.

"We can speed up Albert's mission. The solution to Albert's quandary does not dwell in his current dimension of time. We can bring Albert to Atlantis to help him recall what he has forgotten."

Johann squinted, trying to make sense of this proposition. "Go back to *where*?"

"Albert is a Child of Light," Akhenaten explained. "He has been chosen to bring the Atlantean technology of space-time to his own era to further the evolution of science. The compass he carries is a beacon with intense energy from Atlantis. Once he completes his mission, the power of the compass will sleep until it's time for the next Child of Light to come forward."

"In another time, Albert was a priest-scientist named Arka, who worked with the power crystals in Atlantis and understood their space-time functions," Moses added, picking up the narrative. "His spirit in this lifetime is receptive to this knowledge, but he is experiencing difficulty bringing it fully into his conscious mind."

"Perhaps we could transport him in his soul body to Atlantis," Jesus suggested, "while he is recuperating from this incident at school."

"Hmmm. Yes, I believe that could work. What do you think?" Moses asked, turning to Akhenaten.

Nodding with a smile, the pharaoh who had introduced the concept of the One God to the Egyptians agreed.

The three Mystical Travelers set their gaze on Johann. "You must travel with Albert in soul form to Atlantis.

With Ezekiel, you will assist him to enter the sacred gateway and transport his spirit through the dimensions of Light to the correct moment in Atlantis history where he will find himself. The healer of Light will be intuitively expecting him to appear."

"Me? If Ezekiel's going to be there, why do you need me? I think this is way beyond my experience," Johann protested.

Jesus placed his arm around the lightworker in training. "You can provide something that Ezekiel can't." Johann looked up at the Master, "Friendship. A familiar face will help him feel comfortable through an exercise that is sure to challenge him."

Johann swallowed his protest.

* * *

A red-haired woman in a white nurse's uniform quietly loomed over Albert as he lay sleeping in the hospital. Privacy curtains ringed Albert's bed, so her presence went unnoticed. With a satisfied smile, Countess von Baden checked the syringe she held, making sure it was filled with the lethal liquid. She leaned over Albert's arm, the needle poised to find a vein. She almost pitied him. The agony the serum would deliver before it finally snuffed out his life, would be unspeakable. Suddenly, the etheric form of a young boy materialized in the space next to her. "What are you doing?" Johann cried out.

Startled, the Countess dropped the syringe, and its glass cylinder smashed on the hard floor, the liquid it held spilling out on the tiles. With a frightened curse, she bolted from the room.

"It appears our arrival is quite timely. The Light still protects my friend," Johann observed, speaking into the Infinity Portal he had secured to his belt. The holographic images of his three fellow travelers showed their relief.

"Are you ready, Johann?" Moses asked.

Johann gulped in affirmation. The trio clasped hands and closed their eyes in devotion. Jesus instructed, "Johann, focus your awareness on the love in your heart. We will aid you with our love. Now we will pray for Albert's soul to leave with you."

The travelers said in unison, "We call forward the Light of God from the Highest Realms to surround, fill, and protect each of us, Ezekiel, Johann, and Albert. We pray for Ezekiel as he supports Albert Einstein in his mission for his entry to Atlantis. All this is for the highest good. So be it."

A brilliant sphere of glowing light enveloped Albert as his etheric body floated up and hovered over his physical form still in the hospital bed. In his new state, Albert's gaze was drawn to Johann, and he drifted to be next to him. "Johann?" Albert attempted to touch his friend, but his hand moved right through him. Suddenly, Albert noticed his body below him on the bed. "What...? How...?" Albert's voice was a mere whisper. "Johann am I... dead?"

Johann shook his head rapidly from side to side. "Take it easy, Albert. You're not dead. I can explain." Johann took in a deep breath, trying to figure out how to explain the situation to his skeptical friend. "Okay, do you recall what Pater Benjamin told you?"

"Of course, I remember," Albert said. "But what he suggested sounded like madness. I am a physicist, not a philosopher. It's... it's... not scientific! It flies in the face of the scientific method—observing, postulating, creating a mathematical proof."

"Yes, I know, Albert. Just give your obsession for tangible proof a rest for a moment. I know how your research has been consuming you."

"Well—" Albert said, preparing to defend himself, but Johann interrupted him.

"Relax, Albert. I have good news. The Mystical Travelers have appointed me to accompany you to a place where you will be reawakened and given answers you have been seeking."

"Relax— Where are we going? Will we take the train?"

"No, Albert. We are going to travel back in time—to an age when you lived in Atlantis as a priest-scientist. A train can't get us there."

"Back in time? How is that possible?"

"Look, just take my hand, Albert. Trust me."

Still skeptical, Albert grasped Johann's hand, and they vanished...

Chapter 28
Atlantis 10,000 BC
Arka

*A*rka was preparing for his morning meditation when he noticed a messenger striding toward him from across the garden. Dressed in black linen trousers and shirt with the Black Sun symbol on each collar, the female soldier from Aryan came to a stop in front of the priest-scientist and stood at rigid attention.

"Sorry to interrupt, sir. General Tora-Fuliar ordered me to deliver this to you immediately." She extended a paper bearing the seal of the Aryan High Command. Arka thanked the soldier and dismissed her. His eyes widened, as he read the message from his twin brother, Raka, who had been missing for some weeks.

My Dear Brother,

I expect you may be wondering what has become of me since my recent disappearance from Atlantis. I assure you, I am fine... no, better than fine. In fact, I am prospering on Aryan in my new position as Supreme High Commander of all Aryan forces.

You might wonder how I was able to accomplish such a feat considering your low (and inaccurate) opinion of me. Let's just say that I had a little help from the Draconian DNA. (I presume you are aware that I had taken it.) With my innate intellect and savvy, I was able to "convince" the Aryan leadership that I was the man (loosely speaking) for the job. As you can imagine, I am so much more than a man now.

Please accept this letter as notice that, under my leadership, the Aryans will be assuming control of the temples and power crystals of Atlantis. I look forward to our next meeting, where you may kneel at my feet out of respect for my accomplishments and in awe of my power.

Your loving brother,
Raka

Arka's face went pale. His brother had fallen from God's grace into the darkness of greed and power. *Not only is Atlantis in danger, but the entire planet is also doomed if Raka gets ahold of the Firestone Crystal.* As he folded the letter and put it in his tunic pocket, Arka tried to hold back his feeling of fear. Before he could consider next steps, he needed to center himself and align with his higher self. Despite his brother's revelations, he was eager to prepare for the day. He recently had been made aware through meditation that he would be receiving an exceptional guest today.

* * *

As Albert and Johann clasped hands, Ezekiel uncloaked the Atlas, exposing its Light from the Holy of Holies. He touched the screen of the Crystal Lux Portal. The holographic gateway opened, and the illumination beam pulled their etheric bodies into the vessel.

The silver-haired pilot focused on manipulating the craft's holographic controls, motioned for his passengers to sit behind him. Albert was trying to look everywhere at once. Then, he heard Johann cleared his throat. "Uh, Albert."

"Yes. What?"

With a wry look, Johann pointed to their still-clasped hands.

"Oh, right," Albert laughed, letting go. "But... look at this... whatever it is," he said, gesturing to the glowing interior of the craft.

"This is an energetic vessel called an Ark, Albert." Ezekiel completed his course setting for the ship as he spoke. "It is something of a metaphor, actually, and allows us to travel through the constructs of time and space."

The pickup accomplished, Ezekiel gestured over the control panel, and the golden ship disappeared into another dimension of time.

"But... How?... What?..." Albert tried to formulate a complete question.

Ezekiel held up a hand. "Easy, my friend. Let me try to make sense of things for you."

"Yes, that might help." Albert tried to relax

Johann leaned forward to listen as well. While he had a fair amount of experience being on the inner realms of Light, this travel through time was new to him.

"Okay, let's see," Ezekiel said with an easy smile. "First off, my name is Ezekiel. Like Moses, Jesus, Akhenaten, and others, I am what's called a traveler, or Mystical Traveler. We have a specific role to play in the spiritual evolution of mankind."

Albert's eyes widened. "Wait, Ezekiel, as in 'Ezekiel saw the wheel' Ezekiel?"

Ezekiel's laugh was friendly. "Yes, that would be me."

Having now worked with several spiritual masters, Johann was not surprised. Albert, on the other hand, was still working on it. "Uh, o-o-o-kay..." he said, trying to process it all.

"You, Herr Einstein," Ezekiel continued, "also have a part to play in the unfolding evolvement of humanity. That's why you are here."

"I think you've made a mistake," Albert interjected. "I'm just a student."

"Yes, that's what you're doing now...well, at least at this moment in your present time and space. But you have a destiny, Albert, and we travelers are assigned to assist you in realizing it."

"Destiny? I'm not so sure I believe in that."

"Reasonable enough," Ezekiel responded, "but let me ask you a question. What is consuming you? I know it's not studying outdated science."

Albert rolled his eyes. "Of course not. I am working on proving certain theories of light, time..." Albert was suddenly struck by where he was and that he was moving in a dimension other than his own. "...and space," he concluded haltingly.

Ezekiel smiled as he watched Albert's realization unfold. "So, do you know why you have such a burning interest in these things?"

Albert could only shake his head, his mind still struggling to grasp the immensity of what he was experiencing.

"Well," Ezekiel said, "like destiny, this may challenge your scientific beliefs and your typical demands for tangible proof in the material world."

"Go on," Albert said.

Ezekiel chuckled again. "Well, suppose—just suppose—that you are getting glimpses into a past life you had."

Albert started shaking his head, but Ezekiel continued. "And in that life, you were a scientist working with light, time, and space. Suppose you have been having memories about what you learned in that lifetime."

"I'm going to need some time to think about that," Albert declared, rubbing his temple to try and alleviate a headache beginning to pound in his head.

Ezekiel felt only compassion for his new student. "Take all the time you need. I know this challenges your analytical mind. But I think you're getting a sense that there's a lot more going on than what the mind can readily grasp. Why don't you relax for a bit and digest everything?"

Albert was relieved to be able to retreat into his thoughts and consider everything he had heard. After about twenty minutes, the pilot beckoned Albert and Johann over to watch as millennia of time passed on the Crystal Lux Portal.

Albert was struck with a thought as he watched. "If things are as you say, then shouldn't we be able to move through time instantaneously?"

Ezekiel nodded approvingly. "Excellent, Herr scientist. But remember, this craft is only a metaphor. It would be too distressing to the conscious mind to have things appear simultaneously, so we operate in conjunction with the constructs that the conscious mind accepts."

Albert was satisfied for the moment, and Ezekiel announced that they had arrived at their intended destination; Atlantis 10,400 BCE, by his reckoning. Albert watched as the traveler manipulated the holographic controls of their craft and it came to rest in a luxurious botanical garden with flowering trees, a lily pond, and water fountains. As the craft's port opened, the smell of jasmine greeted Albert's senses.

Ezekiel remained in the craft as Johann and Albert exited and looked around. For Johann, Atlantis was not all that different from the inner realm school environments where he had been studying. But Albert was awed by the scene in front of him. In one location, tall Atlanteans walked a labyrinth in devotional reflection. In other areas, people walked and talked as they made their unhurried way to the temples of learning and healing that dotted the landscape. An aura of peace and tranquility pervaded.

Their attention was drawn to a blond fellow in a short emerald tunic who was sitting in a meditative posture in a grotto near where they were standing. As they watched, the man's etheric body extended from his physical space and approached them. He waved, saying, "Welcome to Atlantis. My name is Arka."

Albert scratched his perpetually unruly brown hair and looked up in awe of the Atlantean.

Remembering his assignment, Johann pulled himself together. "Thank you for coming to receive us. My name is Johann, and I am studying with the travelers." Urging his friend forward, he said, "May I introduce Albert Einstein?"

Arka extended his hand and looked Albert in the eye. When their palms and gaze met, Albert felt a gentle jolt. "Nice to meet you, Arka.... But I feel like I already know you."

Arka smiled and inclined his head as he guided the boys to a nearby bench. "I understand, Albert. And I need you to listen to what I have to say with an open mind, as best you can."

Albert shook his head ruefully. "I'm getting that a lot today." He took in a breath and said, "Just go ahead, and I'll see how I do."

Arka launched into his explanation. "Do you accept the idea of reincarnation—well, re-embodiment, actually?"

Albert shrugged. "I have heard the concept. I can't say I believe it."

"Fair enough. Now then, many people who think of such things believe we are a body that has a soul. But the fact is, we are souls having a human experience. Our souls extend into human bodies throughout time to gain knowledge. Can you, for the time being, accept that?"

Albert looked at Arka and considered the question. "Until today I would have said no. But I feel like the whole foundation of what I believe is being shaken, so, for the moment, let's say that I will entertain this idea."

Albert could only nod and retreat into his thoughts to consider what he had heard.

"Okay, good." Arka rewarded Albert with a smile. "So, here's the situation: our souls are gaining experience through us while we are alive, and it is gaining experience through you when you are alive."

Albert blinked as he silently absorbed what Arka had said. "So, you're saying..."

"Yes, we share this soul. And it is bridging ideas from

your past to your awareness in your time."

Despite Albert's dazed look, Arka continued. "Before a soul reembodies, a spiritual plan is agreed upon. It includes many things, like which experiences the soul will need to progress, and which parents will be able to provide those experiences."

Johann, who had been studying these things, knew his friend was having a hard time coming to grips with all this information. He had confidence, though, that Albert would come to see the truth of it all.

"I believe you have been brought here, Albert, to quicken your awareness of the principles of light, space, and time," Arka finished.

"So," Albert said, "this is like a class for me, so I can bring the information to my time and then expand on it?"

"Well, yes... and no," Arka said. "We are discussing all of this in our etheric bodies. I am doing it consciously, but, as I understand it, you are not doing it intentionally. So, what you will learn here will go into your unconscious and subconscious mind, where it will present itself to you from time to time. In a sense, you will experience it as inspiration or intuition."

Arka was struck with an idea. "I know all of this is challenging for you, Albert. How about I give you a small demonstration of some of the work we are doing here on

Atlantis. Would you like that?"

Albert nodded. "Something tangible would certainly help."

Arka reached out. "May I see your arm, Albert?"

Albert slowly extended his damaged arm toward the priest-scientist. "It's pretty badly burned, so please be careful."

Arka tenderly unwrapped the gauze bandage. "While I work with your etheric body, Albert, the results will filter down to your physical body in your own time." Arka could now clearly see the large, crusted scab forming on Albert's scorched arm. It was clear there would be quite a scar. Arka closed his eyes and quietly prayed, "I call forward the Light of God and the Masters of Light and healing." The priest-scientist was fully relaxed as his love poured forth from within his sacred heart and he held his palm over Albert's damaged arm. "I ask if it is for the highest good for Albert, that his arm be healed." Almost immediately, the angry red skin under the scab began to take on a healthier pink glow. Arka gently touched the crust and saw that it was no longer attached to Albert's arm. He carefully lifted it to reveal utterly normal skin underneath.

Bewildered, Albert looked up at Arka. "Oh, how did you do that?"

"Love is the healer. I simply made a request."

Albert looked at Johann. "Unbelievable!"

"Believe it, Albert." Johann smiled. "You are enough of a scientist to observe evidence, even when it goes against your beliefs."

Arka was gazing intently at Albert, checking the boy's aura to make sure the healing was complete and integrated. Suddenly, his eyes narrowed.

"Something wrong, Arka?"Albert inquired.

"Has anything strange happened to you recently, Albert?" the priest-scientist asked with a concerned look on his face.

"You mean like getting blown up in a lab accident? Would that qualify as 'strange'?" Albert's sarcasm was palpable.

"The travelers had asked me to warn Albert to be careful around one of his professors," Johann jumped in, "but, as you know, we are not allowed to provide any information that will alter a person's destiny. So, what I could tell Albert was limited."

"So, you could know something bad was about to happen, and yet you couldn't tell me?" he asked his friend incredulously.

"It's complicated, Albert," Akra interjected. "The laws of space and time, as you are learning, are filled with paradoxes and contradictions."

"But we're talking about my life!" Albert exclaimed.

"Stop and think about it, Albert. Unexpected things happen to people all the time," Arka pointed out.

"Yeah, like people getting pushed in front of trolley cars," Johann aid wryly.

"It's not fair!" Albert declared.

Now Johann took the lead in explaining things to Albert. "There is no such thing as 'fair.' We embody to gain experiences so our soul can progress. Nothing is exactly good or bad—there are just experiences. It's what we do with them that determines whether we *think* they're good or bad."

Albert wasn't buying it. "But you died so young, Johann."

"True," Johann shrugged, "but look where I am and what I'm doing now!" He gestured to the idyllic scene around them. "Just today, I traveled ten thousand years through time and countless kilometers in space."

"That's true." Albert considered his friend's words and found the anger leaving him. "I can't argue with that."

"And I'm as close with you as I have ever been," Johann concluded with a flourish.

Albert had to smile at that. "Well, that's very true."

Arka had been watching the conversation with interest. He leaned forward to focus the two boys on the matter at hand. "Okay, now that you're on board, Albert, let me explain what I'm seeing. I am detecting my brother Raka's frequency in your aura."

"What does that mean?" Albert was baffled.

"We don't have much in the way of understanding about the energetic bodies in the time we come from, Arka," Johann offered. Then he turned to his friend. "Albert, let me explain. We have these energy fields around our bodies."

"Energy fields? You mean like electromagnetic energy?"

"Yes, very much like that. And a person skilled in reading these energy fields—or 'auras'—can tell a lot about a person."

"Like what?" Albert was interested despite the conflict with his rigid scientific views.

"Well, like the health of a person's physical body, or some of their thoughts that are represented symbolically, or even the influences of people who have been around them."

Albert turned to Arka. "So that's what you meant by your brother's 'frequency'?"

"Yes," a sad expression replaced his normally cheerful demeanor. Earlier today, I received some very troubling news about my brother. He has transformed his entire physiology with genetic material from a reptilian species that we have become allied with. It is a terrible misuse of his power."

"Rept... What in the world did he do?" asked Albert, aghast at the idea.

"He stole some DNA that we use in our healing work, helping people regenerate organs and limbs. But Raka used a much larger quantity—enough for hundreds of medical applications. He has taken a massive overdose of this genetic material. If our projections are correct, and if he survived the dosage, the DNA will transform him not only into a powerful reptilian but into a shapeshifter, allowing him to take many different forms."

Johann had a worried look on his face. "Arka, I don't think we can tell Albert too much about this without interfering with his purpose."

"I understand, but what he figures out on his own will be permitted," Arka said with confidence. Turning to Albert, he added, "I believe we are still in safe territory to say that you must be very careful around others. People whom you think you know well, may not be who they present themselves to be."

Understanding dawned on Albert's face. "Hmmm. Professor Meiss certainly seemed to change a little while ago. But why would he—"

Johann jumped in again. "It's the compass. It's extraordinary and essential."

"But what could be—" Albert started. Johann held up

his hand to stop him.

"This is another one of those things we can't tell you too much about, Albert. Just trust me, you need to be very careful."

When he heard Johann mention the compass, Arka realized something. "Now it is starting to make sense." Turning to Albert, Arka said, "Look, Albert, I don't know the details either, but I do know my twin brother, Raka—"

Albert interrupted, "Wait, the bad guy is your twin brother?"

"Yes, I'm afraid so. Raka was lazy and didn't study. Then he became resentful of me, feeling that my accomplishments were a result of favoritism, not hard work." Arka looked chagrined. "Apparently, he took a shortcut with this Draconian DNA—and has also learned to travel through time."

Seeing that Albert was furiously trying to process all this information, Arka decided to shift gears. "Look, I know this is a lot to take in all at once. Let's take a break and get on with the real purpose of your visit, Albert."

"I think that would be good." Albert looked gratefully at Arka.

"Let's begin with the Temple of Poseidon," Arka beckoned the boys to follow him. "Throughout the tour, we can address some of the ideas that I understand you are bringing forward in your time."

Albert immediately agreed. "I'd really like that."

Arka guided them around the wall of pure gold that surrounded the temple. As they walked, Albert felt a sense of peace settle into him.

Arka enjoyed telling guests about his beautiful home. "Atlantis is a place of wisdom and healing. People here interact with one another with caring, respect, and love."

"I believe it," Albert agreed. "I can actually feel the peace."

"The peace you experience is not passive, submissive, or indifferent, Albert. Rather, it is a dynamic, active peace that enriches the quality of life within the individual, in society, and the world at large. People come from all over the world to meditate and rejuvenate," Arka said proudly. "The land, its waters, vegetation, and wildlife can all be used to tap into the part of you that is calm, loving, and peaceful. I think it will help you accept what you've been hearing."

"It must be working," Albert smiled. "I feel serene."

Arka smiled back, then pointed up. "The sacred Temple of Poseidon is 98 feet high, with foils of silver over the limestone. And notice the golden statuary. The contrast of elements is in keeping with the esoteric principle of honoring opposites. The spiritual equilibrium—

in this case, gold representing the sun and silver representing the moon—represent the ultimate expressions of male and female energies; solar being male and lunar, female."

Albert and Johann were drinking in their surroundings and the information. As they reached the facade of the temple, the glass doors opened like magic. With such wonders around him, Albert forgot his troubles. He put his hand on Johann's shoulder. The two could only stare in awe and wonder as they strode into the thirty-foot-high atrium. At the center of the sanctuary, they passed the solid metal orichalcum pillar into which the laws of Atlantis had been engraved. Healers and priests in bright tunics walked about, tending to their tasks.

Arka guided his guests into the Gathering Hall and over to a square, a twenty-foot topographic map of Atlantis that hung on the west wall. As he pointed to the three archipelagoes, he said, "The island with concentric circles of land on the far left is Poseidon, where we are. The more massive island is Aryan, and the smallest is Og." The boys took it all in as Arka continued. "In millennia past, Atlantis was one vast continent stretching nearly to the coasts of the eastern and western continents. But over time, a series of earthquakes have reduced Atlantis to three islands."

"The formation of Poseidon is certainly interesting,"

Johann observed.

Arka nodded. "Yes, Poseidon has ten provinces, one on each ring, with sacred shrines on each of them. It is our purpose to bring humankind into accord with cosmic harmony by observing the ebb and flow of opposites." Arka turned to Albert.

"Now, let 's address what interests you most, Albert." The young scientist leaned forward in anticipation. "To understand energy and light, you must learn how we are implementing the principles of natural forces. Our temples are not solely for religious worship. Each is dedicated to one of the arts or sciences or professions. In our Temples of Learning, each student on Atlantis learns not only the details of their chosen field but also how to access their creativity through alignment with the spiritual heart. When in harmony with God, the flow of inspiration and creativity is pure, and higher light pours forth with divine love."

Arka pointed to the Temple of Light on the map. "Albert, we have discovered that sound waves imperceptible to the human ear are emanating from the Earth. Our Temples of Light capture those sound waves, amplify them, and direct them as energy sources."

"You use the energy of the Earth as a power source?" Albert was fascinated.

"Yes, our Firestone crystals are near the center of the

island's land mass and serve as a focal point. They modify the energy moving out of the inner core into the shafts we have created in the Earth itself. They allow the highest frequencies to radiate out of our network of pyramids." Arka gestured, and a holographic image of the Earth appeared in front of them. "We have Temples of Light around the Earth in a power network."

Albert's eyes widened, and he pointed to what was known as Egypt in his time. "Wait, are you saying the pyramids here are part of your network and have something to do with transmitting light and energy to other pyramids?"

Arka nodded. "Yes, there are pyramids here, here, here, and here," he said, pointing to what Albert recognized as Mexico, China, Antarctica, and the United States of America. Then he turned and motioned for the boys to follow. "Come on. I'll take you to the Temple of Light."

Johann leaned over and whispered to Albert as they followed Arka, "Are you doing okay with all of this?"

Albert shrugged, "I don't know what to think. A lizard monster wants my compass. They use sound waves to produce electricity. Pyramids broadcast energy around the world. How could I *not* be just fine?" he smirked.

Johann gently punched his friend's now healed arm. "You'll get used to it, Albert... I did."

Exiting the temple, the trio boarded a silver, cylindrical-shaped hovercraft. As the craft gently lifted off, an impressed Albert commented, "This is so quiet! And I feel almost no acceleration."

Arka smiled, "This craft uses anti-gravity. It produces virtually no waste emissions and its flight is very smooth."

Flying low, they passed over the Temple of Healing, where a green dome of malachite shone in the afternoon sunlight. Then Arka indicated another building. "That's the Temple of Tablets."

From their vantage point, they could see a central courtyard with a gleaming circular marble basin. In the center of the pond, they saw floating lotus plants and a glow of crystal-white light. Arka pointed to several slabs of lapis lazuli spaced along the courtyard. "Inscribed on the lapis stones is the entire history of Atlantis."

In just a few minutes, the hovercraft gently lighted on a pedestal near an elliptical, two-story marble building with a dome that was transected by an opening, much like a modern-day observatory, and the passengers disembarked.

At the entry to the building, Arka swiped his palm on a lighted panel on the wall, and a marble door receded, beckoning them in. The group stepped into the temple, the ground floor of which was more a platform that ringed the lower levels.

Albert felt his compass tingle in his pocket when he entered the inner chamber. He drew out the etheric construct of the compass and studied the twelve glowing gems.

Arka glanced at the gems on the compass's cover. "Hmm," he said approvingly. "We will need that soon," Albert responded to the comment with a puzzled glance but did not question Arka, who guided the boys to a hovering platform where they descended into a vast subterranean chamber housing the six-sided, twenty-foot, Blue Larimar Tuaoi Stone. As they entered the massive chamber, the platinum dome opened, allowing the stone to receive the energy of the sun.

Arka checked a holographic gauge that measured the energies of the power source. Then, glancing aside to Albert, who still held his compass, Arka said, "Your compass is responding to the emanations from the stone, which is directing the solar and terrestrial energies."

Albert glanced at his compass, which was indeed glowing brightly.

"This stone," Arka said reverently, "is the power source for the planet. It receives rays of light from the sun and the stars, then concentrates those energies. As the stone vibrates with our Earth's frequencies, it broadcasts them to satellites that then rebroadcast them to power everything from our hovercraft to our great engines of manufacturing to the lighting in our homes."

Albert was in awe. "This is amazing. Where do I go to learn? Who will teach me?"

Arka put his hand on Albert's shoulder, saying, "We will not give you books to read, Albert. Instead, we will show you how to reach into the light source of your spiritual heart, so you can receive the inner knowledge and create with the divine moving through you."

Albert nodded. "That would be wonderful. I have practiced doing thought experiments: I imagine the possible solutions to a problem." He frowned, "However, I have been having trouble with my theory of light."

Arka smiled again. "Yes, you are using your mind. But that will only take you so far. To truly gain understanding, you must expand into a greater awareness of the Light within your spiritual heart. That is why you are here."

Albert felt a great sense of rightness with what Arka had told him. "I would be very grateful for whatever you can teach me," he said with uncharacteristic humility.

Arka asked Johann to wait outside, then led Albert to a pair of mahogany chairs that faced each other and gestured for Albert to sit across from him.

Arka said, "Lay your compass in your open left palm,

then close your eyes, sit back, and relax." Albert did as he was told, and Arka continued with his lesson. "Take a deep breath and hold it. Now let the air go." Albert did as he was instructed several times, then he heard Arka say, "Realize the love in your heart. Envision a presence of Light shining from deep within you. Imagine the sound of your spirit singing to you."

Albert found himself flowing with the sound of Arka's voice as the priest-scientist guided him deeper and deeper into his self.

After an indeterminate time, Albert heard Arka say, "Now open your eyes and put your compass next to your heart."

Albert, with a serenity that bordered on reverence, did as instructed.

"When you go into your thought experiments, hold the compass next to your heart, and it will reconnect you to this blessing. As that happens, you will be free to expand in a greater way to the inner source of your creativity."

Albert's skin tingled. His brown eyes glowed with a gentle light. He struggled to speak but could not, so he just relaxed back into his chair.

"In time, you will do this without the compass," Arka said.

Albert just nodded in acknowledgment.

Arka respectfully allowed Albert to bask in this Light of his own essence and went to bring Johann back into the room. As Johann entered, he took one look at Albert and declared, "Albert, you look radiant."

Albert took in a deep breath and inclined his head, acknowledging his friend, then turned to Arka. "I have never experienced anything like that."

Arka nodded in understanding. "You went beyond your mind, Albert, into a purer state of being. Your compass will assist you in reaching such a state when you return to your own time."

Albert turned his attention to the compass and frowned. "That will be great, Arka, but, other than that, how do I make it work? There have been several occasions when it came awake, and I don't know why."

"Do you recall what was going on when that would happen, Albert?" Arka wanted to know.

Albert thought for a moment. "The first time was when Johann and I were children. I showed it to him and told him how my papa gave it to me. Suddenly, it lit up like magic."

"Okay, show me what you did," Arka replied.

Albert thought for a moment, then held the compass in front of his chest as he had done when he showed it to Johann so many years ago. "It was something like this."

The priest knew he would not be permitted to explain

the Shamir Stone, so he answered, "Yes, the compass responds to the loving in your heart. When you're ready to create a situation, hold the device near your heart, close your eyes, and breathe in love with your thoughts. You will transcend into your intuitive knowing, where you may see pictures or symbols." Then Arka asked another question. "Have you seen the symbol 33?"

"Yes. The last time was just before the accident in the lab at school. The number 33 flashed moments before the explosion. That's why I only burned my arm, instead of getting my head blown off." Albert paused. "The 33-warning saved me from the full blast."

"The compass is sacred and for you alone," Akra stated. "It is attuned to your destiny pattern and has an energy field that can sense imminent danger. Your connection with Johann has always been deep, but from now on, I strongly encourage you not to show the device to anyone—not even your wife or children, should you marry."

Albert saw the wisdom in what Arka had told him and promised to show the compass to no one.

"Good," Arka said. "Now, since you are in danger from my brother, Raka, I am going to program your compass with the number 666. When my brother is within 15 meters, a musical tone only you can hear will sound to alert you to see who might be near. If he comes within five meters, the number 666 will flash. If that happens, look around to see who's nearby."

"Got it," Albert said.

"Good. Remember, Raka may *appear* to be a man, but he is no longer human," Arka said as he pressed the center of the compass and placed a blessing as he hummed a tone into the Shamir.

"This is what the alarm sounds like." Arka pressed the crystal at the center of the compass.

Albert listened to the melodious sound, but Johann looked puzzled. "I don't hear anything," he said. Arka grinned. "That's because the frequency is tuned to Albert. It wouldn't be much of a warning device if Raka could hear it, would it?"

"I guess not," Johann said, rolling his eyes at his own naivete.

"What should I do if Raka comes near me?" asked Albert.

Arka stood and guided the boys toward the elevator. "Move quickly to a place of safety. Maybe the best thing would be to get into a crowd of people. He would not want to reveal himself. If he gets within two meters, the compass will vibrate, and you should be able to identify who's setting off the alarm." Then Arka paused and became serious. "But there's a chance you may not be able to get away. You may have to get creative and find a way to defend yourself."

"Okay." Albert was now feeling more than a little concerned.

Arka remained solemn. "Be aware also that Raka may have allies who might also want to hurt you. They may not be obvious either. Watch out for anything that seems suspicious."

Albert heaved a deep sigh. "I'll do my best to keep myself alive so I can fulfill this 'mission' of mine," Albert said with a hint of sarcasm. "You know, I can't say I would have believed any of this earlier, but now..." he cast a significant glance at his healed arm.

"I'm sure you'll do fine, my friend," Arka said, attempting to buoy Albert's spirits.

As they exited the temple, Arka took an alexandrite crystal from his pocket. He held the violet-green stone up to the sun and prayed, "I call forward the Portal of God's gate with the Holy Spirit into the realms of Light to open."

In a moment, the Ark materialized nearby, and the three walked over to it.

"I'll do my best to remember what you've told me, Arka," Albert promised as he approached the craft.

"Because we have engaged you so fully, I believe you

will retain more of this in your conscious memory than you might have under other learning circumstances. And I believe the unusual healing of your arm will be a conscious trigger for you."

As Johann followed his friend into the craft, Arka patted him on the shoulder. "You are doing an excellent job, Johann. Albert is blessed to have a friend like you to assist him."

Johann beamed.

Just before he reached the craft, Albert turned. "Arka, wait! When can I return here? There is so much to see and experience."

Arka inhaled deeply. "I am truly sorry, Albert, but I don't think you can return. With Raka threatening to unleash the Aryan forces to take over the fire crystals, we will be more than occupied."

Albert's crestfallen look touched Arka deeply. "But remember, Albert, you are learning to access your inner wisdom. Truly, all you need to know is within you."

Albert and Johann moved to the Ark, and Ezekiel touched the screen of the Crystal Crystal Lux Portal. The holographic gateway opened, and the illumination beam pulled Albert and Johann through the astral door. In a heartbeat, the golden ship vanished.

Once back in his own time, Albert's etheric body was

reintegrated with his physical one, while Ezekiel and the Atlas returned to the travelers in the astral realm. Johann remained with Albert in ethereal form.

After a moment, Albert opened his eyes. He was a little groggy, but still immediately recognized Johann, even in his less-than-solid presence. He sat up with a smile. "I had the most amazing dream, Johann. You were with me. We flew in a golden ship and traveled to an amazing place. Oh, and there is a bad guy who wants my compass."

Johann grinned. "Dream, huh? Then how do you explain that?" he said, pointing to Albert's arm.

Albert looked, then did a double take. The gauze was still on his arm, but he could feel there was no pain or stiffness. The patient gently poked at the bandage, then prodded harder. Shaking his head, he unraveled the gauze and flexed his perfectly healed arm. He looked up at Johann, his eyes wide, and said, "You mean...?"

Johann nodded, his grin growing wider. "Right. Not a dream."

Albert fell back on his bed and heaved a sigh. "My God, Johann, my world is upside down!"

Johann held up a placating hand. "I know it's a lot, Albert. But it will be okay." Then a thought occurred to Johann. "Do you remember what Arka said about how to use your compass?"

Albert turned on his side to face his friend. "Yes, I think so."

"Then that's what matters," Johann assured him. Then his friend became uncharacteristically serious. "Albert, I have completed what the Mystical Travelers wanted me to do here with you. I've got my own mission to deal with. So, I've got to get back to the astral realm and continue my training."

Albert shook his head. "Who would have thought that you and I had important things to do, Johann?"

Johann shrugged, "I never would have guessed. But life is what it is." Then he took a step back and prepared to leave. "It's time for you to go forward on your own, Albert. Be aware that there are those who do not want you to complete your mission. Be brilliant, and be on guard." Johann smiled a wide smile. "You know, Albert, I think you're about to set out on the adventure of a lifetime."

Albert smiled back, though he was a little more rueful. "I don't know what I've gotten myself into, but I'm sure it won't be dull."

Johann nodded at that and said, "Okay, I have to go. Take care of yourself, Albert. And heed the warnings from your compass."

"I will." Albert reached in his pocket and pulled the

compass from his pocket. With the compass firmly in his hand, Albert lay back and began to explore the new worlds that were just beyond the edge of his awareness.

Not too far away, Countess Victoria von Baden was making plans of her own.

Chapter 29
Victoria's Plan

Countess Victoria von Baden's pursuit of the compass weighed on her. She reclined on a tufted maroon velvet Gothic settee and frowned into the gilded mirror she held in her hand.

She did not like what she saw. "I have fawned over and followed that miserable reptile for too many years, and all I have to show for it are wrinkles and graying hair. I'm barely closer to my compass than I was more than a decade ago when we found out where it was." Thinking back to her performance in the hospital, she reflected, "If only I could have poisoned that despicable Jew kid in the hospital, the prize would be mine now."

When that latest scheme to seize the compass at the clinic had failed, she fled her temporary residence in Zurich for her Altes Schloss Castle on Lake Constance. A few days after that, Raka abandoned the human body of Professor Meiss and made his way back in his dragon form to join her and plan the next move.

How many schemes had she listened to? Victoria drained her wine glass and mocked Raka. "We will have the compass this time, I guarantee." Imbibing in a drink or two of claret had turned into an everyday routine, and a way to avoid facing what she had become: a tired, aging woman.

Her compelling, sea-green eyes shone dimmer and were red with the weariness of life. She moaned in sorrow as much as in frustration and yanked on her thinning, long, once bright-copper-colored tresses, now showing streaks of gray. Her sensuous lips that had offered such promise now were thin and disapproving. Victoria sighed. "I can't deny it; I have let myself go."

With that admission, the Countess drew herself to her feet and began pacing. "I am no longer the innocent girl Raka found. It is time for me to take back my power and get rid of that Einstein boy myself." She wandered to the bedroom window and drew back the drapes. From the top floor of her villa, she stared down at the statue of her ancestor, Heinrich von Hohenlohe, a former Knight Hospitaller of St. John in Jerusalem with the Crusades and seventh Grand Master of the Teutonic Order, serving in the mid-thirteenth century. Victoria was the heir of one of the wealthiest and most powerful feudal lords in Wurttemberg.

Herr Hohenlohe had recovered in the ruins of Solomon's Temple the relic Victoria now sought. The twelve-gem-encrusted compass had lain in a dusty chest for centuries until she discovered it and found it attractive, thinking it just a pretty bauble. Her father, completely unaware of what he possessed, took it from her and traded it with other family jewels to the Einstein Electric Company for a new lighting system in their large castle.

"No one had any idea of what power that old relic held," Victoria mused. "Raka is formidable in his own right, yet he seeks this compass. It must be powerful beyond belief." Then her thoughts turned in a slightly different direction. "If a powerful being like Raka has not been able to get the Einstein boy out of the way, is it possible the compass is protecting him? That would certainly explain a lot," she realized. "If the compass protected Einstein, then imagine the protection and power I can wring from it!"

As she considered those possibilities, her lips twisted into an evil smile. "I am a Countess. I am tired of being a handmaiden to a giant lizard. Once I take my compass back, I will be independent of that grotesque toad, and will no longer need to do his bidding." The Countess heaved a deep sigh as if releasing a long-held burden. "Why, I believe I will use the compass's power and have that slimy lizard work for me!"

With a renewed enthusiasm and determination, she began plotting to recover the family heirloom "I will use Raka's cane that has the venomous needles to end that Einstein boy. When I have the compass back, there soon will be statues of *me* all over my kingdom!"

Her gleeful musings were interrupted by a gentle tap on her chamber door. She recognized the soft sound as the rapping of Ana, her handmaid.

"Herr Werner von Wiesel is downstairs for you, mistress," the mousy little woman said.

The Countess had been expecting him. Raka had told her that he had invited the young man to the castle. His note had given the impression that the invitation was from Victoria since the young fool was besotted with her. The only reason Victoria hadn't objected was she knew this was part of yet another plan Raka was hatching to get the compass from Einstein. So, she was willing to play along... for the time being.

Victoria recalled her conversation with Raka. When he had informed her of the invitation, she had inquired what Raka had in mind for the boy. With a gleeful grin, Raka told her he didn't really need the boy, just his body.

Victoria had briefly considered the possibilities of the lizard being in a young and virile body once again, then paused. "But isn't he your friend?" she had asked. Raka had developed a relationship with Werner when he had inhabited one of his more powerful bodies, showering the boy with flattery and implying great things for him. Wer-ner had eaten it up. Even when the boy had failed in his mission to kill Einstein, the dragon, in an uncharacteristic display of forgiveness, maintained his relationship with Werner, stoking the boy's hatred and playing off his need to be respected.

Raka waved his hand as if waving away the notion. "Bah, he is not my friend. He is just useful at times."

Victoria brought her thoughts back to the present and said to her maid, "Take him into the library and provide him with tea and sweets. Tell him I will join him shortly."

* * *

Victoria strode into the library with a teasing smirk, her hair piled high on her head in such a way as to hide the gray. The emerald-green brocade bustier brought out the green in her eyes, so they almost sparkled as they used to. A thigh-length skirt showed her shapely legs to their best advantage, and the three-inch-high heels on her black leather ankle boots with a silver buckle thrust her hips forward and made her appear even taller than she was.

Once a young upstart, Werner now stood six feet tall, with his broad shoulders straining the black leather trench coat he wore. The noblewoman smiled at him co-quettishly and gestured to the snack on the buffet. "You haven't partaken of my hospitality."

Werner removed his fedora and nervously smoothed back his golden hair with his other hand. "My apologies, I have not, Countess. I cannot stay long. My duties with the Secret Police leave me little time for the things I would prefer to be doing." He leaned over and kissed her hand.

The Countess smirked as she sensed the young man's desire. "Indeed? What is this Secret Police you refer to?" she asked with feigned fascination. She knew very well that Werner's father had persuaded the kaiser to let him take over the state enforcement agency with almost un-limited power.

"It is something my father leads, and he has made me a commander in charge of training a hundred young Ary-an men," he said proudly. Gesturing to his coat and hat, he asked, "What do you think of my uniform?" enthusi-asm overcoming his bashfulness.

Victoria nodded in false appreciation while thinking, *Uniform? A black hat and trench coat? What a preten-tious fool.* But what she said out loud was, "You are very handsome in your uniform. You are such a powerful man."

Werner preened at Victoria's praise. "Yes, the Kaiser and my father have charged me with establishing the policy for eliminating those opposed to the German state. You know, Jews and such."

Victoria linked her arm into his and leaned into him conspiratorially. "I know you are a busy man. However, I have a small favor to ask, if I might."

"Why, Countess, I would be delighted to assist you in any way I can." He looked into her eyes, but his gaze could not help but drift to her shapely breasts, which Victoria had made sure would be on display. She stifled a smile of her own as she felt his response to her stiffening against her leg.

Victoria squeezed Werner's arm and said, "I think you might actually enjoy this, my love. The last time our plan to eliminate your schoolboy friend Albert Einstein didn't work out, but perhaps we might be successful with your new authority."

Werner could barely listen. The Countess's feminine presence and her French perfume had him befuddled. With an effort, Werner struggled to bring himself back to what Victoria was saying. Something about the Jew, Einstein. "Oh, well, I was an adolescent when we first met, but now I can offer you so much more." He sought to draw her more tightly to him.

Victoria felt his excitement and added coyly, "Herr von Wiesel, I know your time is valuable, but might I entice you to join me where we may continue this discussion in a more... intimate setting?"

It was all Werner could do to stammer his agreement.

The two strolled out of the castle to a hidden entrance at the rear of the stone building. Dagobert I, the king who had built the Merovingian castle, wanted a secluded den for himself and secure storehouse for his gold and the family jewels.

Victoria opened the ornately wrought iron gate with a matching key she drew from her skirt pocket. She beckoned Werner into the raw, stone passageway and lit a brass lantern. Werner's head almost touched the ceiling as they descended a flight of twenty marble stairs. When they reached the last step, the Countess made as if to stumble. Werner reached out to steady her.

"Are you all right, Countess?" he asked with concern.

Victoria grasped his proffered hand and steadied herself. "It's nothing, Werner, I'll be fine." With the Countess feigning a slight limp, they entered a large, windowless square room that smelled of moisture and must. The Countess lit two torches that flanked the fireplace, then knelt to light the fire that had already been laid.

Werner noticed the silence of the cold, thick stone room. Along the rear wall were a high oak chest and a mahogany square table with four straight-back armchairs.

A Gothic-style ebony sofa sat amid the den. A thick antique rug covered the stone floor. Alone with the Countess where no one could see or hear them, Werner mustered his courage and attempted to sound suave. "My Countess, I have hardly dared dream of having the opportunity to be with you in such a setting."

Victoria turned her gaze from the fire to the young man. "Why, Werner, a handsome and influential man such as you..." she said, leaving the implication to his imagination.

Von Wiesel gulped, and stammered, "I, I don't mean that many young girls haven't expressed an interest in... uh, getting to know me better. But a woman of your worldliness and experience..." He left the sentence hanging.

Victoria frowned to herself. *Is he calling me an old woman?*

Remembering her purpose, Victoria stifled an indignant response and rose, gesturing with a smile to the love seat. "Ah, well, do sit down." She walked to the oak chest and deftly opened one of the bottles sitting next to a tray of wine glasses. She poured two glasses of claret, and as Werner looked around the room, she added a dusting of white powder into one of the drinks. It was, in fact, the very type of powder she had used to subdue Professor Meiss not so very long ago. Not that she couldn't handle the young twit herself, but this would make it all the easier.

Carrying the two glasses to the love seat, she handed the drugged wine to Werner, then sat close to the boy, her hip touching his. She laid her palm on his thigh and murmured, "When we first met, you were so young, Werner. But I sensed you had potential. I can see I was right. You have become the big and powerful man I imagined."

As Werner gulped yet again, Victoria declared, "Let us toast to old times and new possibilities, shall we?" He nodded, blushing, and they clinked their glasses. Victoria sipped from hers, watching Werner take another large gulp, probably to bolster his courage. Werner set the glass onto the floor and turned toward the object of his desire. "My Countess, you have no... no... idea..." He was reaching to embrace the woman, but he found he could not control his arms. "I... I don't... what...?" With a gasp, Werner slumped back.

Raka was watching from behind a wall tapestry the interplay between the Countess and Werner with disdain for the inept boy. When Werner lost consciousness, Raka, in his dragon form, stepped into the room. He could have overpowered the boy when the Countess first brought him down to the chamber, but why exert unnecessary effort. Why watch the kid flail about and scream, when he could just handle things with no fuss?

"Nicely done, my dear," Raka said. "You have consistently been someone I can count on."

Victoria responded, "So sad the little bully won't be able to appreciate what he is undertaking for you."

Raka smiled a lizard grin and poked Werner with his claw. The sleeping boy did not respond. Grunting, the dragon tugged Werner's black shirt away from his pale, white skin, exposing his abdomen. Then, with a long claw, pierced deep into his belly.

The pain was enough to waken Werner, who emitted a blood-curdling scream.

The dragon grinned and glared into Werner's eyes. "That's better. Now, Werner, you will serve me one last time."

Werner gasped when he saw the dragon and recognized his voice. He had heard Raka referred to as The Dragon, but he had not taken it literally. No one had. "Oh my God. What do you mean?"

Victoria patted the still paralyzed boy on the arm. "Don't worry about a thing, Werner. It is a great honor to serve Raka." Then she turned to Raka. "My lord, I seem to have twisted my ankle. You don't mind if I borrow your cane for a while, do you?"

Distracted with Werner, and eager to move on to the next phase of his plan, the dragon waved her off without even glancing at her. "No. Fine. Whatever you need."

Hiding her satisfied smile, she nodded her thanks. She turned and limped over to where the cane rested against the wall and hobbled out of the chamber. As she mounted the stairs, her thoughts turned to how she would eliminate Einstein with a poisoned needle and take the compass for herself. "Once I have the compass, the lizard will not be able to touch me, just as he has been unable to harm Albert while he had it," she mused. As Werner's tortured screams began to emerge from the room below, she was distracted for a moment, but they faded from her awareness as she walked back to her room.

Chapter 30
Spring 1903
An Invitation

*A*lbert threw the letter down on his desk and began pacing. "Fools!"

He was referring to professors Weber and Pernat of the Physics Department at the Polytechnic. They had declined to recommend him for a teaching position now that he had graduated. Albert had sought to locate Professor Meiss who had, at least at first, seemed to understand Albert's passion for cutting-edge work. But he had become distant and then mysteriously disappeared.

As with most of his education, the general physics classes he took at the Swiss Federal Polytechnical School did not engage Albert. As a result, he had alienated mainly the professors there when he embarked on a course of independent study to learn firsthand from the masters. He wished he could have been taught by his idols, James Clerk Maxwell and Ludwig Boltzmann, the pioneers and founders of the kinetic theory of matter.

Albert had often skipped classes, studied the latest research, and then naively wondered why the school's faculty turned him down when he sought a referral to teach. The fact was, his professors understood his genius, but would not tolerate his lack of respect for them or the traditional theories of physics that they taught.

After four years of study, by the end of October 1900, Albert was no longer a student, and he was jobless. He had churned out job applications and letters, and by 1901, had a truly impressive stack of rejection postcards. Albert began to wonder if anti-Semitism played a role in his inability to land a job. The jury was out on that.

Nearing desperation, Albert reached out to his school friend Michael Besso, who had wandered around for a while after graduating and then became an engineer in Italy. Of all the people Albert knew, aside from his fiancée, Besso was his closest friend. But, friendship or not, even he could not help.

Feeling thwarted at every turn, a ray of hope came through his former classmate and college friend Michael Grossman, with whom Albert would often ditch class and go to the cafes to debate "real" science. Michael had learned of an opportunity at the Swiss Patent Office. Michael's father knew the director there and offered to recommend Albert for the position. Although it was not anything close to what Albert had dreamt of as his first position after graduation, he was now at the point of entertaining any possibility. Albert hoped to hear soon whether he was accepted for the job.

* * *

The sun would not rise for another three hours, but Albert was awake. Dressed in his bathrobe and slippers, he was bleary-eyed from too much coffee and not enough sleep. Anxious about his cash running out and still without a job, he sat at the kitchen table piled high with notebooks that were crammed with math equations. In pursuit of an answer to his life's predicament, he drew his twelve-jeweled compass from his bathrobe pocket.

As it often did, the compass triggered memories of the day when his father offered him not just a brass direction finder but also awakened him to the quest to discover the unforeseen forces of the universe. Albert brought the compass closer to his heart and closed his eyes. As Arka had taught him, he repeated the blessing to activate the compass.

Almost as soon as he completed the prayer, Albert heard a guitar playing and a man with a Scottish accent singing a Robert Burns poem, "Comin' Thro' the Rye." As the music became more explicit, an image formed. Albert was shocked to see James Clerk Maxwell, who had studied and reported on electricity as early as 1855. Maxwell's work on electromagnetism, kinetic theory, and thermodynamics won him every scientific honor of his time. His most significant discovery, though, followed his equations for electromagnetism, which were called the second grand unification in physics, following the first from Sir Isaac Newton.

A devout evangelical Presbyterian and elder in the Scottish Church, Maxwell completed his song, then said to Albert, "Aye, boy-o, what you seek is beyond math. What principles of the many disciplines that you have learned have you mastered? The Lord sees the universe in harmony. Find the unity in all."

As the first light of dawn hit his eyes, Albert was startled awake from his reverie, the compass still gripped securely in his palm. Inspiration struck him like a physical blow, and he exclaimed, "Oh, I understand how to merge my work on capillarity to Boltzmann's theory of gases!" Albert hurriedly put the compass back in his pocket and started scribbling away in his notebook.

* * *

As it turned out, the senior Grossman's recommendation did the trick, and Albert was hired at the patent office. While he was relieved to have an income, science was still Albert's first love. As a patent clerk, he analyzed technical designs and often collaborated with inventors by making recommendations on their experiments. Oddly, since Albert was fresh with contemporary theories and a new approach to step outside the box and formulate a new direction in physics, the Swiss Patent Office became the ideal laboratory for his experiments.

One day, while working at his desk, Albert received a letter. Picking it up, he felt an uneasiness in his stomach and wondered if it contained bad news. Had something happened to his parents or his beloved fiancée, Mileva, so far away?

He regarded the envelope of expensive white linen, his name and address in elegant calligraphy and written in black India ink. When he turned over the letter, there was a red wax seal with an unfamiliar family crest. Albert carefully broke the seal. As he withdrew the folded stationery, the subtle scent of French perfume wafted out. Even more puzzling. He unfolded the paper and read the message, which had been written in a delicate feminine hand.

Herr Einstein,

I wish to know more about your visionary work in science.

Would you be so kind as to join me at 1:00 p.m. on Tuesday next at 69 Dalmaziquai to discuss how my family's trust fund might support your work?

Kindest regards,
Countess Victoria von Baden

Baffled, Albert refolded the letter and set it among his notebooks and papers.

Chapter 31
Cat and Mousetrap

*A*lbert hummed mindlessly as he shaved then dressed in his best, though slightly threadbare, tweed suit. He had arranged to take the day off work so he could meet with the Countess, though the address in the note seemed odd. He could not remember an inn or hotel along Dalmaziquai; only a desolate park and empty waterfront warehouses. It was not the best section of town. As he tied his necktie, he mused about just who this Countess might be and how she might help him further his efforts into the nature of light and the fundamental connection between space and time.

Albert wondered why the meeting place was at the Maison De Fleur in the obscure waterfront. He shrugged and dismissed his thought as he locked the door to his flat.

Victoria waited impatiently for Albert to arrive. Two days earlier, she had taken the short trip from Baden-

Baden to Bern and secured a hotel room. With a black veil shrouding her face and using the name Frau Schmidt, she had arranged with the proprietor of the Maison De Fleur for a buffet. If the man had been at all puzzled by her mysterious ways, he did not show it. Bern's elite often used the nondescript accommodation for their secret liaisons. There were ten suites in a row along the avenue, each with a private street entrance.

Wanting to avoid a poor first impression, Albert arrived fifteen minutes early. He checked to make sure his clothes were correctly arranged, took a breath and knocked on the black wooden door adorned with the brass number 69.

When the Countess opened the door, the scent of the exotic French perfume from the letter he had received greeted him. Standing in a draped black silk gown and holding an ornate, golden-handled cane, she motioned for her visitor to enter. Albert stepped into the salon while she closed the door and locked it with a skeleton key. Albert took note, but quickly let any concerns slip from his mind as he looked around the large room. The intimate parlor had an antique Chippendale sofa covered in Chinese yellow satin, a low coffee table in front of it with a bottle of claret and two crystal wine glasses. At the end of the coffee table, two popular magazines and a neatly folded newspaper were tastefully arrayed. Beyond the couch was a rectangular walnut dining table with a sumptuous spread of cold meats, cheeses, fruit, butter, and bread next to two more bottles of wine and two crystal goblets. A pair of yellow satin-covered armchairs and a beautifully hand-carved desk with some papers neatly stacked on it sat in the other corner of the room. Paintings of land-scapes and Oriental tapestries adorned the walls, and fresh flowers on the desk and side tables provided the suite with an additional level of elegance. To top thing off, a majestic, eight-foot-tall potted philodendron sat in a delicately ornate porcelain planter against the wall near the desk.

Victoria prepared for her performance. *I will play with my prey before I deliver the coup de grâce*, she thought. Albert stood near the dining table and felt his heartbeat quicken as his beautiful host limped with her cane toward him.

She smiled at him. "Thank you for coming to see me, Herr Einstein. I hoped we might relax and enjoy a quiet talk. I dislike noisy restaurants with so many nosy people. I much prefer a more... intimate setting." She paused, letting the sentence hang, fraught with implication. Albert swallowed, starting to feel a little uncomfortable.

The Countess pressed on. "Please, help yourself to this modest fare. Would you be so kind as to pour me a glass of wine?"

"Of course, Countess," Albert walked over and, poured two glasses of claret and handed one to his hostess. The food was impressive, but Albert's only hunger was for financing his research. "Perhaps I will enjoy the repast later," he said, taking the wine bottle and his glass and moving toward the armchair at the end of the dining table.

"As you will," the Countess said, taking the second bottle of wine. Victoria strode to the armchair opposite her guest at the head of the dining table. She took another sip of wine as Albert opened the conversation. "I was surprised that anyone outside the scientific community knew of my work. Is there something specific that interests you?" Albert took a taste of wine and waited to hear the Countess's answer. Victoria settled back into the armchair feigning nonchalance and gestured toward Albert with her wineglass. "I am interested in talent, Herr Einstein.

Albert waited, not sure where the Countess was going with this.

"Have you heard the works of Maestro Travalio?"

Albert nodded and took a small sip of his wine.

"Good. I encountered the Maestro just out of the university when he was still naïve and enthusiastic, aspiring to do wondrous symphonies. As his patroness, I paid him to compose music. I even managed his early concerts. Otherwise had I not taken him under my wing, he would have been compelled to accept dull-witted music students or take a job waiting tables. His spirit would have been crushed, and he would, today, be a nobody." Victoria took another sip of her wine and watched Albert over the rim of her glass.

Albert raised his eyebrows. "I have heard of Herr Travalio. But I am no musician."

The Countess nodded, taking a larger sip of her wine. She was enjoying enticing the young fool into her web of deceit and lies. "No, but my friends say you are a gifted scientist. What if you didn't have to be a clerk in a patent office? What is your real passion?"

How much could the Countess understand? Albert wondered. His mind raced, then he decided to just plunge in. "My research involves unifying concepts of electromagnetism, kinetic theory, and thermodynamics to discover unique approaches of using light and energy." He paused, waiting for her reaction.

The Countess smiled attentively pretending to understand at least part of what he had just said. She began savoring the game and planned to prolong it a while longer. "That sounds fascinating Herr Einstein. But I am no scientist. Could you explain your research in layman's terms?"

Albert grimaced, but if what he had just stated did not turn the Countess away, maybe there was hope of her funding his work. Albert smiled and refilled the Countess's wine glass. The scientist took in a deep breath and continued his lecture of the essential components of his work.

As Albert droned on, the Countess found herself losing patience. The chase was becoming tiring. Even so, she told herself that she must suffer to the conclusion of his commentary to affect her plan. To endure the boredom, the Countess filled her wine glass time and again. By the time Albert had reached the end of his discourse, Victoria had decided it was time to get on with her plan to seize the compass despite having become woozier than she had planned to.

Taking the last drink from her glass, she set it down and looked at the young man. "Thank you for clarifying your work Herr Einstein," Victoria said slightly slurring her words. "I believe the Einstein Theories are more than worthy of assistance from the Von Baden Trust."

Albert could not hold back a smile. "I ... I'm honored, Countess." *Even though I suspect the wine had more to do with her decision than my discourse,* he thought.

The Countess rose from the armchair holding the cane in her right hand. She took a few unsteady steps over to the carved desk and beckoned to Albert. "Please, Herr Einstein."

Albert walked over to her as she pointed to the papers before her. "My lawyers prepared a contract," she said, signing at the bottom of one of the pages. "You simply need to endorse this, and we will proceed." She nudged the document toward Albert. "Please, give this your fullest attention. I expect you'll find the terms satisfactory."

Excited by this change of fortune, Albert bent over the document and began reading. Next, to him, Victoria readied her lethal cane. The legal language was as alien to Albert as his scientific discourse had been to the Countess. Albert raised his head, and with a sheepish grin, he replied, "I'm certain everything is in order, Countess."

"Herr Einstein, please, take your time." She gestured toward the documents, drawing out the anticipation a few minutes more. The playing with her prey was one of the best parts of a plot like this. Albert turned his attention again to the papers, but they made no more sense to him now than before After reading only a few lines, he took the fountain pen Victoria had left on the desk and began to sign his name. Before he could complete his signature, the number 33 flashed in front of Albert's eyes. Startled, he dropped the pen and with a puzzled expression turned to Victoria. He was stunned; the number 33 confirmed his life was in jeopardy. "What is really going on here, Countess?"

Victoria was sneering, rocking slightly as she leaned toward the desk to steady herself, "You fool. I care nothing about your science. I have you here to regain my compass!"

Albert shook his head. "What do you mean *your* compass?" Sweat began to form on Albert's brow as he began to realize the Countess might be mad and he might be in real jeopardy.

Victoria said as she waved her arms, "I am the reason *that* compass exists."

Albert frowned trying to make sense of the woman's ravings. "W-what do you mean?"

Victoria spat, "If it had not been for my father's ignorance of the power of the compass your father could never have robbed me of it."

Albert's sweaty brow furrowed, "What does my father have to do with this?"

Victoria answered, "My father traded my compass to your father for installing electric lights in our castle. "

Understanding dawned. "So, you want to take back the payment that my father earned? That's crazy."

Victoria rolled her eyes, "This is not about mere payment, Herr Einstein. It is about *power*. My mentor, Raka, is the most powerful creature on earth. He and I have been stalking you for years to regain my compass."

As he heard the name, Raka, a vision of Arka and Johann flashed in his mind so strongly that he staggered backward, away from the desk and the Countess. Memory flooded his mind, and he began to realize how much danger he was in. Fighting to regain his composure he said, "I realize that Raka has been near me many times…"

Victoria's eyes widened, "You know of Raka?"

Albert's heart was now beating so hard he thought it would jump out of his chest. He wanted to run, but the Countess had moved between him and the door. He gulped and nodded.

Victoria responded with delight, "How droll. Raka has been my teacher for many years. He has shown me how to snare the weak and helpless," she shook her head as if in pity, "like you. And execute them. I came after you myself because I tired of failure after failure and grew weary of waiting. So, here we are. I. Will. Have. My. Compass!"

The Countess raised the cane and slid back the metal plate that concealed its trigger. Cackling, she, pointed the stick it at a fern near the sideboard. "Here is a preview of the fate that awaits you, Herr scientist," she said as she pulled the trigger. Albert stared, confused. Why was she pointing that cane at the plant he wondered?

A venom-coated needle struck a tall, vibrant philodendron in a large pot several feet away. Albert shook his head in bewilderment as he glanced at the Countess. Her eyes were firmly set on the plant. Albert turned to the plant again. In front of his eyes, it began to wilt. Then it blackened, its leaves shriveling and its stem drooping to the floor. As Albert watched terrified but fascinated, the plant's vitality and life force evaporated, and it disintegrated into a pool of a viscous liquid in a matter of seconds.

Now horrified, Albert shifted his gaze back and forth between the plant and the Countess.

Victoria held out her right palm and declared, "Now hand over the compass, or you will end up like that houseplant,."

Shaken and confused, Albert glanced over to discover the unsteady Countess pointing her cane at him. Without thinking, Albert picked up the silver serving bowl cover from the nearby dining table and hurled it at the crazy woman. Drunk, the Countess reflexively held up her hands. As the massive metal dome hit her, it jarred the point of the cane down, and her finger slid along the trigger. With a snick, another needle left the tip of the rod and embedded itself in the top of her foot.

Victoria screamed in frustration and agony, "NOOO!" She flung the cane away and fell to the floor, clawing at the needle, pulling it from her flesh. Frantically she began kneading the top of her foot, squeezing out blood and venom. As the crimson pool beside her foot grew, her breathing calmed. "I think I have gotten the poison out in time. She looked up at Albert who was frozen, staring at the scene with horrific fascination.

"I will have my compass yet," Victoria snarled at the young man, reaching toward him as she started to rise. Albert took a step backward and could only point.

The Countess frowned then looked to where Albert pointed. "Aaiieee!" she screamed as she saw that her foot was turning black and oozing with ichor. She began beating at the appendage, hoping to expel more of the toxin, "No, no, no, no…"

Despite her efforts, the blackness began crawling up her leg, accelerating with each ragged breath. In moments the foulness had traveled up her body, and Albert saw the flesh of the Countess's neck shrivel and blacken. Her body could no longer support her, and the Countess collapsed as the toxin relentlessly ate away at her flesh, blood, and bones. In moments her body was reduced to a putrid-, gelatinous puddle, a sheer black dress in its midst.

The peril gone, Albert, horrified and nauseated, struggled to regain his wits. Emotionally exhausted, he plopped himself in the dining chair, ran his shaking fingers through his hair and strived to make sense of the horrible events of the last hours.

In a flash of insight, he realized that he needed to get out of this place and remove any trace of his having been there. The last thing he needed was to be connected to the Countess's death – though he wondered if anyone would even know that the mess on the floor had been a human being, let alone the Countess Victoria von Baden.

Moving into his scientist persona, Albert began methodically erasing all evidence of his presence. When he had wiped clean all surfaces and objects he had touched, he snagged the dress from the puddle of slime with the Countess's cane and carefully wrapped it in a newspaper from one of the tables. Looking over the room one last time, he satisfied himself that nothing remained that could connect him with the place. He went to the door and picked up the key from the table where the Countess had left it. He unlocked the door and cautiously glanced around. Seeing no one, he dropped the key into the bushes next to the entry and, with the cane and newspaper-wrapped dress, he stepped out onto the deserted street and walked away. In a short time, he came to an alley and threw the newspaper and clothing into the dirt.

He started to toss the cane after it but hesitated. It was beautifully crafted, and its length suited his stride. After a moment's thought, he decided that there was no harm in keeping such a beautiful walking stick. It was an acceptable payment for spending an unproductive afternoon surviving an attempt on his life. Yes, he decided, he had earned the cane.

At the Countess's castle, Raka, in his fresh young body, was becoming restless. He had plans to put into motion. He required his apprentice to run errands for him. Glancing at the clock for the tenth time, he bristled and wondered where she had flown.

Chapter 32
Raka's Plans Go Awry

"**W**here is she?" roared Raka. He had been waiting nearly a week for Countess Victoria von Baden to return to her castle.

Now that Raka inhabited Werner von Wiesel's body, he was impatient to put the final stages of his plan into action. But to do that he needed Victoria to travel with him to Bern, Switzerland. There he could trick Werner's old schoolmate into giving him the compass. He had to get to Einstein before the Countess eliminated him. The delay was infuriating.

Raka was glad to have finally shed the feeble body of Professor Meiss. Yet, even in the newly acquired body of the young, strong Werner, he mused how human shapes and temperaments were so diverse. Over the years, he had occupied the physical form of a German businessman, the aging and decrepit physics professor Meiss, and now young Werner von Wiesel. Each had been different, and each had its infuriating limitations. The raging hormones of Werner's body promoted an almost unbearable impatience.

In a state of frustration, Raka, dressed in starched brown linen trousers and a black shirt, entered the kitchen of Von Baden's castle. He greeted the Priscilla the cook indifferently. "Any word from your mistress today?"

The middle-aged matron dressed in a simple white muslin smock and cotton cap glanced up from her kneading dough and replied, "I'm sorry, Herr von Wiesel, nothing yet," she responded. "I don't understand why she invited you for a visit and then left so mysteriously."

Raka frowned. "Let me make sure I understand. Vic... the Countess left a week ago, saying she might be gone for a while?"

"Well, sir, she did not tell me directly. Ana, her handmaid, announced that the Countess had business out of town and would be gone for an unknown period."

Raka rolled his eyes. "Why am I just now learning this?" He stormed off, leaving the puzzled cook shape the dough into breadsticks.

He searched for the handmaiden or any hint of where he could find Victoria... or his cane, for that matter. He vaguely remembered her limping and asking if she could use it when he was finishing off Von Wiesel. He strode past a mirror mid-search and stopped dead. His reflection showed hints of his dragon self. He'd have to get his fury under control before he did something rash. With effort, he finally regained his composure.

Raka found Ana in the library dusting the Countess's desk. The stout, brown-eyed, thirty-something dressed in a white dirndl and a cotton cap heard Werner enter and leaned her feather duster on the sideboard. She looked up at the tall, handsome Werner, smiled and politely asked, "Can I help you, sir?"

Restraining his impatience, Raka advanced toward to the timid woman. "Yes. I understand you were the last person to see the Countess before she left. Is that correct?"

"I believe so, sir. My mistress said she would be gone for a while, but if she did not come back within a week's time, to give you a note."

"I see. Did you notice if the Countess carried a cane with her when she left?" Raka asked.

"Why, yes. I noticed my mistress had a beautiful, gold-handled cane with her when she got into her carriage for the train," Ana replied.

"Train?" Raka stammered, now growing suspicious and angry. "It's been long enough. Give me the note your mistress left for me."

"C-certainly sir, I... I will be right back, sir. Please wait while I fetch it." Ana scurried out of the room.

Werner's blue eyes narrowed with suspicion. Bern? Had Victoria tried to pull something?

A million questions ran through his mind. He had trusted the Countess, at least to some degree. What had she done? Why had she taken his cane?

Things began to fall into place, and he was now convinced the stupid woman had betrayed him. Raka's mood grew dark. *Will I need to rescue her or eliminate her?*

Ana returned with the Countess's message. The note was written in Victoria's hand in black India ink with the family crest burned onto a red wax seal. Raka impatiently snatched the paper and broke the crimson seal. As the note unfolded, the fragrance of Victoria's signature French perfume wafted to his nose.

My Darling Werner,

I have traveled ahead to Bern to see if I can learn more about the Jewish scientist. However, if you have received this note, something has gone awry, and you must come to Bern with all speed. You should expect to find me at the Hotel Schweizerhof.

Yours,

Victoria

A violent snarl escaped Raka's lips as he crumpled the paper in his fist and stalked from the library, leaving a bewildered Ana shaking in fright.

Furious and disturbed, Raka retreated to the guest room where he spotted a stand of walking canes in the entryway. Reminded of his own golden treasure, and wondered, *what could Victoria want with my cane?* The dragon knew she was aware of the poison needles it carried. He'd shown that little feature to her one night in a moment of vulnerability and dearly regretted that now. *Was it possible the fool had planned to use the device to destroy Einstein and gain the compass for herself?* His anger roared to new heights and hastened to get to his room and figure out what to do next.

Inside his guest suite, Raka gave vent to his rage. He threw a priceless crystal decanter against the stone wall, shattering it into a thousand glistening shards. He kicked a handcrafted oak chair halfway across the large room. Then he threw himself onto a velvet upholstered couch and pondered the situation, convinced the Countess had done something incredibly foolish in direct opposition to his orders. Clenching his teeth to stifle more roars, Raka took from inside his boot a razor-sharp silver dagger. In his mind, he considered slicing the flesh from her bones in small pieces as she screamed in hideous agony. He indulged himself the fantasy for a few moments, then returned to contemplate the situation. *The Countess is merely as valuable as the services she renders. Maybe I will eliminate the strumpet and assume her body. Hmmm, yes. Now that has possibilities.* The thought immediately deflated his anger. Calmly and precisely, he replaced the knife in its hidden compartment in his boot and prepared for a journey to Bern.

* * *

The service staff nodded obsequiously to Raka as he marched into the Hotel Schweizerhof as Werner von Wiesel dressed in his severe black trench coat and fedora. The very image of cold authority, he strode past them without deigning to acknowledge their presence as he stepped up to the front desk.

"The Countess Victoria von Baden," he demanded of the diminutive, bespectacled, and balding clerk.

"And you are, sir?" the hotel desk clerk responded politely.

"I am a man who is rapidly losing patience," Raka spit out, glancing at the insignia on his coat collar.

Visibly paling, the desk clerk nodded and swallowed. "Of course. I understand. Just a moment.

Let me check for you." The clerk nervously thumbed through the guest register that sat on the tall counter that separated the two men. "She is in suite 309."

The clerk gave a little shake of his head. "One more moment please, sir." The clerk searched for a few seconds through a small pile of papers, then pulled one from the stack. He frowned as he read, then looked up at Raka. "I thought the number was familiar. Housekeeping has reported her bed has not been slept in for several nights."

Raka's eyes narrowed, and he snapped his fingers impatiently. "Key. Give me the key to her room."

"Yes, her room key. Of course." The hotel desk clerk opened a cabinet behind the counter and sorted through the keys while Raka drummed his fingers on the marble countertop. In a moment, the clerk held up a key. "Ah, here it—" Raka snatched the key and rushed up the grand stairway to Victoria's suite on the third floor. Growing angrier by the moment, he fumbled with the key in the lock, then threw open the door. Inside the elegant three-room suite, his eyes scanned the opulent appointments, finally coming to rest on an envelope propped up on the intricately carved oak mantelpiece. He strode to the mantel and tore open the note.

My Mentor,

I have gone to number 69 Dalmaziquai to secure Herr Einstein's compass for you. If you are reading this, things have gone badly, and I may be in trouble. I know you will come to rescue me.

Your ever-faithful,

V

Ever faithful. Indeed, he snorted, stuffing the note into his coat pocket. Briskly making his way back to the front desk, he glared at the desk clerk, who was still recovering from their earlier encounter.

"Did you find anything that would assist you, sir?" the clerk asked in almost a whisper.

"Number 69 Dalmaziquai," Raka spit out. "Where is it... and what is it?"

"Oh, uh, yes. The Countess requested we recommend a discreet place where she could conduct a special... encounter. The address is the Maison De Fleur, exclusive accommodation for the upper class..." The clerk glanced down, not meeting Raka's eye. "...if you know what I mean, Sir." Raka turned and stormed out of the hotel. He spotted a carriage for hire and barked at the driver to take him to the Maison De Fleur as quickly as possible. *Oh, Victoria, whatever have you done?* He wondered as he fidgeted in the carriage.

After what seemed like an interminable ride, though in truth it had only been a few minutes, Raka threw some money at the driver and raced to the black door with the number 69. He struggled to open the latch with no luck. The door was locked. He looked around. Seeing no one on the street, he grasped the door handle and squeezed hard. His anger-fueled strength disintegrated the handle and lock completely, and he made his way into the suite.

Inside, the spotless room was uninhabited. Raka detected the faintest hint of the Countess's perfume amid the scent of cleaning soap. It might just be enough for him to track her to where she'd been taken.

He glanced quickly around to see if his cane was there. Not seeing it, he cautiously withdrew, following the faint remnants of the Countess's perfume to the riverbank, where he saw a rubbish dump not far away. The scent trail led him past small piles of garbage to a newspaper partially concealing an elegant black dress soiled beyond redemption by a viscous goo. He recognized the garment as one he had seen the Countess wear and detected her essence in the liquid.

"Fool!" he snarled. He could envision the scene where Victoria had tried to use the cane, and it had somehow backfired on her. It was likely the idiot Einstein boy now had the walking stick and the compass. Raka cursed the Countess for having fouled his scheme so wholly.

Raka closed his eyes and saw his brother the high priest of Atlantis Arka shaking his head in disapproval. *So many years of planning,* he fumed, *destroyed so quickly by her stupidity. How dare she!* He could no longer contain his fury. *There was no way I am going to lose the compass! I will get that compass if it's the last thing I do!*

Chapter 33
Time Revealed

*S*till inhabiting Werner's body, Raka had been surreptitiously observing Albert's routine for a week now. *The fool is so methodical,* he thought.

I could set my watch by his movements. Satisfied he knew the boy's exact daily route to work, Raka placed himself strategically near the Bern clock tower to intercept Albert on his way to the office. Now, all he had to do was wait. Raka allowed his mind to wander in delicious anticipation of what was to come. His enhanced dragon senses had confirmed that the Shamir was in fact in Albert's possession. Raka's excitement grew as he thought about finally possessing it. The dragon in human form glanced at his boot where he had secreted his silver dagger in preparation for the encounter to come.

The fallen dark angel yearned for vengeance, not just on his youthful nemesis, but also on Arka, his brother, who had become a high priest in Atlantis. Raka scowled at the thought of how Arka had so severely undermined his progress in Atlantis before he had taken on his dragon form. He would show them all just how accomplished he now was. And how dare this Einstein person kill his servant Victoria—using Raka's own cane and venom, no less! Raka attempted to calm himself with thoughts of what he could do, what power he would wield, once he had the supernatural Light source. But the hormones in this young body and the anger raging within him clouded his judgment and made rational thought and emotional restraint virtually impossible. Exerting tremendous willpower, Raka forced himself to be patient just a little while longer and sought something... anything... to divert his mind. He began watching the small crew of workers across the cobblestone square. They were preparing the coals in a massive brazier that had been erected in front of the clock tower. Apparently, they were planning to cook meats for some local festivity. The sturdy metal structure was massive, at least fifteen feet long and about six feet wide. The long metal gratings that would eventually be set atop the hot coals leaned against the base of the brazier. Raka curled his lip at the scent of the kerosene that the workers were liberally splashing on the large bed of coals. He flinched and moved back a step as the coals were lit with an enormous flash and an audible *whoosh*. Almost instantly, he could feel the heat from across the square, and he did not like being anywhere near flames.

* * *

Not long after the sun rose, Albert roused himself from a deep sleep and prepared himself for the day of work at the patent office. For some reason, he had awakened with a feeling of anticipation. Albert sensed something momentous awaited him. He had been staying up nights working hard on his theory of light and was sure he was close to a breakthrough. He shrugged off the feeling and completed his ablutions, then dressed suitably for the pleasant spring weather.

On his way out the door, he grabbed the gold-handled walking stick he had acquired in that bizarre encounter with Countess von Baden. He had almost thrown it away along with the Countess's dress, but he couldn't bring himself to discard something of such fine craftsmanship. The handle was indeed a work of art. Having kept it, he quickly became fond of the ornate cane with the ruby-eyed dragon grip that so comfortably fit his palm. He considered it to be his reward for fending off the crazy woman who sought to steal his compass and kill him. Making a final check of his clothing, Albert opened the door and stepped out of his two-story apartment building and walked down the stairs to Kramgasse Street. The sunny day and warm spring air put a bounce in his step. The cane swung forward and back, aligning grace-fully with each footfall.

As he did every day, Albert strolled a few blocks to the Bern clock tower where he would board the streetcar to work. He was enjoying the spring air and letting his thoughts wander to his theories. In the last few weeks, the budding scientist had returned to his preoccupation with the velocity of light. When he was 16, Albert imagined himself running alongside beams of light. Now, he under-stood that in Maxwell's equations at least, light always traveled at the same speed.

What's more, it would be impossible for an observer to attain that velocity. No human could move at the speed of light. Albert could see no solution to the velocity prob-lem.

He was frustrated and sometimes considered giving up. As he rounded the corner toward the medieval fif-teenth-century clock tower, Albert's compass rang out the alarm tone that Arka had programmed into it. Star-tled, Albert halted in his tracks and spun around. The morning commuters and women with their shopping bags dotted the broad boulevard. He surveyed the crowd and spotted a tall, youthful man in a black leather trench coat and black fedora who looked vaguely familiar. He seemed out of place. Albert turned the corner and tucked himself behind the thirty-foot-high bear that defined the Zahringen water fountain.

Raka scowled. He thought he'd glimpsed Einstein by the fountain; now he was gone. He scanned the crowd, then slowly made his way toward the monument. Albert peered around the statue. His eyes widened as he recognized the man in the trench coat as his childhood nemesis, Werner von Wiesel. As Werner approached Albert's hiding place, Albert's compass flashed the number 666. Albert's eyes narrowed as he tried to remember what the warning meant. He knew it wasn't right and had to try and get away.

Looking around, he spied the entrance to a narrow alley and scurried toward it. Raka sensed Albert's movement and recognized his prey. Noting that the crowd had thinned, he confidently strode toward the passageway into which Einstein had run.

Entering the alley, Raka laughed. It was a dead end. Yards away, Albert was ineffectively trying to climb a pile of trash to reach a window high above. Hearing Werner's derisive snicker, Albert ceased his futile attempt at escape and slid down to the backstreet floor to face his enemy.

"Why are you pursuing me, Werner?"

"Maybe I just like the sport of it, Jew boy."

Albert scowled. "I had almost forgotten that's what you used to call me. What do you want? You and I were never friends. Then, when you destroyed my friendship with Johann, you became my enemy."

"Oh yes, Johann. I noticed you at his funeral," Raka bragged in Werner's body. "You looked so pathetic. Have you figured out that I was the one who pushed Johann into the trolley? He was such a goody-goody. I begged him to get the compass for me." Werner snickered. "When the fool told me there was no way he was going to betray you, I got mad and went after him. Well, the rest you know. What do you think of that?" he taunted.

Until this moment, Albert had thought Johann's death had been an accident. He had no idea Werner had murdered his friend. Anger and pain welled up inside him, and he moved threateningly toward his enemy.

Raka sneered, reached down and whipped the silver dagger out of his boot, pointing the sharp point toward Albert. "Easy, Einstein. I wouldn't make any rash moves."

Albert stopped his advance, eyeing the glistening blade. In a flash, Albert remembered what the 666-warning meant. "What do you want, Werner? Or should I say... Raka?"

Now, it was Raka's eyebrows that shot up, while his rising anger threatened to overwhelm him. "What do you know of..." He realized it didn't matter. Only the compass mattered. What Einstein knew was of no importance; he would soon be dead.

Raka took a slow breath, calming himself, and smiled an almost friendly smile toward Albert. He knew his possession of the compass and the Shamir would change the course of history. His triumph was mere moments away. "What I want is the compass. If you turn it over now, I will go easy on you." Of course, he meant not a word of what he said, but maybe the assurance would prompt the boy to surrender the prize without a struggle. Albert couldn't possibly win a fight with him, and it would be so much easier to dispose of the boy's body if he could avoid a messy conflict.

For the first time, everything became clear to Albert. He was dealing with something terrifying, evil and magical. Despite his otherworldly adventures with Johann and the travelers, Albert felt utterly unprepared...and he was terrified!

Raka took a threatening step toward his victim, and Albert reflexively raised the cane to defend himself.

"You can't stop me with my own venom," Raka snorted.

Albert was confused. *Venom? What is Raka talking about?*

As Raka started his move toward him, Albert took a step back and lost his footing on a piece of wet trash. As his elbow hit the ground, Albert's finger slid against the hidden trigger and a dart shot from the cane, hitting Raka in the chest. Raka roared in pain as Werner's flesh instantly began melting from his body. His hand holding the dagger lost its form, and the silver blade fell to the back lane floor with a dull click. The leather trench coat slid off his body as his shoulders slumped and dissolved. The black fedora slipped down over Raka's surprised eyes, then fell to the ground.

Albert was unable to look away, but unlike Victoria, who had melted into a pool of scum, something strange was happening with Werner's disintegrating body. Amid the pile of clothing on the ground, greenish-black scales began to appear, and a reptilian form began to take shape in the slime. Albert realized the danger was not over. He sprinted past the resurrecting dragon, but Raka reached out to grab him. But he had not re-formed completely, and Albert was able to elude his grasp. Barely.

Albert ran out of the alley as fast as he could and frantically sought a place to hide. Now a fully formed dragon, Raka slowly picked himself up out of the puddle that had been Werner. Albert spotted a door in the side of the Gothic clock tower and ran toward it. The dragon cleared his head with a massive shake and set off in pursuit. There was nowhere Albert could go, Raka smiled.

Albert reached the door and pushed, still clutching the cane. The door was jammed. He pushed harder, then threw his full weight against the weathered wooden window. It opened with a pop and Albert fell inside. He found himself in a chamber housing some of the gears and levers that powered the ancient timepiece. He saw a wooden staircase and ran toward it, desperately making his way up the six very high floors of what had been a castle's guard tower. At the top of the stairs, he found another door. This one opened more easily into a room above the clock face. He closed the door, wedging it shut with a piece of wood, and looked around. Thick dust covered everything, and it swirled into the air as Albert moved further inside.

The tiny room only had a small window leading out to a deck above the clock face and no other way out. Albert prayed the door would be strong enough to protect him and that the dragon eventually would be forced to abandon his pursuit. Albert was sure the monster would not want to raise a commotion and be discovered.

As surreptitiously as he could in twelve-foot dragon form, Raka darted quickly toward the tower. He made it without attracting a glance and disappeared into its interior. Once inside and out of view of the citizenry, he stormed up the stairs taking them two steps at a time, his talons crashing onto every second wooden step with a thud.

He reached the door to the chamber where Albert cowered and listened intently. Inside, Albert fidgeted nervously. He had heard the dragon thundering up the stairs and fancied he could hear him outside the door. Albert stepped further into the room and drew in a breath, inhaling a nose-full of dust that had stirred up with his movement. In terror, he clapped his hand over his nose and pinched, hoping to forestall a sneeze. Feeling the tickle subside, he relaxed. That was when a sniffle escaped his nose. With the sound, Albert gasped and paled, fearing he may have given himself away.

He held his breath and waited. When nothing happened for a moment, Albert allowed himself to start breathing again and began to relax.

Suddenly, the door exploded off its hinges, and Raka burst into the room. Spotting Albert pushing himself up against the wall, he smiled. Shaking his head in mock pity, the dragon reached out for the young man, but Albert batted the claws back with his cane and started inching along the wall.

Raka watched, enjoying the cat-and-mouse game. He knew Albert didn't have a prayer. And Raka exulted, imagining his brother, Arka, experiencing the same terror.

He laughed when, in desperation, Albert smashed the window with the cane and tumbled out onto the deck of the clock tower. Chuckling, Raka leaped through the opening and landed on the stone ledge. He turned toward Albert, his back to the waist-high railing wall. When his eyes found his victim, his grin widened. "Seems like there's no way off this tower, puny human." He glanced at the ground far below. "Unless you can fly."

Albert looked around frantically, seeking any way off the tower short of jumping. *Puny human is right*, he thought.

At that moment, the clock's life-sized cast-iron automatons began their hourly dance, the chimes sounding and the brass bell clanging out a deafening peal.

Raka screamed in agony and clapped his clawed hands over his highly sensitive ears. He could not stand the thundering blast of sound. His reptile senses were on overload. He stepped back and bumped into the wall that was waist-high for Albert, but barely knee-high for the monster. Unbalanced, the dragon flailed his short arms, trying to regain his balance. Albert recognized the opportunity and ran toward the beast. With his full weight,

Albert shoved the shaft of the cane into Raka's chest. The dragon snarled in pain and disbelief, and reached toward Albert, grabbing the rod to steady himself. Albert pushed again, then let go of the stick and scurried back out of the dragon's reach. He watched as Raka tumbled backward over the edge of the stone wall. Screaming, Raka made a desperate twist and caught the minute hand on the clock's zodiac face. His fall arrested, he took in a deep breath and looked up, snarling at Albert, who was peering over the wall. "Say your prayers, Herr Einstein, because I will be up in a moment to deliver your fate."

Raka reached over to make his way along the metal hand to the clock's center. But his weight was too enormous and, as he reached for a more solid grip, the long metal hand broke off from the face of the clock with a snap. A look of disbelief crossed Raka's face when he fell back away from the clock's face and plunged toward the blazing inferno of the brazier far below.

Raka's roars filled the air as his body twisted in pain. His small, vestigial wings were useless now. He crashed down into the middle of the brazier. Raka's body ignited with a flash of light and a burst of heat.

People in the square, attracted by the screams, shielded their eyes, then ran toward the commotion. Peering over the edge of the ledge, Albert surveyed the scene. His eyes widened at the sight of Raka writhing on the red-hot coals, his body aflame. Not wanting to be seen, Albert backed away from the wall and quickly made his way through the window and down the stairs. In moments he was out on the square, melting into the crowd. Undiscovered, he paused to watch what would happen next.

The crowd muttered in horrified fascination, not sure what they were seeing amid the red-hot coals and sparks and cinders flying everywhere. Albert bit back a gasp as the dust and cinders settled, just as the indistinct dragon form transformed into that of a tall, blond-haired man.

At sight, Albert was transported in memory back to his visit to Atlantis when he had met himself in his previous incarnation as the priest-scientist Arka. The face he saw in the fire was the same as Arka's, and Albert realized that he saw Arka's identical twin, Raka, in his natural form, before he had fallen from grace and become the treacherous dragon.

Sadness filled Albert then as he watched Raka's human body writhe in agony, and finally become entirely consumed by the unspeakably hot coals.

"Who was that?" a man wanted to know.

"Don't recognize him," another said, shaking his head.

"Poor fellow. How...?"

The crowd could only speculate as they cowered back from the terrible heat and flying cinders.

"What was he doing in the clock tower?" a man wondered.

"No idea," another commented.

"I'm sure the authorities will figure this all out," a woman suggested, shaking her head as she glanced at the now charred husk in the brazier.

Still running on high adrenaline, Albert tried to make sense of what had happened. He turned to a man next to him and asked, "Uh, what did you see?"

The man shook his head. "I don't know. I heard screams and saw that fellow disintegrate in the fire."

"You didn't see anything else?" Albert asked hesitantly.

"Like what? All I know is some poor man fell into the brazier."

The sounds of the fire brigade approach brought Albert back to his senses, and he heard the trolley approaching. Despite the extraordinary events of the day, he still had to get to work. As most of the would-be riders remained behind to see how this remarkable event would play out, Albert climbed aboard the empty train and found a secluded seat at the back of the car. Sitting down and taking a few breaths to calm himself, he drew his compass from his trouser pocket. He paused a moment, then held the device close to his chest with gratitude. The compass had saved his life. Albert silently repeated the compass blessing, and a bright hologram appeared before his eyes. As he gazed at it, he was lifted into a higher level of intuitive awareness. He turned his attention out the trolley window and saw translucent, ghost-like images of people in all modes of travel; some walking, some in carriages, a few on bicycles. As if viewing a movie in his mind, Albert watched them moving at different speeds and observed that the objects around them in were different sizes—some truncated; others elongated. Puzzled at first, he had a flash of inspiration: time and space were different for him and different for each observer he passed. Time depended, he realized, on how quickly you are traveling. Albert realized that the faster you go; the more time slows down.

As the revelation dawned, he suddenly understood that as you approach the speed of light, space distorts. Things would appear shortened. Everything was relative! Albert gasped as he became aware that he had the fundamentals of his new theory of light. Instantly, he felt the warm hum of the compass cease. He saw the crystals, once bright and sparkling, go dim. After all these years, the compass had gone silent.

Putting the compass into his pocket, Albert settled back and closed his eyes, relaxing into the steady rhythm of the wheels clacking on the metal track. *I now know how time works*, he thought to himself. *Now all I must do is figure out how to prove it.*

Chapter 34
Relinquishing the Compass

As Albert rested, half-asleep, half-awake, he felt himself disengage from his body as he had when he'd done his thought experiments. Though there was almost no one on the trolley, he sensed a presence next to him. He hadn't heard anyone come all the way back to where he was, so Albert reluctantly opened one eyelid. To his surprise, he found a grinning Johann sitting next to him.

His friend nodded at him. "Well done, Albert. I knew you could do it."

"Do what? Defeat a 12-foot monster dragon? I wouldn't have put money on that."

"Maybe not that, but I knew you would find answers to your questions about light and energy."

"I think I have more questions than answers," Albert laughed. Then, becoming serious, he asked, "And speaking of twelve-foot dragons, Raka seemed to be invulnerable. What happened back there?"

"There are cosmic laws that prevent even powerful forces of Light from interfering with the forces of darkness as long as those laws are observed."

Albert nodded as Johann continued. "The travelers and I could assist you, but only up to a point—as long as Raka didn't personally attack you."

"So, you mean—" Albert started.

Johann nodded. "Raka's lust for power finally overrode his judgment, and when he finally made his move against you, he became vulnerable." Johann shook his head. "I can't believe it. He'd been around for thousands and thousands of years, easily avoiding fire... until he crossed the line and violated the cosmic law."

"I couldn't believe it when I saw him transform back to his natural human form. I kind of knew he had been my twin in that Atlantis lifetime, but seeing that face was... sad."

Johann put a hand on Albert's shoulder. "It is sad when someone chooses to work against the Light. But he had to be held responsible for his choices."

Albert sighed and nodded. "I guess."

The two sat silently for a moment, then Albert asked, "What's next?"

"Well, there are great things for you, my friend," Johann said with a big smile. "Believe it or not, your work will revolutionize science."

Albert shook his head. "I know my theories are important, but change the world? I don't know."

Johann patted Albert's arm. "You'll see, Albert. You will bring new light to the world. But..." Johann became unusually somber as he looked out the window. He motioned with his head toward a youthful boy dressed in a brown shirt and knickers. "The world is in for some challenging times."

At Albert's questioning look, Johann reluctantly continued. "Look, I can't say much, but the forces of darkness are on the move. Raka was just a foreshadowing of what is to come."

"Let's not talk about these things," Albert shuddered, still exhausted from the morning's events. "They are not here now, and we are together for the moment."

Albert nodded, and the two friends sat together agreeably for a moment. "Johann, you say I'll be changing the world, but what of you?"

Johann got a faraway look, then, almost embarrassed, he said, "Um, well, apparently my work with you was, um, acceptable, and, uh..."

"Johann, you're blushing!" Albert laughed. "Come on, spit it out."

"The travelers have said they want me to work with others who will be leaders in changing the world."

Albert squeezed Johann's arm. "Really? That's wonderful!"

"It's amazing is what it is," Johann said, looking at the trolley floor. "I think they made a mistake."

"Well, I don't. You'll do great." Then Albert paused as a thought occurred to him. "But... will I see you again?"

Johann shook his head very slightly. "Probably not— or not very often, in any case. But it's okay, really," he assured his friend. "We are in each other's heart and as close as a thought. And if you ever really need me, I will find a way to get to you."

Albert nodded sadly. "I guess we both have important work to do now."

"Who would have thought we would end up here from such an innocent meeting all those years ago in my father's newly electrified barn." Then he turned toward Albert and held out his hand, palm up.

A puzzled look crossed Albert's face. "What?"

"I have a final task with you, Albert."

Comprehension dawned, and Albert reached into his pocket and withdrew the compass. One last time he gazed at the gems, no longer glowing, and its ethereal warmth, gone. "I don't know how I will do without this. It's been my constant companion for most of my life."

"You'll do fine," Johann said. He closed his fingers around the device and, as he slowly began to fade, he said, "God bless you, Albert. You have been more than a brother to me."

The clang of the trolley bell announced Albert's stop. He stood and looked at the now empty seat where Johann had just visited him. "Goodbye, my friend," he said. Then, turned and walked toward the trolley door. He emerged into the sunshine of a beautiful spring day and headed down the sidewalk to change the world.

About the Authors

Grace Blair is an award-winning self-help and motivational author, and podcast host, who has assisted thousands to find their spiritual wisdom to solve everyday challenges. Throughout her adult life, Grace became a serious student of the spiritual. She found that, often, psychological principles and practices were incomplete, but could be filled out by adding the missing spiritual component. Her approach was always to see practical applications for what she uncovered in the mystical. It was through immersing herself in this field of study and experience that she came up with her idea for her book, *Einstein's Compass*. She lives in Lubbock, Texas, with her husband, Dr. John Blair.

Laren Bright is a three-time Emmy nominated award-winning writer who has written nearly 100 children's animated cartoon scripts. He has spent the majority of his professional life over the last two decades assisting authors to produce topnotch books with titles and other promotional writing indistinguishable from those of mainstream publishers. During that time, in addition to *Einstein's Compass*, he also co-authored a young adult fantasy series and several books for young children about positive values. Laren lives in Los Angeles with his wife, computer, and two granddogs.

DATE DUE

Made in the USA
Coppell, TX
12 February 2022

73447803R10236